D1396691

MURDER IN
MURRAY HILL

Center Point
Large Print

Also by Victoria Thompson and available from Center Point Large Print:

Murder in Chelsea

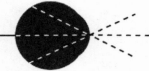

This Large Print Book carries the Seal of Approval of N.A.V.H.

MURDER IN MURRAY HILL

A Gaslight Mystery

Victoria Thompson

CENTER POINT LARGE PRINT
THORNDIKE, MAINE

This Center Point Large Print edition
is published in the year 2014 by arrangement with
The Berkley Publishing Group,
a member of Penguin Group (USA).

The text of this Large Print edition is unabridged.
In other aspects, this book may vary
from the original edition.
Printed in the United States of America
on permanent paper.
Set in 16-point Times New Roman type.

ISBN: 978-1-62899-226-7

Library of Congress Cataloging-in-Publication Data

Thompson, Victoria (Victoria E.) author.
 Murder in Murray Hill : a Gaslight mystery / Victoria Thompson. —
Center Point Large Print edition.
 pages ; cm
 Summary: "When facing injustice, the residents of nineteenth-century
New York City's tenements turn to midwife Sarah Brandt and Detective
Sergeant Frank Malloy to protect their rights. Now the two must track
down a cruel criminal preying on the hopes and dreams of innocent
women"—Provided by publisher.
 ISBN 978-1-62899-226-7 (library binding : alk. paper)
 1. Brandt, Sarah (Fictitious character)—Fiction.
 2. Malloy, Frank (Fictitious character)—Fiction.
 3. Women detectives—New York (State)—New York—Fiction.
 4. Murray Hill (New York, N.Y.)—Fiction.
 5. New York (N.Y.)—19th century—Fiction. 6. Large type books. I. Title.
PS3570.H6442M8655 2014b
813´.54—dc23
                                                              2014019473

To all my friends at the LSS Foundation

MURDER IN MURRAY HILL

1

Being rich wasn't nearly as much fun as Frank had always been led to believe. Of course he wasn't really rich yet, and he was in no hurry about it either. Oh, the money would be nice, he supposed. Never having to worry about the future sounded appealing. And, of course, he'd have Sarah as his wife. The rest of it, though, that's the part he didn't like. His life was going to change in a hundred ways, only a few of them good, and he couldn't do a damn thing about it.

"Malloy?"

Frank looked up from the paperwork he'd been pretending to work on at one of the battered desks in the detectives' room at Police Headquarters.

The desk sergeant had trudged up the stairs to find him, and he didn't look happy about it. "There's a man here says his daughter's gone missing. Wants to report it."

Frank almost smiled. A case. Maybe his last one, but a case. "Send him up."

The sergeant motioned to someone in the hallway, and a neatly dressed, middle-aged man stepped into the doorway. He was average height and a little too thin. His brownish hair barely covered his scalp, and he had a little brush of a mustache. "This here is Detective Sergeant Frank Malloy," the sergeant said. "He'll take care of you."

The sergeant didn't wait for a reply and disappeared back down the stairs to his post.

Frank rose and pulled over a chair from one of the other desks. "Have a seat, Mister . . . ?"

The man approached cautiously, obviously appalled by the unkempt condition of the large room full of old desks covered with the detritus of scores of unfinished reports and half-smoked cigarettes.

"Thank you," the man said as he gingerly sat in the rickety chair. When he was fairly confident it would hold him, he relaxed slightly but not completely.

Now Frank could see the tension radiating from the man and the unspoken fear in his eyes. His daughter was missing, the sergeant had said. Frank knew how that felt. He reached into his coat pocket and pulled out his notebook. A pencil stub lay on the desk. He picked it up, licked the tip, and said, "What's your name, sir?"

"Livingston. Henry Livingston." Frank took in the details of his appearance with a practiced eye. A good quality suit, but not extravagant. His shirt was crisp, his tie proper. His shoes showed wear but not heavy use. The hands nervously clutching the brim of his bowler hat were clean and not callused.

"Where do you live, Mr. Livingston?"

He gave Frank an address on Fortieth Street, in the Murray Hill neighborhood. Once the location of millionaires' mansions, it had fallen out of fashion as the wealthy moved farther uptown. Now comfortable middle-class businessmen were building modern brownstones there.

Maybe he and Sarah should think about moving to Murray Hill when they got married.

"The desk sergeant said something about your daughter?" Frank prodded when Mr. Livingston offered nothing more.

"Yes, Grace. That's her name, Grace. She's gone missing."

"How long has she been gone?"

"Since yesterday. Overnight. I mean, I wasn't too worried about it until she didn't come home last night. She never stays out all night. She's not that kind of girl, Mr. Malloy."

He seemed very anxious for Frank to believe that. Frank nodded. "How old is she?"

"She's . . ." He closed his eyes, squinting them in his effort to remember. Or maybe he was doing the math. "She's twenty-eight. Not a flighty young girl, my Grace. Very sensible. Not the kind of girl who stays out all night without saying a word to anyone."

"Have you looked for her?"

"Of course I did," he almost snapped, then caught himself. "I'm sorry. Yes, I contacted all her friends, but none of them had seen her. I went to the church to see if she'd been there. She volunteers, you see, and I thought perhaps . . . Well, if she'd been taken ill and no one knew . . ."

"But she wasn't there."

"She wasn't there or at the library or any other place she might have gone."

"She's not married?"

"No. An unclaimed blessing we always said. She'd make some man a wonderful wife, but . . ."

"Does she have any gentlemen friends? Anyone she might've eloped with?"

Livingston's pale blue eyes widened. "Eloped?"

"Maybe you didn't approve of him, so they decided to run off together. It happens."

For a moment hope sparked in his eyes, but it died quickly. "No, I'm afraid not. Grace doesn't have any gentlemen friends, suitable or not."

Of course, if the gentleman was unsuitable, Grace probably wouldn't have brought him home to meet her father. But Frank would find out for sure from her friends. He hoped that was it, because the other reasons a young woman might go missing in New York City weren't good.

"When did you see her last, Mr. Livingston?"

"Yesterday morning. We had breakfast together. I asked her what she was going to do that day, and she said she had some errands."

"Did she say what the errands were?"

"No. I've been racking my brain all night trying to recall, but that's all she said. Just errands."

"Did she say anything to your wife?"

A shadow crossed his face. "My wife died several years ago. Grace is our only child."

"I'm sorry," Frank murmured. "What about your servants?"

"I asked them, of course. We live very simply, with just a cook and two maids. They said she went out around eleven o'clock."

"Did she tell them where she was going?"

"She had some errands, she said. That's all."

So, plainly she had something important to do that she didn't want anyone to know about, Frank thought, but he said, "I'd like to question them myself, if you don't mind."

"Of course I don't mind. I'm sure they'll be happy to help. They love Grace."

Frank would reserve judgment on that until he'd talked to them himself. "I'll also need to see her room."

"Her room? Her *bedroom?*" The very idea shocked him.

"She may have left something behind that would tell us where she was going. She may even have left a note."

"A note? I didn't think of that."

Frank doubted that she had, but he wasn't going to tell Mr. Livingston. "Maybe she was going someplace she didn't think you'd approve of, so she left you a note."

"Do you really think so? My goodness, we should go right now, then, shouldn't we?"

Frank saw no reason to delay. The two men left Police Headquarters, walked down Houston Street and caught the Third Avenue Elevated Train up to Forty-second Street. While the El rattled uptown, Mr. Livingston explained that he didn't keep a carriage. The cost and bother was too much in New York City, where you could usually walk faster than a horse could pull you through the streets.

Frank decided he wouldn't keep a carriage either, when the time came. But maybe Sarah had other ideas about that.

Livingston didn't want to discuss his daughter on a crowded railway platform or in an even more crowded railway car, so they rode the rest of the way in silence. A short walk from Forty-second Street Station brought them to a fairly new brownstone in a row of equally new brownstone town houses.

A maid came rushing down the hallway as they entered, but she stopped dead when she saw Frank enter behind her employer. She was a young girl with no claim to beauty and probably not much wit either.

"Have you heard anything from Miss Grace?" Livingston asked.

"No, sir. I was hoping . . . that is, when I heard the door . . ." Her anxious gaze darted to Frank and away again.

"This is Detective Sergeant Malloy from the New York City Police," he said. "He's going to help us find Miss Grace."

"The police?" she said, wringing her hands.

Like most people in the city, she obviously believed that nothing good ever happened when the police were involved.

"Mr. Malloy is going to ask all of us some questions. I want you to tell him everything you know."

Her eyes widened. "We don't know anything about where Miss Grace went, Mr. Livingston. We already told you that."

Frank stepped forward and gave the girl his friendliest smile. "Yes, you did, but she may have said something that would give us a clue as to where she went, something you don't even remember or maybe something that didn't seem important at the time."

His smile obviously didn't reassure her, and his words only seemed to upset her more. "I don't know anything, I tell you."

Frank nodded. "Maybe you could show me Miss Livingston's room first, then."

"Her room?" She glanced at Livingston for his opinion of such an outrageous request.

"Please take Mr. Malloy up to Miss Grace's room, Daisy."

Daisy pulled a face, but she took Frank's hat, then led him up the stairs.

"Should I come, too, Mr. Malloy?" Livingston called when they had reached the first landing.

"Why don't you look around downstairs and in your own room to see if she left you a note," Frank said.

Livingston nodded and turned away, as Frank had hoped.

Frank caught Daisy giving him a disapproving frown. "She didn't leave no note," she whispered.

"I know, but he needs something to keep him busy."

Daisy sniffed her disgust and climbed the rest of the stairs, reluctance radiating off her like a bad smell. They reached the second floor, where the parlor and other public rooms would be, then continued up to the third floor and the family's bedrooms. Frank figured the servants would occupy the fourth floor, where they'd freeze in winter and bake in summer. She took him to one of several doors opening off the short hallway.

"This here's her room, and I know everything that she's got in there, so if any of it goes missing, I'll tell Mr. Livingston."

"Thank you for the warning," Frank said, trying not to take offense. After all, lots of cops would think nothing of helping themselves to whatever they found.

"Don't get smart with me," she said. "And don't

think you can get any money out of Mr. Livingston either. He ain't rich, and he never paid a bribe in his life."

Frank had no intention of asking for a bribe, of course, but she couldn't know that. Bribes were the only way most cops could earn a living, since the city didn't pay them enough to survive. "You can watch me, if you want, but you should know, I have to go through everything. You can complain about what I'm doing, but I still have to do it."

She sniffed again, but she opened the door and stood aside for him to enter.

Grace Livingston's room surprised him. He'd expected white-and-gold French furniture covered with flounces and ruffles and wallpaper with buxom shepherdesses. Instead he found a neatly made single bed covered with a rather worn quilt and plain pine furniture—a wash-stand, a wardrobe, a dressing table, and a nightstand. A faded rag rug covered the center of the floor, and a slipper chair had been pulled up near the grate. Its small footstool bore a needle-point pattern too ancient to make out. Except for the once-vibrant colors in the quilt, the room was all in shades of brown.

Frank glared at Daisy. "You were supposed to take me to Miss Livingston's room."

"This *is* her room."

Frank looked around again, then turned back to

Daisy, giving her a glimpse of how angry he could get.

"You can call Mr. Livingston if you don't believe me," she said, wringing her hands again. "I know it ain't pretty, but that's how Miss Grace wanted it. She never was one for fancy things."

Still not convinced, Frank strode over to the wardrobe and threw open the doors. A paltry few items of women's clothing hung there. Several shirtwaists. Two skirts—one brown, one dark blue—and matching jackets. A black mourning dress that looked a bit dusty, as if it hadn't been worn recently. A pair of ladies' boots sat slumped in the bottom of the cabinet, and some battered carpet slippers lay beside them.

Grace Livingston didn't waste a lot of time or money on her personal appearance any more than she did on her bedroom furnishings. "What's missing from here?"

Daisy came over and looked, staying as far from Frank as she possibly could and still see into the cabinet. "Just the clothes she was wearing yesterday, looks like."

She hadn't packed then, which meant she hadn't meant to be gone very long. He pulled out his notebook and a pencil. "And what was she wearing yesterday?"

"What's it to you?" She was back to being snippy.

Frank sighed. He appreciated her loyalty to

Miss Livingston, but he didn't have time for this. "It might help us identify her if we pull her out of the East River and the fish have eaten her face."

Daisy widened her eyes again, going chalk white this time, and she swayed on her feet.

Frank grabbed her arm and steered her toward the slipper chair. "Take deep breaths," he said as he settled her into it.

After a few moments, she looked up at him with tears in her eyes. "Do you really think she's dead?"

"I have no idea, but if she's not, I'll need all the help I can get to find her. Now stop protecting her and tell me what she was wearing."

"It was her Sunday best," Daisy said, no longer reluctant at all. "A bottle green skirt and matching bolero jacket and a white shirtwaist with ruffles on the front. Her nice shoes, too, all polished up."

"Did she usually dress up like that to run errands?"

"Oh no! She wasn't one for dressing up at all, except for church on Sunday, which is why I thought it was strange. Oh!" she added, clamping a hand over her mouth.

"What is it?"

She lowered her hand an inch or two. "I just told you something I didn't know I remembered."

He rewarded her with a smile. "That's good,

Daisy. That's very good. What else do you remember? Did you say anything to Miss Livingston about being dressed up?"

"Oh no, I'd never do that. I did ask where she was going, though. I thought maybe she was visiting somebody special."

"What did she say? What did she say *exactly?*"

Daisy frowned in concentration. "She said, 'I have some things to do today, and I won't be home for luncheon.' "

"Was it unusual for her to be gone for lunch?"

"She'd sometimes go to visit a friend. She knows some ladies from her church. But not real often."

"And when she did go out, would she tell you or the other servants where she was going?"

"Yes, always," Daisy said, surprising herself again with the knowledge. "But not yesterday."

Frank nodded. "Daisy, would you help me by going through Miss Livingston's dresser drawers? Her personal things? You know what's supposed to be there, and you'll know if something's missing."

To his relief, Daisy hopped right up and scurried over to start her search.

"And let me know if you find anything that shouldn't be there, too."

"Like what?" she asked in alarm.

"Letters, books, jewelry, whatever. You said you know everything she has. If you see any-

20

thing you didn't know about, I need to see it."

She nodded and went to work.

Frank went to the nightstand and pulled out the top drawer. A slender packet of letters tied with a yellow ribbon lay there among the stray buttons and hairpins and other odds and ends of a young woman's life. They were addressed to Miss Livingston but at a post office box, in a distinctly masculine hand. He almost sighed with relief. An elopement then, with an unsuitable young man. At least there was a good chance they'd find her alive.

But when he picked up the packet, he found the small scraps of newspaper clippings beneath it, and he knew the young man might be far worse than just unsuitable.

"Oh, Mrs. Brandt, I don't know what to say." Mrs. Ellsworth had let her coffee grow cold in its cup while Sarah told her next-door neighbor about Frank Malloy's amazing good fortune and their plans to marry. "Except that I'm so very happy for you both. Or for all of you, I should say. My goodness, you'll have quite a family, won't you?"

"Yes, we will. Catherine is so happy that Mr. Malloy's son is going to be her brother."

"I'm sure she's happy that Mr. Malloy is going to be her father, too. She adores him so."

"Yes, she does." Sarah adored him, too, but she

supposed Mrs. Ellsworth had known this for a long time, so she didn't bother to mention it.

"Will Maeve be staying on?"

"Yes." They were sitting in Sarah's kitchen, the back door standing open to the late spring afternoon. Sarah got up to get the coffee pot off the stove. "She's especially excited that I'll finally be able to pay her wages for being Catherine's nursemaid."

"I guess you'll be able to adopt Catherine, too. I know it will be a relief to know she's legally your child."

Sarah topped off their cups. "Yes, it will. We've been through so much since I brought them both here from the Mission."

"You can probably . . . Oh dear!"

"What is it?" Sarah asked, setting the coffee pot back on the stove.

"I was going to say that you could probably find work for a few more of the girls from the Mission—what is it they're calling it now?"

"Daughters of Hope."

"That's right, and they probably have some more girls there like Maeve who could be maids or cooks or whatever, but . . ." She glanced meaningfully around Sarah's modest kitchen.

"Oh, I see. You're right, we don't exactly have room for servants' quarters here, do we?"

"Or even for Mr. Malloy and his son. Well, I suppose Mr. Malloy will share your room, and

22

Brian could share with Catherine, until they're a bit older at least, but you'll certainly be wanting a larger house very soon."

"We haven't really talked about it, but I guess you're right."

"And it would be selfish of you not to provide employment for a few servants. Heaven knows, there are far too many young people on the streets for lack of honest work as it is."

Sarah wondered if Malloy would agree. She'd grown up with servants, of course, but he'd had a far different life.

Mrs. Ellsworth sighed. "My goodness, I just realized that if you move, I won't be able to see the girls every day anymore."

"I hope you know you'll always be welcome, no matter where we might live. The girls would miss you terribly!" A lonely widow, Mrs. Ellsworth had been making sure Maeve and Catherine were learning everything they would need to know to run a household. Since Catherine was only four years old, the lessons hadn't been particularly advanced yet, but everyone had enjoyed them.

"Thank you for that, Mrs. Brandt, but it won't be quite the same if you aren't right here anymore, will it?"

"No, I suppose not."

Sarah hadn't realized how many people would be affected by the changes in their lives.

"And what about Mr. Malloy's job at the police

department? I don't imagine he'll continue to work there . . . or anyplace else for that matter. He'll be a gentleman of leisure, won't he?"

"That's something else we haven't really discussed. I mean, he won't have to earn his living anymore, but I can't see him spending his afternoons reading the newspapers at his club."

"But he won't be a police detective anymore, will he?"

Sarah sighed. "I don't see how he can. Once they find out, well . . ."

"Yes, I'm sure things will change for him," Mrs. Ellsworth said, sipping her warmed-up coffee. "No one would understand his wanting to work, and everyone would be jealous of his not having to. They would make him miserable."

"I hadn't thought of it that way, but I'm sure you're right."

"And he won't want you running around the city at all hours delivering babies either, will he? I never knew a man yet who didn't want his wife home in bed with him every night."

Sarah felt certain Frank Malloy would agree with that sentiment. "I can't live like my mother, though. I love her dearly, but I'll go insane if I have to spend my days visiting other rich ladies and trading gossip."

"Oh, I don't think you'll have time for visits and gossip, although I hope you'll think of me if you do," Mrs. Ellsworth added with a twinkle that made Sarah smile. "You've got your work at the Mission, and you'll probably have a few children of your own."

Yet another thing she and Malloy needed to discuss. She wasn't going to mention her concerns to Mrs. Ellsworth, though. "Yes, I'm sure I'll manage to keep busy. Now that I think of it, there are a lot of good works I'd do if I didn't have to worry about how to finance them."

"And now you're in that enviable position. How much longer do you think Mr. Malloy will be working for the police?"

"Until they find out, I suppose. He hasn't even told his mother yet."

"What!" Mrs. Ellsworth almost spilled her coffee. "What is he waiting for?"

"I don't know, but I suspect he's waiting until he hasn't got any other choice. The attorneys are still settling the estate, so Mr. Malloy doesn't actually have access to the money yet. I think he's a little superstitious and doesn't want to tell her until he knows for sure it's going to happen."

"So she doesn't know that you're engaged either?"

"Not yet. We're going to tell her together."

"I'd like to be a fly on the wall for that," Mrs. Ellsworth said with a smile.

Frank gingerly picked up the small scraps of newsprint. There were about a dozen of them, one column wide and a half-inch or so long, all clipped from the "lonely hearts" ads in a newspaper. A quick glance told him they represented the romantic yearnings of modest young men of comfortable means looking for respectable young ladies with matrimony in mind.

Maybe some of them actually were modest young men of comfortable means looking for a wife. The problem, of course, is that anyone could place a newspaper advertisement. No one checked to see if an advertiser was an upright young man or a rapist. Even if the newspapers made the individuals come in person to place their ads, no one could tell simply by looking at someone if he was a rapist. That would only become apparent when a young woman had placed her trust in the young man and let him take her someplace where her cries for help could not be heard.

Frank looked at the handful of ads. Which one had she answered? Perhaps all of them. He looked at the packet of letters. Which one had replied to her? There was only one way to find out.

He made his way over to the slipper chair, which he found remarkably uncomfortable for a man of his size.

"What have you got there?" Daisy asked from where she was leaning over a lower dresser drawer.

"Some letters I found in the nightstand."

"Miss Grace never got no letters."

"They're addressed to a post office box. Did you know she had a post office box?"

"I never heard of such a thing. Why would she need that?"

"To get letters she didn't want her father to know about, I expect."

"Miss Grace isn't like that. She . . . she'd never go behind her father's back."

She was trying to sound certain, but Frank heard the trace of doubt. "And still, here are the letters, addressed to her at a post office box."

Daisy looked as if she might cry. "You shouldn't be reading her letters."

"I know, but I've got to see who was writing to her. She might have gone to meet this person."

Frank laid the scraps of newsprint on the footstool and spread them out.

"What's that?" Daisy asked.

"Newspaper advertisements. Have you seen them before?"

"No! I never look at the newspaper. What would she be wanting with newspaper advertisements?"

"They're from young men who are looking for a wife."

"Pshaw! They ain't any such thing! Who would advertise in the newspaper for a wife?"

Frank chose one and held it up. "See for yourself."

She took it from his fingers as cautiously as if she feared it would burst into flames at any second. While she read it, Frank untied the yellow ribbon and checked the postmarks on the envelopes. They all seemed to be addressed in the same handwriting. At least he'd only have to locate one man.

"I never heard of such a thing," Daisy repeated when she'd finished. "If this fellow is as fine as he says, why can't he find a wife on his own?"

"Maybe because he's not as fine as he says."

"You mean he's lying?"

"I hope it won't shock you to find out that young men often lie when they're trying to impress a girl."

Daisy sniffed. "I know that, but to put it in the newspaper . . . it just ain't right."

Frank had to agree, but if he tried to arrest every bounder in the city, the jails would be full by nightfall. "Did Miss Livingston ever say anything about wanting to get married?"

"She's not a one for talking, at least not to us. She keeps herself to herself, if you know what I mean. I guess she's like every other girl who wants to have a husband and children, though, but she never complained."

"Did she have many suitors?"

"Oh no, sir. Not Miss Grace. She's . . . well, she's a plain-looking girl, and she doesn't do anything to make herself prettier."

"I could tell that by her clothes."

Daisy nodded, gratified to find someone who agreed with her on this subject. "Not that she'd ever be a beauty, but she could fix her hair and wear prettier clothes. So, what's in them letters?"

"I have to read them first," he said, and started to do just that, beginning with the oldest one.

Dear Miss Livingston, it began in a firm masculine script. *Thank you for being so kind as to answer my advertisement. There is no need for you to apologize for what you called your lack of beauty. As I said, I care nothing for that. I am seeking a wife who possesses the virtues of honesty and a pure heart. I can tell from your letter that you do.* It went on to explain that he was nothing much to look at himself and that he hoped she would not find him too unattractive. He mentioned her virtues a few more times and then asked her to write again if she was interested in learning more about him.

Apparently, she had. His next letter told her all about his family (sadly, all dead now, and how convenient), and the prosperous business he had inherited from his father, although he never actually mentioned the nature of the business. Her reply to his first letter must have told him about her family and situation as well, because he asked several questions. He wanted to know if she got along well with her father and if she had any other close family in the city.

29

Frank didn't like this one bit. The next letter carried on the same interrogation, asking more personal questions. The fellow never crossed the line into anything inappropriate, but if she'd answered all his inquiries, then he knew an awful lot about her. Had she told him her father was well-to-do? That he'd provide a dowry? And was this fellow interested in a dowry or a ransom?

The last letter was about what Frank had expected. This fellow suggested that they meet in a park, in a very public place. He wanted her to feel comfortable, he said. If they got on well, perhaps she would consider having lunch with him at a nearby restaurant. He would be wearing a brown suit with a yellow handkerchief in his breast pocket. If she didn't like his looks, she could walk on by, and he would never know who she was.

Not likely, Frank thought. A young woman in that situation would be anxious and excited and looking at every man in the park. She'd be easy to pick out of the crowd, so if she turned out to be too shy to approach him, he would approach her. And Frank had a feeling this man wasn't as homely as he made out. Probably, he was at least presentable, so when he did speak to the young lady, she'd admit she was the one he was to meet. He would be charming, too, quick with a compliment and never at a loss for words.

Where would he take her then? Not to a

restaurant, Frank was certain. Or at least that's not where they'd end up. He'd closed the letter with a suggestion that they arrange to meet at eleven-thirty yesterday, the day Grace Livingston had gone off wearing her Sunday best and expecting to have luncheon out.

When he'd stuffed the last letter back into its envelope, he looked up to find Daisy watching him warily. "What did it say?"

"Do you know anyone named Milo Pendergast?"

She scowled, chewing her bottom lip. "No. Is that his name? The fellow from the newspaper?"

"That's the name he signed to the letters."

"Did he say where he lives? Did she go there? Is that where she is?"

"No." Frank gathered up the letters and the clippings and pushed himself out of the chair. "Keep looking through her things. Take the bedclothes off the bed and turn the mattress up. Look everywhere, and if you find anything that doesn't belong, let me know."

Frank was pretty sure she wouldn't find anything else, but that would keep her busy. He went back downstairs, where he found Mr. Livingston in a room that must have been his study. A large leather armchair sat near the fire, and bookshelves lined the walls. Livingston was standing by a window, staring out as if he could make his daughter come down the street by the simple force of his will.

"Mr. Livingston?"

He jumped slightly, but his expression lifted a bit when he saw Frank in the doorway. "Did you find something?"

Frank made him sit down before giving him the letters to read. While he did, Frank looked through the clippings again, trying to figure out which one she'd answered. The solution turned out to be embarrassingly simple. Each ad gave a box number in care of the newspaper to which interested ladies could reply. The newspaper would then forward the replies or else the man would go to the newspaper office to pick up his mail. Frank simply had to match up the box number on the return address to figure out which ad was Milo Pendergast's.

Miss Livingston had obtained a box at the post office, probably, as he'd told Daisy, so her father wouldn't know what she was doing and perhaps also to protect her from harassment if one of the men with whom she corresponded got too eager in his pursuit.

She hadn't given him her address, but she'd gone to meet him in person and had probably gone off alone with him somewhere or else she would have come home yesterday, safe and sound.

"I don't understand," her father said when he'd finished the last letter. "She never said a word to me about this. I know she was disappointed not to be married by now, but this is so . . . so unlike her!"

"You do understand that she probably went off to meet this man yesterday, and since she didn't come home, we have to assume she is still with him."

"With him? Dear God, you mean he kept her overnight? He seduced her?"

Seduced wasn't the word Frank would have used, but it would do. "It seems likely. I'm going to go to this park and see if anyone saw them there. Do you have a picture of Miss Livingston that I can show?"

"What? Oh, yes, of course." He crossed to where a desk sat against the far wall and picked up a picture frame. He stared down at the photograph for a long moment. "If he's harmed her in any way . . ."

"We'll find her, Mr. Livingston." Frank took the picture from him. "Send word to me at Police Headquarters if you hear from her or if she returns."

"Do you think she will? That she'll return, I mean?"

The desperate hope in his face made Frank want to wince, but he only said, "We'll find her."

Frank just hoped they would find her alive.

2

The "park" was one of the small patches of green found tucked here and there in the city. Not even large enough to have a name, it served as a place for children to run around or courting couples to sit for a while. When Frank arrived, he saw a nursemaid—a plump Irish girl in a starched uniform—push a baby buggy over to one of the weathered benches and sit down.

He strolled over and glanced at the sleeping infant. "Cute little fellow."

"It's a girl, and she's got a face that would stop a clock. Lucky for her, her da's got money." The maid smiled, showing gapped front teeth. "I never saw you here before."

"I've never been here before," Frank said, trying his hand at flirting. He was more than a little rusty. "Do you come here a lot?"

"And what's it to you if I do?" she countered with a smile that told him she was flirting back.

"Nothing at all, but I wondered if you'd ever seen a friend of mine here. He told me it was a good place to meet a lady."

"I don't think you'd meet many *ladies* here, but if you're looking for a *girl,* you've already met one."

"So I have. I guess Milo was right."

"Milo? Is that his name?"

"Yes. Nice-looking fellow. Wears a brown suit with a yellow handkerchief in his pocket."

"Oh, him," she sniffed.

The faintest hope flickered in his chest. "You know him, then?"

"I've seen him. Can't say I know him. He's too good for the likes of me."

"What makes you so sure?"

"Because he said so."

Frank didn't have to feign his astonishment.

"Yeah, I was that put out with him myself," she went on. "I just tried a little friendly conversation, and he told me to be on my way and not to bother him. He had bigger fish to fry."

"He told you that?" Frank could hardly believe his luck.

"About the fish? Not right out like that, but I took his meaning pretty quick. Wasn't but a few minutes later some woman comes up, and he's making over her like she's the Queen of Sheba or something."

Frank swallowed down his desperation and managed to sound just mildly interested. "When was this?"

"Oh, a month or two ago. Maybe longer. He's not a very nice man, your friend."

"He treated you badly."

"Oh, I don't mean how he treated me. I mean he's always with a different woman. I've seen him here at least three times, and each time some woman comes up and it's the same thing."

Frank thumbed his bowler hat back as if astonished to hear this about his friend. "That devil! He never let on he was a ladies' man."

"That's not what I'd call him. More like a rotter, if you ask me."

"Were you here yesterday?"

"Yesterday? No, I wasn't."

Frank managed to hide his disappointment. Still . . . He pulled the picture out of his coat pocket. "Have you ever seen her before?"

She stiffened instantly. "Hey, what's this about?"

"This young lady was supposed to meet that fellow Milo here yesterday, and she's gone missing."

"The devil you say! I knew he was a rotter." She peered closely at Grace Livingston's photograph. "Never saw her before, but she looks like the rest. They're all of a piece."

"What do you mean?"

"I mean they're just like little Ethel here." She cocked her thumb in the direction of the buggy. "They'll need a da with a lot of money if they want to catch a husband."

Frank glanced at Grace Livingston's photograph before shoving it back into his pocket. She was right, of course. Grace wouldn't turn anyone's head. "Do you know where he takes them?"

"You're no friend of his, then?"

"No, I'm with the police."

"Gor, the police! I never!"

She looked like she might jump up and start running. Frank put his hands up in surrender. "I'm not after you. Her family wants her back is all. Do you know where he takes them when they leave here?"

She shrugged and got to her feet. She wouldn't want anything to do with the police. "I don't know. All I ever saw was him sitting and talking with 'em. Did you say she didn't come home last night?"

"I said she's missing."

"That'd be like him. Keep a girl for a day or two, ruin her right proper, and then cut her loose."

"You know that for sure?"

"Me? I don't know nothing about him, and I don't want to." She grabbed the handle of the buggy and shoved it into motion. He let her go.

He'd have to come back tomorrow morning if Grace didn't show up before then. He'd see who was usually here at that time. Maybe someone would remember. He started walking. Maybe Pendergast did take them to a restaurant. They wouldn't go far with him, he was sure, so it would have to be someplace close. Maybe someone would remember.

Frank showed Grace's photograph at four places before he got a nibble. The proprietor of the tea shop took Grace's picture over to the front window to get a better look.

"I think that's her," he said. He was a slender, middle-aged man with a carefully groomed mustache. "I didn't pay much attention. She's not one you'd look at twice is she?" He handed the photograph back to Frank.

"She's a respectable young woman," Frank said.

"I can see that, but she's no beauty. I might not've remembered at all if you hadn't mentioned him. The yellow handkerchief, I remembered that."

"Has he been in here before?"

"Oh, yeah, he comes in from time to time. Always with a different girl."

"Do you know who he is?"

"His name you mean? No, never heard it, and I don't have much reason to ask, now, do I? He orders his food and pays for it. I've got no complaints."

Frank glanced around. Only two tables were currently occupied by groups of ladies gossiping over tea and cakes. "Do you keep this place by yourself?"

"My wife helps."

"Is she here?"

He shrugged. "She's always here, same as me."

"Can I speak to her?"

"She won't know any more than I do."

Frank didn't want to frighten the man because he'd probably stop cooperating completely, but he did give him a hard stare that sent him scurrying to the back to fetch his wife.

She came out wiping her hands on her apron and frowning. "What's this all about? We run a decent place here."

"I'm sure you do," Frank said, trying his smile on her. She didn't smile back.

"He wants to know about that fellow with the yellow handkerchief," her husband said.

"Mr. Pendergast?" she asked.

Frank bit his cheek so he wouldn't smile at her husband's surprise. "How do you know his name?" the husband asked.

"How do you think? He told me," she sniffed. "What do you want to know about him?"

"Your husband said he was in here yesterday with this young lady." Frank handed her the photograph.

She squinted at it and shook her head. "Never saw her. But I'm usually busy with the cooking."

"Your husband said he comes in regularly with different young ladies."

"Yes, and I'm not surprised. He's a charmer, that one," she said. "Always quick with a compliment. A woman can always do with a compliment, you know, even if she knows it's a lie."

Frank would have to remember that. "Do you by any chance know where he lives?"

"Lives? Not hardly. Someplace close, I'd think, though."

"What makes you say that?"

She had to think about this. "Just an impression, I guess. I heard him ask one of the girls if she'd like to meet his mother. Then they got up and left. I got a feeling they were going to walk, so it wouldn't be too far, would it?"

"Do you remember which direction they went?"

She shook her head. "Not hardly. It was a while ago, and I'm too busy here to pay attention to where customers go when they leave here, aren't I?"

"They went that way," her husband said, pointing down the street.

"Are you sure?" Frank asked.

"Yeah, I just remembered. He left before I gave him his change. I had to run after him."

Frank thanked them for their trouble and stepped back outside, peering down the street in the direction the man had indicated, as if he could make Pendergast appear. Of course, he couldn't, and even if he could, Frank wouldn't even know him without his yellow handkerchief.

He slipped the photograph back into his pocket and headed over to Newspaper Row.

Luckily, the Livingstons only subscribed to the *World*, so Frank thought the odds were good

Grace had found Pendergast's ad in that paper. Of course, New York had lots of newspapers, and newsboys hawked newspapers on every corner in the city. She might have picked up any of them, but maybe he'd be lucky.

The advertising department of the newspaper was a busy place, with several clerks dealing with customers who had come in to place an ad. A few minutes of observation told Frank most of the customers had no idea what they wanted, so the clerks had to spend a lot of time with each one of them, getting the ad copy down just right. No wonder the line was so long.

Frank quickly lost his patience and asked for the supervisor, earning disgruntled glares from customers who had been waiting much longer than he had. A glimpse of his badge sent the clerk running for his boss, and Frank returned the disgruntled glares of the customers until they found something else to stare at.

An officious man wearing wire-rimmed spectacles and abundant side whiskers appeared at the counter. "May I help you?"

Frank pulled the handful of newspaper clippings from his pocket and laid them on the counter. "Are these from your newspaper?"

He frowned, then adjusted his spectacles and peered at the tiny scraps of paper. He quickly separated them into two groups. "These are," he said, indicating one pile. "And these are not."

"How can you tell?"

"We use a particular style with our lonely hearts advertisements. Other newspapers try to copy it, but I can still tell which are ours."

Frank was happy to see that Pendergast's ads were from the *World*. He separated them from the others. "Can you tell me who placed these ads?"

His frown deepened. "May I ask what this is about?"

"Sure, but I don't have to tell you."

He pulled himself up to his full height. "The people who place these advertisements with us rely on our discretion. We only identify each client by a box number so they may remain anonymous to any individuals whose acquaintance they do not wish to make. How do I know you aren't just a lovesick swain who wants to force his attentions on some unwilling female?"

Frank sighed in exasperation. "Do I look like a lovesick swain?"

"How can I possibly judge? You are becoming angry, which I assure you is an indication of thwarted desire."

Frank definitely felt as if his desires were being thwarted, but he took a firm hand on his temper and said, "If you will look closely at the ads in question, you'll see they are seeking *female* companionship. And just so you understand how serious this is, a young woman who answered these ads and had arranged to meet the man who placed them is missing."

"Missing?"

"Yes, which means that at least one person placing ads in your newspaper is using them to kidnap women."

The fellow swallowed. "You . . . you have no way of knowing . . . I mean, she might have eloped. That's hardly kidnapping."

"If she eloped, then no harm done, but either way, she's got a family who wants to find her. Now get me the name and address of the person who placed these ads."

By now the other clerks had all stopped serving their customers to listen to what Frank was telling their supervisor. Which was fine, because all the customers were listening, too. The nearest clerk snatched up one of the ads and read it. "It's Tom," he told the others, drawing a chuckle or two from the half dozen clerks.

"You know him?" Frank asked.

"Oh, we know him all right," the clerk holding the ad said. "He's in here about every week to pick up his love letters."

"What's his name? Tom what?" Frank asked, pulling out his notebook and pencil.

"Tom Cat," he said, drawing snickers from the other clerks. "At least that's what we call him. Always looking for a new pussy to warm his bed."

"That's enough, Kirk," the supervisor said,

silencing the snickers instantly. "Get this gentleman the name and address of this man."

The clerks exchanged some furtive glances. "That's just it. We don't know his name. Well, we do know the name he uses, because the letters that come in are addressed to him."

"Milo Pendergast," Frank said.

"How'd you know?" the clerk asked in surprise.

"But you don't think that's his real name?" Frank said.

"Do you? It don't sound real, at least. And we don't have an address because he didn't want the letters forwarded. He always comes to pick them up and pay for his ads."

"How do you know which letters are his?"

"Everybody who places an ad gets a box number, so we know which letters go to which box. Most people give us an address, and we forward the letters to them, but not this Milo fellow. He says he doesn't trust the mail or something."

Frank managed not to sigh again. This Milo Pendergast, or whatever his name was, had turned out to be smarter than Frank had imagined. "How often does he come in? You said every week." If he came on a particular day, then . . .

"We put his ad in the paper once a week, but he comes in whenever he feels like it, I guess. Sometimes he comes every couple days and sometimes not for a couple of weeks."

Probably, Frank thought, it depended on whether he'd successfully lured a woman into "meeting his mother." Frank pulled out a card and laid it on the counter. "Let me know the next time this fellow picks up his mail. But don't tell him somebody is looking for him."

The supervisor picked up his card and gave the other clerks a baleful glare. "No one will say anything to him, and I'll notify you immediately if we see him. Now everyone, back to work. We have customers waiting."

Frank glanced around to see all the customers staring in gaping amazement. He wondered if any of them were here to place a lonely hearts ad.

Sarah was relaxing in the kitchen while Maeve and Catherine prepared their dinner. She watched fondly as Maeve patiently instructed Catherine on each step as they carefully stirred flour into the meat drippings to make gravy for the pot roast they'd just pulled out of the oven.

The sound of someone knocking on the front door stopped all three of them.

"I hope it's not a baby," Catherine said.

As a professional midwife, Sarah knew she should hope it *was* a baby, but she couldn't help thinking how little she wanted to leave just now. "I'll get it," she told the girls.

She hurried out of the kitchen, into the front room that served as her office, then through it to the front hallway. By then she'd seen the familiar silhouette through the glass, and she was already smiling when she pulled the door open.

"Malloy," she said.

He was through the door and pushing it closed before she could blink. "Quick, kiss me before the girls come," he whispered.

She did.

They had three or four delicious minutes before their silence alerted the girls that the caller wasn't someone summoning Sarah to a delivery. The clatter of tiny shoes running across the floor signaled them in time for Frank and Sarah to be standing demurely apart when Catherine launched herself at Malloy. He picked her up, and she threw her slender arms around his neck.

"I'm so happy you came!" she said.

"I am, too," Malloy said, giving Sarah a wink over Catherine's shoulder.

"We're just putting supper on the table, Mr. Malloy," Maeve said. "I hope you can stay."

"Did you cook it?" he asked Catherine.

She nodded vigorously.

"Then of course I'll stay. What are we having?"

"Pot roast," Catherine informed him.

"My favorite!"

"Why don't you and Mrs. Brandt sit down out here, and we'll call you when everything is ready," Maeve said. "Catherine, you and I can set the table."

When the girls were gone, Malloy got another kiss before they settled into the chairs by the front window. "I'm so happy you're here," Sarah said, "but I always feel guilty keeping you from Brian."

"I hardly ever got home for supper before, so he doesn't really expect to see me, and my mother would probably die of shock if I got home early. I'll see him before he goes to bed. And you don't have to feel guilty tonight, because I'm here on business."

"Police business?" she asked with open skepticism.

"Of course police business. I need you to write a lonely hearts letter for me."

"A what?"

"A lonely hearts letter. In answer to one of the lonely hearts advertisements in the newspaper."

"I don't think so, Mr. Malloy. One fiancé at a time is all I can handle, I'm afraid."

He smiled at that. "It's for a case I'm working on. A young woman has gone missing, and she'd been answering those ads. I think she went off to meet somebody yesterday, and she never came home."

"Do you think she eloped?"

"I wish I did. So far, I've found out that this fellow she was supposed to meet has been seen with several other females, and he places his ad every week."

"He doesn't sound like he's really looking for a wife, does he?"

"No, and whatever happened to this young woman, I don't think marriage was involved."

"How awful for her."

"Her father is very worried, as you can imagine, and the longer she's gone, the less likely it is that she'll ever come home."

"Wouldn't the newspaper be able to tell you who placed the ads?"

"They know who he is, but they don't know his real name or where he lives. He goes to the newspaper office to pay for the ads and to pick up his mail. They assign each advertiser a box number and either forward the mail or hold it until the advertiser comes in to get it."

"Couldn't you have someone wait at the newspaper office until he comes in?"

"He doesn't come in on a regular schedule, so we can't predict when he might show up, and the city of New York isn't going to pay an officer to just sit there for days, waiting."

"But if a young woman's life is in danger . . ."

"We don't know that for sure. She might really have eloped. Besides, she's just one girl in a city full of thousands of them."

"Sounds like you already asked."

"I did. So my next idea is to write to this fellow and try to set up a meeting with him."

"And you need my help for that?"

"Of course I do. I don't have any idea what a lonely spinster would say to a potential husband."

"And you think I do?"

Apparently, he knew better than to answer that. "And it needs to be in a woman's handwriting."

"I can do that part, at least."

"I don't think it makes much difference what you write, in any case. Tell him you're lonely and not much to look at. I think that's what Miss Livingston said, and that seemed to do the trick for him."

"He's easy to please."

"That's what worries me. According to his replies to Miss Livingston's letters, he says he doesn't care about physical beauty. He just wants a woman who is beautiful inside."

"Oh my."

"That's exactly what I thought. What man wants a homely woman?"

Sarah gave him a disapproving glare that he didn't seem to understand. "But every woman wants to be appreciated for who she is, not what she looks like. He's obviously made a study of how to appeal to females."

"But why? I can understand if he just wants to seduce as many of them as he can, but what does he do with them when he's finished?"

"None of the possibilities are good, are they?"

"No. Even if he just turns them loose, many of them would be too ashamed to go home again."

"We definitely need to find this man and stop him," Sarah said.

Catherine came running from the kitchen and skidded to a halt at Malloy's knee. "Supper is ready," she told him.

"About time, too," he replied, scooping her up as he rose to his feet.

She giggled. "When are you going to come live with us and be my papa?"

"Soon, I hope," he replied, smiling at Sarah.

Sarah hoped so, too.

Supper was a preview of the life that lay ahead of them, Sarah thought as she watched Malloy teasing Catherine and Maeve and making them laugh. Someday their supper would be like this every evening.

"Would you girls mind washing the dishes tonight?" Sarah asked as they were finishing their meal. "Mr. Malloy needs my help with something."

"Can I help, too?" Catherine asked.

"Can you write a letter for me?" Malloy asked quite seriously.

"I can make a C. That's the letter my name starts with. Maeve teached me to do it."

"That's very good," Malloy said, still perfectly serious, "but I need someone who can write the kind of letters that come in the mail."

"Oh. I can't do that."

"Then you can help me with the dishes,"

Maeve said, "and your mama will help Mr. Malloy."

Plainly, Catherine found this less than satisfactory, but she conceded with good grace.

Sarah and Malloy returned to her office, where she found some stationery in her desk and sat down to draft her letter. It was still unfinished, the page marked with many scribbled revisions, when Maeve and Catherine emerged from the kitchen.

"What on earth are you doing?" Maeve asked.

Sarah looked up from where she was hunched over the paper. Malloy sat in a chair on the other side of the desk, frowning in frustration.

"We're trying to write a letter in reply to a lonely hearts advertisement," Sarah said.

"It's for a case I'm working on," Malloy added with a glance at Catherine. They never talked about unpleasant things in front of the child if at all possible.

"Is Mr. Malloy being much help to you?" Maeve asked Sarah.

Sarah smiled as sweetly as she could manage. "Not a bit."

"Maybe I can, then," Maeve said.

"How many lonely hearts ads have you answered?" Malloy scoffed.

"None, but if it involves lying, I'll probably be a lot better at it than Mrs. Brandt."

"You shouldn't tell lies, Maeve," Catherine said.

Maeve ruffled her hair. "You're right, but I was just teasing. I meant I'd make up a story, like the ones in your books."

"What a wonderful idea," Sarah said, jumping to her feet. "I'll take Catherine upstairs, and you can help Mr. Malloy." She shot Malloy an apologetic smile and made her escape with Catherine before anyone could stop her.

Frank watched them go as Maeve took Sarah's vacant seat behind the desk.

She folded her hands like a model schoolgirl and looked him straight in the eye. "Now tell me what this is all about."

Frank sighed, knowing resistance was useless. He explained everything he'd learned about Grace Livingston's disappearance. Maeve glanced over the newspaper clippings of Milo Pendergast's advertisements and his replies to Grace Livingston's letters.

"This fellow is a monster," she said.

"Yes, he is, and I intend to stop him, but first I've got to find him. The letter has to make him think you're somebody like Grace Livingston, somebody lonely and desperate."

"I think I should mention I've got a little money put by, too."

"What? Why?"

"He probably tries to relieve these ladies of their fortunes in addition to their virtue. If he doesn't, he's not as smart as we think he is, so if he thinks I've got some money and that I'm alone in the world, he might come after me quicker. We want him to answer my letter first, don't we? Before he considers somebody else? If he advertises every week, he must get a lot of letters, and judging by how many letters he wrote Grace, it took a few weeks for him to warm her up before he asked her to meet him. I don't think you want to wait that long, do you?"

"No, I don't."

"Well, then, let's see how desperate I can sound. How will you get this to him?"

"The newspaper holds the letters for him until he picks them up."

"You don't want to put it in the mail, then. That will take at least an extra day. Will they put it right in his box if you take it to the newspaper office tomorrow?"

"I don't know why not."

"Good, then I'll explain why I didn't want to wait for the mail." She picked up the pencil Sarah had discarded.

"Don't you want to look at what Mrs. Brandt wrote first?"

She gave him a pitying look, then went to work, her pencil scratching confidently across the paper. She paused a few times to consider her work, then continued. After a very few minutes, she handed him the paper. "What do you think?"

She hadn't crossed out a single thing, he

noticed. *Dear Sir,* it began. *I hope you don't think me unseemly for having delivered my letter in person, but I did not trust the mail to get it to you in good time. Please do not think me forward, but I find myself at the mercy of others. After my dear mother's death several months ago, I have been left completely alone in the city. I want for nothing, as my parents provided for me, but my mother's sister does not think it wise for a female to live alone. She is coming in a fortnight to fetch me. She wishes me to live with her and my uncle out in the country. She claims to have only my best interests at heart, but I fear she only wants control over my legacy. If I could but introduce her to my fiancé when she arrives, I could escape her clutches. I should very much like to make your acquaintance to see if we might suit. I long to hear from you soon.*

Frank looked up to find Maeve smiling at him. "You are amazing."

"Being raised by a grifter has its advantages," she said.

"Your grandfather trained you well."

"He did that. Like I said, I'm a much better liar than Mrs. Brandt."

Frank studied the handwriting. "I'm thinking I should have Mrs. Brandt copy it over. Your handwriting looks too young."

"Good idea. Also, what name do you want to use?"

Frank hadn't given that any thought at all. "What do you suggest?"

"Who's going to meet this fellow?"

"Nobody! I'm not going to put any more women in danger."

"Then how are you going to catch him?"

"I figured we'd wait until he shows up at the meeting place and then grab him."

"How will you know it's him?"

"He'll have a yellow handkerchief in his pocket or some such thing."

Maeve frowned. "And what if he doesn't put the handkerchief in his pocket until he's sure everything is on the up and up? What if he walks by the park and sees a bunch of plug-uglies waiting to grab him and keeps on going?"

"What do you mean, plug-uglies?" Frank asked, affronted.

"You know what I mean. Coppers. A fellow like him can probably spot one a mile away in the dark. If he doesn't see a nervous-looking female waiting for him, he's not going to stop, you mark my words. He might already be a little spooked because this one looks too easy, so he's not going to take any chances. If he's taking advantage of these women, seducing them, and then doing heaven-knows-what with them after, he's learned how to be real careful."

"I'll find somebody."

"I can do it."

"You're too young."

"I can make myself look older. Besides, being young means I don't have much sense. He'll think he can fool me real easy."

"I'm not going to put you in danger."

"No, you're not. You're going to have a bunch of plug-uglies hanging around the neighborhood to follow me. And if you think I'm going into a house with him, you're crazy, so don't worry about that!"

"Maeve, I can't let you do this."

"I'll need a nice dress. Maybe Mrs. Decker can loan me something."

Frank had the sinking feeling he was losing control of the situation. "You can't tell Sarah's mother about this."

"Then you can buy me something. What address will you give for him to answer? We don't have time to get a post office box like this Livingston girl did."

"We're not using this address," Frank said.

"Of course not, but who, then? Not Mrs. Decker's. Her neighborhood's too good. Not yours, because it's not good enough. This would be perfect, except—"

"I told you—"

"Mrs. Ellsworth! She's right next door, and she'd be happy to get the letters for us, and if he goes to her house, he'll find out no young woman lives there, so no one's in danger."

"I don't want her involved either," Frank tried, but Maeve was already on her feet.

"I'll tell Mrs. Brandt to come down and copy the letter."

She was gone long enough that he knew she'd told Sarah her plans, so he wouldn't have a chance to convince her otherwise. Sarah came back alone.

"She's right about using Mrs. Ellsworth's address, you know," Sarah said before she'd even sat down again.

"At least leave your mother out of it," he said. "You can buy Maeve a dress."

"She'll need a hat and gloves and shoes. It might look funny if everything is brand-new, though."

"Wouldn't a girl buy new clothes to meet her future husband?" he asked in desperation.

"I suppose. We'll think about it. My mother's clothes would be too old for her anyway. Let me see what she wrote."

In the end, Frank walked out of Sarah's house with Maeve's letter, copied over in Sarah's handwriting, with Mrs. Ellsworth's return address on it, and signed *Sarah Smith*.

Maybe, he thought as he walked off into the springtime dusk, Grace Livingston had come home today. He'd stop by her house on his way to the newspaper in the morning in hopes of finding her safe and sound.

3

"How exciting!" Mrs. Ellsworth said when Sarah had explained the plan to her over coffee the next morning. "I'm happy to help. That poor young woman. I can't imagine how terrified her father must be. I'll do whatever I can to bring her safely home."

"I know you will, but you must be careful. We don't want to put you in any danger."

"Oh, pooh. What danger could I be in? No one is interested in an old woman like me."

Sarah frowned. "We don't know much about this fellow, but he could be violent, and if he came to your house looking for someone, he might not want to believe he had the wrong house."

"He's not going to come to my house. Someone might see him. He'll meet Maeve in a park like he did all the others."

"You're probably right, but just in case, you shouldn't open the door to anyone you don't know, especially when you're home alone."

Mrs. Ellsworth smiled at that. "I'm hardly ever home at all! I'm usually here with you and the girls. Which reminds me: Would you and Mr. Malloy be willing to live in this neighborhood if you could find a suitable house?"

Sarah had no idea how to answer a question like that, especially because Mrs. Ellsworth was all too easily encouraged to interfere in their lives. "We really haven't had time to think about where we want to live, I'm afraid."

"You need to think about it, then. I'm sure he doesn't want to remain engaged forever, and you'll never fit him and his boy into this place. And what about his mother?"

Sarah suddenly felt a little dizzy. "His *mother?*"

Mrs. Ellsworth nodded knowingly. "Those Irish mothers never want to give up their sons, you know."

Sarah *didn't* know. She suddenly realized she knew very little indeed about Irish mothers. "I've never noticed Mrs. Malloy being overly fond of her son."

"And what about her grandson? She's been taking care of him since he was born. And didn't you say she takes him to school every day?"

Fortunately, Maeve and Catherine chose that moment to join them in the kitchen. Mrs. Ellsworth had found some strawberries at the Gansevoort Market that morning, and she was going to help the girls make a strawberry short-cake.

Sarah was looking forward to eating the first of the summer fruits. Maybe Malloy would stop by later to enjoy it with them.

● ● ●

Frank regretted stopping at the Livingston house the instant the front door opened. Mr. Livingston himself stood there in his shirtsleeves, looking as if he hadn't slept all night. For a second, hope lighted his eyes, but then he saw Frank's expression, and it died instantly, leaving behind the kind of black despair Frank had seen all too often in his career with the police.

"You haven't found her." He stood back so Frank could enter.

"And I don't guess you've heard anything from her."

"Not a word." Livingston pushed the door shut and sighed.

"Can I speak with you privately?" Frank asked, glancing at the servants clustered anxiously at the end of the hall.

Livingston led him into the front parlor and closed the door behind them. "You've found out something."

"I found out this Milo fellow places an ad in the *World* every week, and he's met other women in the park where he probably met Grace."

"Dear God."

"Yes, well, that probably also means he lets them go when he's finished with them."

Livingston groaned and slapped both hands over his face. "My poor Grace."

"I have a plan to catch him," Frank explained

60

before Livingston could fall into complete despair. "I've had a letter written to him that I hope will draw his interest, and when he arranges to meet with the young woman who wrote it, we'll follow him back to wherever he takes her."

Hope bloomed again in Livingston's red-rimmed eyes. "Do you think it will work?"

"It has to. I'm going to take the letter over to the newspaper office this morning. Then we'll have to wait for him to answer. That may take some time."

"And Grace may come home before that."

Frank thought that unlikely, but he said, "Yes, she might. But even if she does, we'll go ahead with our plan. We need to stop him."

"Yes, of course. We can't let him continue to prey on innocent girls, can we?"

"No, we can't. If you hear from Grace, send me word at Police Headquarters. I'll let you know if we hear from this Milo."

A few minutes later, Frank made his escape. He hated giving Mr. Livingston false hope, but whatever happened, he'd need time to grow accutomed to it. Even if Frank managed to rescue the girl, she'd never be the same. No woman ever was after something like that.

On that thought, he headed down the street toward the El. He'd drop the letter off at the newspaper, then stop by the park to see if anyone there this morning remembered seeing Grace Livingston.

Apparently, not many people got up early to place advertisements in the newspaper, Frank observed, walking straight up to the counter, where only one lone customer conferred with a clerk. The other clerks were working at the desks lined up behind the counter, and only one looked up when he rapped on the counter to get their attention.

"It's the copper," the clerk said, springing to his feet and hurrying over. The others followed, coming close so they wouldn't miss a word. "Did you find him yet?"

"Is your boss in?"

"Mr. Snodgrass!" the clerk called, and the prim little man emerged from an office located back behind the desks. "That copper is back."

Frank resisted the urge to grab the fellow by the lapels and teach him some manners.

"May I help you?" Snodgrass asked a little breathlessly. "Have you found him yet?"

"No, and I'll never find him if this is how your people are going to act when he shows up." Frank gestured to the gaggle of clerks unabashedly listening to every word.

"Get back to work," Snodgrass snapped, sending them scurrying to their desks again. "I apologize, Mr. Malloy."

"You'll have to do more than that. A young

woman's life is at stake here, maybe more than one. If your clerks let Pendergast know somebody is looking for him, we'll never see him or the girl again."

"They won't say a word to him, I promise you," Snodgrass said, his face flushing with outrage.

"They don't have to say a word. All they have to do is stare at him the way they're staring at me right now."

Snodgrass jerked his head around and caught them all hastily getting back to work. "I will make sure that—"

"Don't bother. I want to speak to whoever is in charge."

"I'm the editor of the advertising—"

"No, I mean who's in charge of the whole paper. Is Pulitzer in?"

"Good heavens, you can't expect to—"

"I can expect to have your job if you don't let me speak to somebody in charge." The threat was meaningless, but Snodgrass had no way of knowing that.

A few minutes and several whispered conversations later, Frank was escorted to a plush office on one of the upper floors of the enormous building. The office was so far from the presses in the basement, he couldn't even feel their rumble anymore.

"Now what's this they're telling me about a woman being kidnapped?" the well-dressed man behind the huge, shiny desk demanded. It wasn't Pulitzer, who was in Europe, but one of his underlings, Brisbane.

Frank told him how Milo Pendergast had used the newspaper to lure young women and how he had recently taken Grace Livingston.

"And what am I supposed to do about it? I run a newspaper. I can't control what people do when they advertise."

Frank sat back in the comfortable leather chair provided for visitors and gazed out the large windows at the city below. "Well, now, Mr. Brisbane, I was going to suggest that if you got your staff to cooperate, I'd give you an exclusive on the story of how we rescued an innocent woman from the clutches of a fiend. But now I'm thinking you might not want anybody to know this Pendergast used your newspaper to kidnap young females."

"I most certainly would not! People would stop advertising with us altogether!"

Frank nodded, hoping he looked thoughtful and not as angry as he felt. "I'm also thinking that every other newspaper in town *would* want that story. They'd probably run it on the front page, how this evil seducer of women used the *World* to trap his helpless victims but their editors wouldn't lift a finger to help catch him."

Brisbane turned an unbecoming shade of purple. "You wouldn't dare!"

"I know lots of reporters, Mr. Brisbane. In fact, they camp out in the building right across from Police Headquarters every day. I could just shout out the window, and they'd all come running."

For a minute, Frank thought Brisbane might be choking on his own bile, but when he could speak again, he said, "What do you want me to do?"

Less than an hour later, Frank left the imposing *World* building, confident that several of Brisbane's most trusted editors would be spending their days in the advertising department to make sure no one noticed Milo Pendergast when he finally showed up to collect his mail. As a bonus, he had also extracted a promise that Maeve's letter would be the only one found in Pendergast's box whenever he did finally show up.

Now all he had to do was wait.

Frank had no luck in the park, so he returned to Police Headquarters to report in and find something else to fill his time while he waited for Milo Pendergast to pick up his mail.

Tom, the doorman at Police Headquarters, gave Frank an uncharacteristically stiff smile in response to his "Good morning."

"Is something wrong?" Frank asked.

"Oh no, sir. Everything's fine." But he didn't quite meet Frank's eye.

Still puzzled by Tom's odd behavior, Frank

strolled into the lobby. Ignoring the newly arrested felons on the benches lining the walls, he nodded to the desk sergeant and headed for the stairs.

"Malloy!"

Frank turned back to the desk sergeant. "What is it?"

"Chief O'Brien wants to see you."

This was not an unusual request, but suddenly the hairs on the back of his neck prickled and the very air in the room seemed to quiver with expectation. Frank glanced around and realized every cop within sight had stopped what he was doing to stare at him.

They knew.

Slowly, as eagerly as he would have climbed the scaffold steps to his own execution, Frank climbed the stairs to the second floor and the office of the chief of detectives. The cops he passed paused to watch him, their eyes guarded and mistrustful.

They all knew.

Finally, he reached the second floor. He knocked on O'Brien's door, and a voice impatiently bid him enter.

O'Brien looked up from the piles of papers on his desk and frowned. "Shut the door."

Frank did.

"When were you going to tell me?"

"Tell you what, sir?"

O'Brien was a mild-mannered man, God-fearing and normally patient, but not today. "Don't act stupid, Malloy. You're many things, but you're not stupid. The money. When were you going to tell me you're a millionaire?"

"I'm not a millionaire yet." Without waiting to be asked, he gingerly sat down on the straight-backed chair in front of O'Brien's desk.

"What does that mean?"

"It means I haven't seen a cent of the money yet."

"But you're going to. You're going to be richer than a Vanderbilt, aren't you?"

"I don't think so."

O'Brien sighed in exasperation. "But you're going to be rich enough that you don't need to work here anymore."

This is what Frank had been dreading. "I suppose."

"And I suppose that you won't be *able* to work here anymore, not another day. Not with every cop on the force envying you and hating you. You see that, don't you?"

He did, of course. He probably would've felt the same way about anybody who suddenly found himself almost as rich as a Vanderbilt through no fault of his own. "How did you find out?"

"Is it supposed to be a secret?"

"No, but it's not exactly public knowledge either."

"It will be soon. Some reporter got wind of it. He's going to break the story."

Frank thought about the way he'd just strong-armed the editor at the *World*. Still, that would be fast work. "Which newspaper?"

"The *Sun*."

But the *World* would pick it up and sensationalize it even more after the way he'd treated Brisbane an hour ago. That reminded him of Grace Livingston. "I'm in the middle of a case. A young woman is missing . . ."

"Tell whoever's around to pick it up. Here's your pay packet, although I don't guess you really need it now, do you?"

Frank took the envelope, thinking how he'd never imagined leaving the police force like this. He'd expected to retire as an old man and get a gold watch, and his friends would have a party for him and tell stories about the cases he'd solved and . . .

"I'm sorry to lose you, Malloy. You're a good man, but millionaires aren't cops."

"Thank you, sir."

A small crowd had gathered outside O'Brien's office, but they instantly dispersed when Frank stepped out. Nobody made eye contact with him. He walked down the hall to the detectives' room. Several men were lounging there, feet up on the desk and cigars smoldering in their teeth while they lazily traded lies.

All conversation ceased abruptly when Frank came in. Their hostile gazes told him they'd already begun to hate him. "I've got a case. A missing girl. Who wants it?"

For a long moment, nobody moved. Frank thought he was going to have to get mad, but finally, Bill Broghan dropped his feet to the floor and said, "I'll take it."

Frank wouldn't have picked the old drunk to handle *any* of his cases, but Broghan was probably the only volunteer he was going to get. Frank pulled the letters and clippings out of his pocket and placed them on the desk in front of Broghan. As he started to explain what he knew and what he had discovered, the rest of the detectives silently stood up and filed out. Frank ignored their cold stares, and Broghan looked after them with an ironic smile.

"They'll never forgive you, you know," Broghan said when they were alone.

"I know. I'll probably never forgive me either."

That made Broghan's smile even wider. "Still, they say a million dollars makes up for a lot of unhappiness."

"Do they? I'll let you know if it's true. Now, about this girl . . ."

When he'd finished telling everything, Broghan shook his head. "You know we're not going to find her, don't you? Girls like that, they never go back home. End up in a bawdy house, too ashamed to face their families."

Frank didn't want to argue. "Like I said, I've got a girl who'll meet this Pendergast character. I'll let you know when he answers her letter."

But Broghan shook his head again. "She won't want to be found. You mark my words."

Frank was tired of marking people's words. "I'll let you know."

He started the long walk out, his footsteps unusually loud in the hallway. Of course, every other time he'd walked down this hall, all the other people there and in the adjoining offices had been busy working and talking and moving around. Today, they were just there, waiting and watching, as he made his way out of the building where he'd worked for so many years. He made a point of looking each one of them in the face, and they had the good grace to look away. Envy wasn't a very honorable emotion, but they'd turn the anger they felt at themselves on him, so he didn't bother to speak to anyone. Men he'd known for over a decade turned away. Even the shackled felons in the lobby downstairs were silent as he passed.

Tom opened the door for him and gave him a little salute as he stepped outside. "We'll miss you, Mr. Malloy."

"Thank you, Tom. I expect I'll miss you, too."

"Think about us now and then, won't you?"

Frank smiled at that. "Oh, I'll think about you more often than that."

His heart thudded in his chest as he walked down Mulberry Street, not daring to look back. He needed to see Sarah. He'd have to make one stop along the way, but then he'd see her. She wouldn't understand, not really, but she'd listen.

The girls had just taken the cakes out of the oven when someone rang Sarah's doorbell. Catherine's little face crumpled in disappointment.

"Maybe it's not a baby," Mrs. Ellsworth said.

"If it is, we'll save you some, Mrs. Brandt," Maeve called after her as she went to answer the door.

Sarah swallowed her disappointment. She couldn't help thinking that when she and Malloy were married, she'd never have to drop everything to go deliver a baby. The knowledge should have thrilled her, but how many times had she been grateful her life had a real purpose? Her parents might be glad she was going to return to the kind of life she'd known growing up, a life where women were cosseted and safe, but she also knew most women in that world were bored and unhappy, too.

She was so lost in thought that at first she didn't realize she recognized the shadowy figure visible through the glass. "Malloy," she said when she'd thrown open the door. But her smile froze

71

when she saw the expression on his face. "What's happened?"

"I got fired."

"From the police? Whatever for?"

"They found out about the money."

Before Sarah could even register this amazing statement, Catherine exploded out of the kitchen and raced into Malloy's arms. Maeve and Mrs. Ellsworth quickly followed. The next few minutes passed in greetings and in reporting to Malloy how they were making strawberry shortcake and would he like to have some? He readily agreed, only to be told by a solemn Catherine that the cakes were still too hot, so they'd have to wait awhile.

"That's all right," he said. "I need to talk to Mrs. Brandt about something, so by the time we're done, the cakes should be cooled down enough. Mrs. Brandt, maybe you'd like to go for a walk with me."

"I, uh . . ." Sarah considered the possibility of having a private conversation here with Mrs. Ellsworth and the girls lurking nearby, and said, "Let me get my hat."

A few minutes later, after Sarah had changed into something more appropriate for the street, she and Malloy set out down Bank Street, heading toward Washington Square.

"How did they find out?" Sarah asked as soon as they were safely away from the house.

"A newspaper reporter went to Headquarters asking questions about me. O'Brien didn't give me any details, just that the fellow works for the *Sun*. I'm guessing it'll be in the paper soon."

"I suppose it is an interesting story."

"For people who don't have anything important to think about, I guess."

"And they just fired you for that?"

"You should have been there. Every cop in the place was staring at me like I was a sideshow freak at the circus."

"I'm so sorry." She tried to think of something more to say, but words couldn't take away the hurt he must have been feeling at being so unceremoniously booted out of a job he'd done all his adult life. He looked so beaten, she wanted to put her arms around him, but that would be highly improper on a public street. She settled for touching his arm. He took her hand and tucked it into the crook of his elbow as they continued down the street. "Are you going to be all right? I know you haven't gotten the inheritance yet, and—"

"I went to see the attorney today. He said they're still selling off the various businesses, but he put some money into an account for me to use in the meantime."

"That's good."

"Yeah. He said he hoped it would be enough to last a month or so until everything is settled." He cast her a sidelong glance. "It's ten thousand dollars."

Sarah smiled at his consternation, somehow managing not to laugh out loud. Ten thousand dollars was more than two years' salary as a police detective. "Oh my."

"I thought I'd buy you an engagement ring."

"You don't have to do that." Only rich people bothered with engagement rings.

He raised his eyebrows.

"Well, if you insist, that would be very nice," she allowed. She was going to have to get used to being rich again.

"You know what this means, don't you?" he said when they had crossed MacDougal Street and reached the edge of Washington Square.

"It means everything will change," she said, trying to imagine things she hadn't even thought of yet.

"It means I have to tell my mother."

"I suppose you do, because if she finds out from the newspapers . . ."

"My life won't be worth living. So I have to tell her today."

"Yes, we do."

Frank frowned. "Are you sure you want to be there? My mother is bad enough when she's happy, and I don't think this news is going to make her very happy."

"I'm sure. She'll be worried about what our

marriage will mean to her and Brian, and I want to be there to answer her questions."

He frowned. "What *will* it mean to her and Brian?"

They'd reached a bench, and Sarah stopped. "That's what we need to sit down here and discuss."

A remarkably short time later, Frank and Sarah got up and started walking back to her house, having made some of the most important decisions of their lives.

Frank enjoyed the strawberry shortcake, but he enjoyed eating it with Sarah, Maeve, and Catherine even more. By the time they'd gotten back to Sarah's house, Mrs. Ellsworth had discreetly taken her leave, which Frank found remarkable. She must have been dying to know what he and Sarah had discussed, and yet she'd decided to wait until she could wheedle it out of Sarah tomorrow. That showed remarkable restraint, Frank thought, for a woman whose life revolved around knowing everything about her neighbors.

After a simple supper of cold ham and biscuits, Frank and Sarah made their way over to Frank's flat on the other side of town. He hadn't let himself think about what his mother was going to say to his news. She might be pleased or horrified or something else entirely. Of only one thing was he certain: She was not going to like the way her life was going to change.

As he followed Sarah up the stairs to his second-floor flat in the tenement where he lived, he heard the door open. Brian would have sensed his arrival, as he usually did. Even though the boy was profoundly deaf and couldn't possibly hear him coming, he always knew when Frank was near.

"Francis?" his mother called.

"It's me, Ma."

She must've given Brian a sign it was all right to go, because he started running to the stairway. He skidded to a stop when he saw Sarah, though, and his small face lit with joy at the surprise of seeing her. He threw his arms around her as she reached the landing, and she hugged him back. His joy bubbled out of him in incoherent sounds he didn't even know he was making. After a few moments he released her, and his small hands started making the signs he'd learned at the school to which Frank had sacrificed to send him.

"Who's that with you?" his mother called.

"Mrs. Brandt," he said, knowing his mother wouldn't like that one bit.

"Good evening, Mrs. Malloy," she said, giving his mother her best smile as they approached. Rich women learned early how to smile at people who hated them, and Frank was glad Sarah had that training. She'd never needed it more.

"If you've come for supper, I don't know what I can give you," his mother said, her hands clutching each other as if she had to stop them from going for Sarah's throat. But maybe that was just his imagination.

"Thank you, but we've eaten," Sarah said, ruffling Brian's hair affectionately. He gazed up at her adoringly, which couldn't have made Frank's mother any happier.

"We need to talk to you, Ma, about something important," Frank said. He reached down and lifted Brian up for a kiss. The boy wrapped his slender arms around Frank's neck as if he would never let go. When Frank looked back at his mother, he saw the color had drained from her face, and the light had vanished from her eyes.

"I guess you'd better come in, then," she said, her voice flat with despair.

He exchanged a glance with Sarah, who shrugged. Sarah had noticed, too, but there was nothing for it but to tell her. They'd known it wouldn't be easy.

Frank and Sarah sat down together on the sofa, and Brian crawled up into Sarah's lap. A worn shawl covered the seat to protect it from wear and dirt, because heaven knew when they might ever be able to replace it. The antimacassars lying across the back protected it from the hair oil that might rub off and stain the fabric. Frank glanced around the rest of the room, really seeing it for the first time he could remember. The furnishings were cheap and a bit worn, but his mother kept the place immaculate, even though she had her hands full with a five-year-old boy, and for the past year she'd been taking him to school every day, too. He'd never really appreciated her until this moment.

His mother perched on the rocking chair that was left over from when Brian had been a baby. She didn't rock, though. She sat forward, as if preparing to make a quick escape if necessary, her hands clutching the arms like claws.

"Well, what is it?" she demanded when no one spoke. She sounded almost desperate, and Frank felt the sting of guilt for putting her through this.

"I should've told you sooner, but I didn't want you to worry until we had everything settled."

Her troubled glance darted to Sarah and back to him. "So it's settled now, is it?"

"Ma, you remember when Mrs. Brandt's daughter, Catherine . . . Well, when her father tried to claim her."

"Of course I remember. Do you think I'm touched in the head?"

He was making a botch of this already, but they'd agreed he would tell her this part, so he soldiered on. "Catherine's father was a very wealthy man, and he wanted to make sure she was well taken care of after he died."

She glanced at Sarah again, this time with disdain. "So he left the girl well fixed, did he?"

"Not exactly. He didn't want anyone to take advantage of her, so he left the money to someone else, somebody he named as her guardian."

She stiffened. "Better still. Now I guess you're rich, Mrs. Brandt, and you can take care of a family of your own."

Sarah gave her a sweet smile, acting as if she didn't notice the sarcasm behind the words. "He didn't leave the money to me, Mrs. Malloy. I don't think he trusted a mere female to handle it."

"He left it to me, Ma."

She blinked several times before she said, "To you?"

"Yes. He named me Catherine's guardian, and he left me enough money to take care of her."

"He had a lot of respect for Mr. Malloy," Sarah added. "He thought he could trust Mr. Malloy to do what was best for his daughter."

Mrs. Malloy nodded slowly, her expression bleak, her jaw clenched as if bracing for a blow. "I guess what's best for her is for you two to get married, isn't it?"

This was Sarah's part, so Frank sat back with a sigh and gratefully let her do it. "Mr. Malloy has done me the honor of asking me to be his wife, and I have accepted. We're looking forward to making a home for Catherine and for Brian."

His mother closed her eyes for a moment as a

shudder ran through her, but Sarah continued before she could reply.

"We're very concerned about Brian, because you've taken care of him since he was born. His life will change when we get married, but we don't want to upset him anymore than necessary, so we are hoping that you will come to live with us, too."

Frank didn't know what he expected, but he hadn't expected his mother to sit there like a stone, staring at Sarah as if she'd suddenly sprouted horns. After a very long, awkward silence, she said, "Live with you?" Her voice was so faint, he could hardly make out the words.

Sarah, of course, pretended not to notice anything untoward. How on earth did she manage it? "Well, not at my house, of course. Neither one of us has a place big enough for our new family. There's the three of you and the three of us, and we'd want you to have your own rooms so you could have your privacy when you needed it. And Maeve—that's Catherine's nursemaid—will need her own room, and the children could share a room now, but they'll each need their own eventually, so as you can see, we'll need to find a much bigger house."

Amazingly, his mother nodded, as if this made perfect sense, although he had a feeling she really had no idea what Sarah was talking about.

"And don't think we want you to do anything

but look after Brian," Sarah went on. "Mr. Malloy will be able to afford to hire some help."

"Help?"

"Servants, Ma. She means servants."

"Servants? You can't afford servants, Francis."

"I can now, Ma. I told you, Catherine's father left me some money."

She narrowed her eyes and looked at Sarah again. "Where is this house you want to live in?"

"We haven't found one yet. We haven't even started looking. I would appreciate your opinion, though. Since you'll be living there, too, I'd like you to see it before we decide for sure."

"You'd have to leave here, Ma," Frank said, wondering if Sarah realized what his mother was really asking. The neighborhoods in New York were like islands divided by streets instead of water. People might live in one neighborhood their entire lives and never even meet people living two blocks away. A person could disappear completely and start a brand-new life simply by moving to a new neighborhood. Leaving the place she'd lived since she'd come to America would literally mean giving up everything and everyone familiar. "You could always come back to visit your friends, though."

His mother glared at him, and for once he was happy to see the familiar expression on her face. "Francis, exactly how much money did this man leave you?"

"I don't know *exactly*. They're still figuring it out."

"A guess, then. You must have an idea if you're planning to buy a house with it."

"Like I said, they don't know for sure, but they think it's . . ." Frank could hardly bring himself to say it. "They think it's around five million dollars."

This time the blood really did drain from his mother's face, and from her head, too, because she slumped to the floor in a dead faint.

4

"Stop fussing over me, Francis. You're scaring the boy."

Frank glanced at Brian and saw that she was right. He got up from where he'd been kneeling in front of his mother, who now sat in the rocking chair again. Her faint had only lasted a moment before he and Sarah had helped her back into the chair.

Sarah pressed a glass of water into her slightly unsteady hands, and she obediently took a sip. "Thank you," she said with apparent sincerity.

"I know this has all been a shock to you," Sarah said, sitting back down on the sofa and gathering an uncertain Brian into her lap. She gave him a reassuring smile, and then he turned to his grandmother and made some signs.

She handed the glass to Frank, who still hovered over her, and signed back to the boy. "He wants to know what we're talking about. I'll have to tell him all of this," she said to them. "About you getting married and about us moving. I don't know the right signs yet, though."

"Maybe they can help you at the school," Frank said.

"Of course they can help me at the school," she snapped.

Frank gritted his teeth, reminding himself how difficult this must be for his mother. "I know it'll be hard for you to leave the old neighborhood."

"No, it won't. I can't stay here if my son's a millionaire. Nobody'll even speak to me unless they want money. You should know that, Francis."

He knew that only too well. "They'll find out pretty soon, too. A reporter from the *Sun* has been snooping around, and it'll probably be in the newspapers in a day or two."

She muttered something incomprehensible and turned back to Sarah. "The boy'll like having the little girl to play with."

Sarah smiled her rich woman's smile. "I hope he'll like everything about his new family."

"Oh, he already likes you well enough, if that's what you're worried about. More women to fuss over him. He'll be in heaven. Did you say you have a nursemaid for the little girl?"

"Yes, Maeve. And you won't really have to take care of Brian anymore either, not really. Maeve is certainly capable of looking after both children, especially with Brian in school. We can even get someone to take him and bring him home, if you like."

"Oh, I'll keep doing that. They need my help at that school. They're forever telling me they can't do without me."

"I hope you don't let them take advantage of you," Sarah said.

His mother smiled. She *smiled!* Frank could hardly believe his eyes. "It's me taking advantage of them. We pay them to teach the signs to the boy, but I learn for free."

"I hope you can teach them to all of us, too. We'll all want to be able to talk to Brian."

"It won't be no trouble to teach the young ones. They pick things up so quick."

"That's true," Frank said. "Catherine already knows some just from playing with Brian a few times."

His mother frowned up at him. "Don't just stand there, Francis. Get Mrs. Brandt some tea. It's steeping on the stove."

Frank didn't know why she was still annoyed with him. He'd just told her they were millionaires. And sure enough, he found a pot of tea on the stove. He took a few minutes to heat it up a bit while he listened to the two women making plans like they were old friends. What had come over his mother? She'd always hated Sarah Brandt. Or so he'd thought. No, he couldn't have been mistaken about that. And he would've bet a year's salary she hated the thought of him marrying her. Maybe Sarah could explain it.

Frank carried a cup of tea out to Sarah just as she was saying, "Why don't all three of you come over on Saturday so you can get to know Maeve?"

Sarah gently moved Brian from her lap to the

seat beside her and took the cup from Frank. "Thank you." Her blue eyes twinkled with mischief. She must be loving this, Frank thought.

"I can't speak for Francis, but Brian and I will come. Did you only pour one cup of tea? What's wrong with you, Francis?" She jumped up and bustled off to the kitchen, leaving Frank to shake his head.

When they'd covered all the important topics, including Frank and Sarah's wedding plans (none yet) and Catherine's attitude toward having a brother (ecstatic), Sarah took her leave. She gave Brian a big hug and a kiss after Mrs. Malloy explained to him that his father had to escort Mrs. Brandt back home. Holding him close, she savored the feel of his tiny arms locked around her neck. She had a son now. What an amazing miracle. Then she took Mrs. Malloy's work-roughened hand in hers, glad to see her eyes no longer held the slightest hint of the fear she'd always had of Sarah. "Thank you for being willing to come live with us. I know it's going to be a big adjustment for you, and I appreciate it so much."

Mrs. Malloy blinked her suspiciously moist eyes. "It's what's best for the boy."

"I think so, too. I'll tell the girls to expect you on Saturday. I know they'll be thrilled."

They were out on the street and lost among the

throngs of pedestrians still enjoying the spring evening before Malloy finally exploded. "What did you do to her?"

Sarah couldn't help laughing at his disgruntled frown. "I didn't do anything except not steal her son and her grandson away from her."

"What does that mean?"

Sarah sighed, more than a little relieved that things had gone so well. She'd been hoping their decision to invite Mrs. Malloy to live with them would placate her a bit, but even Sarah had been surprised at Mrs. Malloy's reaction. "It means that . . . Well, I've always suspected that her dislike of me was actually the fear that we would marry and take Brian and leave her all alone."

"Of course it was. But why does she suddenly . . . ?" He gestured vaguely.

"Like me?"

"It's more than that. I never saw her be that nice to anybody."

"Certainly not to you," Sarah had to admit.

"Oh no. Wouldn't want me to get a swelled head."

"In that case, it's a good thing she's coming to live with us, because with all the money, you'll definitely be in danger of that."

"I just hope it lasts. Her being nice to you, I mean."

"It will. She knows it was my decision to invite

her. But I just realized, we didn't tell her you'd lost your job."

"Plenty of time for that."

"I suppose. Oh dear, I just remembered the poor girl you were looking for. What will happen with her?"

His jaw tightened, and Sarah's heart sank. "I had to give the case to Broghan."

"But surely—"

"Surely, they'll let me keep working on it? No, they won't. They won't even think it's important."

"Didn't you tell them Maeve is willing to—"

"I told them everything, but it won't make any difference."

"Is it because of you and the inheritance?" she asked, oblivious of the startled looks the word *inheritance* drew from the people walking nearby them.

"Partly, and partly because it isn't the kind of case anybody cares about."

"Her father cares!" Sarah said, outraged.

He sighed with what sounded dangerously like despair. "Sarah, these cases never have a happy ending. Her father wants her back. The families always do, but they want the girl they know back. After something like this, the girl is never the same, though. Sometimes the family even blames her for what happened to her and for embarrassing them. And that's if we find her at all. Sometimes these girls kill themselves because of the shame, or they end up on the street because they think they can't go home. And that's if the man doesn't murder her when he's done with her. However it ends, no one is happy, and even if we catch the man, the girl never wants to tell anyone what happened to her, so most of the time he isn't even charged with a crime because the girl and her family don't want anyone to know about it."

"That's horrible!"

"Of course it is, but that's why the police don't care about cases like this." Malloy took her arm to guide her through the crush of wagons clogging the intersection, carefully dodging the piles of horse dung.

"So are you saying *you* don't care if they find her or not?" she asked when they reached the relative safety of the opposite curb.

"Of course I care. I don't want to find out she's dead or selling herself in Hell's Kitchen, and I'd really like to catch this Milo Pendergast, too. But I know better than to think Pendergast will go to jail or that Grace Livingston will live happily ever after."

"Will they even let Maeve try to help find her?"

"I don't know."

They walked on in silence for a time, and Sarah tried to think of a way to help Grace Livingston. By now she should have been used to the injustice in the world, particularly when it involved females, but she hoped she would never become so jaded.

"Will you at least see her father and let him know what's happening?"

He sighed again. "First thing tomorrow."

Sarah tried to imagine what he would tell the poor man and decided she didn't want to know.

Saturday morning finally arrived, and Catherine woke up before dawn, too excited over the pending visit from the Malloy family to remain in bed. Sarah had spent two sleepless nights with a mother whose baby had been reluctant to enter the world, and she had been hoping to sleep in a bit. Maeve, bless her, had spirited Catherine off to the kitchen to keep her busy, but after what seemed only a few minutes of respite, someone again tapped on her bedroom door. Maeve stuck her head in.

"Mrs. Brandt? So sorry to bother you, but Mrs. Ellsworth is here. She got a letter from that Pendergast fellow."

Instantly awake, Sarah threw off the bedclothes and snatched up her robe. Rubbing the sleep from her eyes, she padded barefoot after Maeve. Mrs. Ellsworth and Catherine sat at the kitchen table, chatting about the menu for the day's planned festivities. Catherine was reminding their neighbor of all the things they'd been baking the past few days, even though

Mrs. Ellsworth had been present for all the preparations.

The letter lay on the table between them, giving no indication that it might mean life or death to a young woman.

"Good morning, Mrs. Ellsworth."

"Good morning, Mrs. Brandt," she said with barely suppressed excitement. "This letter came for you in this morning's mail."

"Why did you get a letter for my mama?" Catherine asked.

"It came to me by mistake, my darling." She glanced back at Sarah. "I thought you'd want to see it at once."

"Thank you so much." Sarah picked it up, noting the neat handwriting. Milo Pendergast had learned penmanship in school. "Catherine, would you keep Mrs. Ellsworth company for a few minutes while I read my letter?"

Using the last reserves of her restraint, Sarah walked out into the front room, when she really wanted to rip the envelope open instantly. Maeve followed, her hands clutching each other anxiously until they reached Sarah's desk. Sarah found her letter opener and slit the envelope. The cheap paper yielded easily to the blade, and inside Sarah found one sheet of matching letter paper. She unfolded it with unsteady hands and read with Maeve looking over her shoulder.

My dear Miss Smith, it began. *I am most grateful*

for your prompt reply to my advertisement. I am flattered that you feel I might make you a suitable life mate. I understand your desire for haste, but even a man as anxious as I am for a suitable wife would find it difficult to woo and win a bride in a fortnight. I do enjoy a challenge, however, and I must confess I am curious to meet you and to learn if we might suit. If you are agreeable, may I suggest we meet on Sunday afternoon at two o'clock? He went on to describe the location of the park where he had met Grace Livingston. He had signed it *Milo Pendergast.*

"It worked," Maeve said in wonder.

Sarah could hardly believe it herself. She actually felt a little breathless. "He must have picked up your letter not long after Malloy left it. I guess no one bothered to let him know."

"And the fellow didn't waste any time getting back to me. I knew it was a good idea to mention my inheritance." Maeve took the letter and reread it, excitement bringing color to her cheeks. "Mr. Malloy has got to let me go meet him tomorrow."

"It isn't up to him anymore," Sarah reminded her.

"But surely . . ."

"There is no *surely* about it. Mr. Malloy doesn't work for the police department anymore, remember?"

Maeve's sigh echoed Sarah's own disgust. She only hoped Malloy could assure them someone who still did work for the police would be following up on Grace Livingston's disappearance.

By the time the Malloy family arrived a few hours later, Catherine had practically worn a path from the kitchen to the front window while watching for their approach and dutifully reporting back to Maeve and Sarah every five minutes that she'd seen no sign of them yet.

The girl had thrown open the front door before they'd had a chance to knock or even mount the front steps, and Brian broke into a run and raced up onto the porch to hug her, heedless of his grandmother's efforts to restrain him.

By the time Sarah and Maeve had reached the front hall, they were inside. Mrs. Malloy had worn her Sunday best, a black bombazine gown at least a decade out of style but whose condition was so good, she had clearly given it impeccable care and saved it only for special occasions. Her hat appeared to have recently been spruced up with new flowers. Sarah felt oddly touched that she had taken so much care with her appearance.

"Mrs. Malloy, I'm so glad you could come," Sarah said, taking her hand.

Mrs. Malloy's faded blue eyes had been taking in every detail of Sarah's modest home, and she seemed to relax just slightly at the sight of the utilitarian office area. "Thank you for having us."

Only when she was sure Mrs. Malloy felt adequately greeted did Sarah turn to Malloy, who gave her a tentative smile. "Malloy," she said, returning it. She gave him both her hands, which he squeezed reassuringly. Or at least she thought that was what the squeeze meant.

She glanced down at Catherine and Brian, who were communicating in some mysterious way that seemed to make them both very happy. It made Sarah very happy, too. Then she noticed Maeve hovering expectantly. "Mrs. Malloy, may I present Maeve Smith, the young lady I told you about?"

"Maeve takes care of me when Mama has to deliver a baby," Catherine said.

Maeve gave Catherine a smile and nodded to Mrs. Malloy. "Very pleased to meet you, Mrs. Malloy."

"Mrs. Brandt speaks highly of you," Mrs. Malloy said, taking the girl in with her sharp gaze.

"We think it will be wonderful having Brian to play with all the time, don't we, Catherine?"

Catherine nodded vigorously. "Except when he has to go to school. Will you teach us how to talk to him?"

Mrs. Malloy finally smiled. "I certainly will."

"Please come in and sit down," Sarah said, remembering her manners. She hadn't entertained in so very long, she'd grown rusty. "I'm sorry I don't have a proper sitting room, which is just one of the reasons we'll need to find a larger house."

They had brought some of the kitchen chairs out to the front room where the two upholstered chairs sat by the front window. The girls served everyone lemonade, and they made polite conversation about the weather and inconsequential things until the children grew restless.

"Why don't I take them upstairs to play?" Maeve said.

"Mrs. Malloy, would you like to come up with us to see my dollhouse?" Catherine asked. "I arranged it just for you to see."

"I would love to see it," she said, following Maeve and the children up the stairs.

Malloy took the opportunity to remind Sarah that they were engaged by kissing her rather enthusiastically for a few minutes. When he seemed to feel sufficiently appreciated, she showed him the letter from Milo Pendergast.

"What are you going to do?" she asked when he'd read it.

"I've got to show it to Broghan."

"Will he let Maeve meet this man?"

He frowned, slapping the letter against his leg. "He can't stop her from meeting him. The question is whether he'll assign men to watch her and follow them back to his house."

"But that's the only way we'll find him, isn't it?"

Malloy nodded, still frowning.

"What is it?"

"I was just thinking. It's Saturday, and I probably won't be able to find Broghan until Monday."

"But that will be too late."

"Yes, it will. So what's to stop us from following her ourselves? We can see where he lives, and then Maeve can have a sudden change of heart and run off, and we can tell Broghan where the fellow lives, he can go there and arrest him and be a hero."

"Oh, Malloy, do you think that will work?"

"Why wouldn't it? I'll need to tell Mr. Livingston, too. That way he can go down to Headquarters and insist they raid Pendergast's house and find his daughter. They'll be annoyed that I interfered, but since I'm letting them get the glory, they shouldn't mind too much."

"He should offer a reward, too, shouldn't he?"

"That would help. Can you go with me to keep an eye on Maeve? I think it would be easier if we looked like a couple out for a stroll."

"Of course. I'd feel better if I were there anyway, instead of sitting here and worrying about her. I'll ask Mrs. Ellsworth to watch Catherine tomorrow."

"And I'll go see Livingston later today and tell him what we're doing."

"I'm sure he'll be happy to hear we've finally

heard from Pendergast. He must be nearly out of his mind with worry."

"I just hope we find his daughter. She's been gone nearly a week now. Anything could've happened to her by now."

Sarah took his hand. "You did the very best you could."

He didn't look convinced.

They heard footsteps on the stairs, so he quickly tucked the letter into his pocket.

They both rose when Mrs. Malloy came into the front room.

"Maeve seems like a clever girl," she said.

If she only knew, Sarah thought. "We're very lucky to have her. Did Catherine show you her dollhouse?"

"Oh, yes. She has . . ." She caught herself, and Sarah realized in surprise that her voice had broken, as if she were fighting tears. She cleared her throat. "She has a doll that she said is me and one for Brian. She said she needed them so she would have her whole family."

"Oh my, I had no idea," Sarah said, feeling the sting of tears herself.

Mrs. Malloy cleared her throat again and resumed her usual dignity. "And you're absolutely right, Mrs. Brandt. Your house is entirely too small for all of us."

"Oh, please call me Sarah," she said briskly, glad to be back on familiar ground. "We really need to talk about where we want to live in the city, don't we?"

By the time they had eaten luncheon and devoured all the delicacies Mrs. Ellsworth had helped the girls make, Maeve and Mrs. Malloy were allies and Catherine had learned a dozen new signs to use with Brian.

As they were leaving, Malloy said, "I'll be over before luncheon tomorrow so we can make our plans."

Maeve smiled with a little too much satisfaction. "I'll be ready."

Sarah tucked her hand into the crook of Malloy's arm as they strolled slowly down the street. The little park was up ahead, and Maeve sat there on a bench, clutching her hands together and glancing around with apparent nervousness. Sarah knew that Maeve really felt eager anticipation at the opportunity to fool this Milo Pendergast as he had fooled Grace Livingston and other women before her. Maeve looked like an eager maiden in her Macy's finery, purchased for the occasion. They'd had a lovely time choosing the light blue outfit, which Maeve had pointed out would be easy to follow in a crowd and which also happened to suit her perfectly.

Sarah paused and pretended to look for something in her purse, annoying the people behind them, who cast impatient looks as they had to swerve to avoid knocking them down.

"Where could he be?" she said.

"He's probably here already. He's been here for a while, watching to see who comes and goes."

"I don't see anyone watching."

Malloy sighed. "That's the whole point."

Before Sarah could think of a reply, a tall man bustled past them as if he were late for an appointment. He wore a nicely tailored brown suit and a derby hat. Sarah hadn't gotten a good look at him, but his vigorous stride and the way his head kept swinging from side to side, as if he were looking for something, made her think he was young. Her heart started racing.

"Could that be him?"

"Shhh."

Malloy tucked her hand through his arm again, and they started down the street behind him. He stopped at the park, looked at Maeve for a second, then glanced around again. Maeve gave him a hopeful smile, but he didn't notice. He was too busy looking around. Apparently satisfied, he straightened his shoulders, then reached into his breast pocket and tugged out a piece of cloth until it was clearly visible. A piece of *yellow* cloth.

Maeve half rose and spoke to him, her lovely face twisted into a questioning frown. He nodded and replied. They were too far away to hear, but she could clearly see Maeve's relieved smile and the young man's answering bow as he greeted her. After a moment, he sat down beside her. He glanced around again, still obviously anxious, but then he turned his attention to her.

"What do we do now?" Sarah asked.

"We walk past and don't look at them. Pretend you're talking to me."

"What should I talk about?"

"Explain to me what's happened to my mother."

This surprised a laugh out of Sarah in spite of her anxiety for Maeve.

"I'm serious. All my mother could talk about on the way home yesterday was how lucky I am to get you and how smart Maeve is and how good it'll be for Brian to have a sister. Do you think it was the dollhouse?"

Sarah bit back a smile. "It's a very nice dollhouse."

"Why didn't she get a doll that's supposed to be me?"

Sarah had to choke back a laugh at his disgruntled frown. "She already had one."

"She did?" He seemed delighted.

"The house came with a family, so it had a mother and father. She never told me it was supposed to be *her* family, though."

They were passing the bench where Maeve sat with the young man. Sarah managed to catch a glimpse of him without actually looking at them.

He was presentable, although not what Sarah would have called handsome, and he seemed awfully nervous for someone who'd done this many times before.

"Something's wrong," Malloy whispered when they'd passed them.

"I know. He doesn't seem . . . confident."

"No, he doesn't."

"Maybe that's how he tricks the girls. Maybe he acts more nervous than they are."

But Malloy was shaking his head. "He's a charmer. The women I talked to the other day both said so."

"But Maeve isn't his usual kind of girl. He usually goes after plain girls. Maybe he changed his . . . his method for her."

Malloy didn't look convinced, and he didn't look happy either. They'd reached the corner, and they turned, stepping out of sight and stopping near the wall so the other pedestrians could easily pass them. Malloy pulled a small mirror from his pocket and positioned it so he could see down the street.

"What are they doing?"

"Talking. Usually, he takes them to lunch, but it's too late in the day for that. I'm hoping he tries to take her directly to his house."

"With that story about meeting his mother?"

Malloy nodded, never taking his gaze from the mirror. "Most girls would agree to that. There's only one reason a man introduces a woman to his mother."

"You warned her not to be too eager."

"I hope she can do it. I know how anxious she is to catch this man and find Grace Livingston."

"I've learned to never underestimate her."

They stood in silence for a while, earning puzzled glances from the many pedestrians out to enjoy this lovely Sunday afternoon who must have wondered why they were standing there with Malloy holding a mirror around the corner. Sarah desperately wanted to walk back down the street to check on Maeve, but if Pendergast had noticed them before, he'd think that strange. They couldn't afford to spook him, not when they were this close. And if they scared him off this time, they'd probably never get another chance.

After what seemed an hour, Malloy said, "They're getting up."

"Oh, good!"

"Wait, what . . . ? They're going the wrong way."

"What do you mean?"

"The man at the restaurant said Pendergast always heads uptown when he leaves with his lady friends, but he's heading the other way. Come on. We need to catch up."

The plan had been to wait until they passed, then fall in behind them. Instead, Frank and Sarah were headed back the way they'd come. Luckily,

Maeve's suit really was easy to spot as they strolled along the crowded sidewalk, so they didn't need to follow too closely.

"I just hope Maeve keeps her promise not to go inside with him," Sarah said.

"She's too smart to do anything else."

Malloy quickened his pace when Maeve and Pendergast turned down a side street, disappearing from sight. Sarah was nearly running by the time they reached the corner, but to her relief, the couple was still in sight. Maeve, she noticed, had taken his arm. A nice touch. He'd think she trusted him.

Malloy slowed down again, not wanting to catch them, just keep them in sight. This street was quieter, lined on both sides with comfortable rows of modest town houses. Trees struggled to thrive here with varying degrees of success, their newly unfurled leaves soaking up some of the city noises and providing intermittent patches of shade.

Up ahead, Maeve and Pendergast stopped in front of a house. Pendergast gestured that she should precede him up the steps to the front stoop, but Maeve hesitated, backing away slightly. Malloy quickened his pace again. They wanted to be close if he tried to force her. They were still a block away, unable to hear the words, and Maeve took another step back, apparently uncertain. He leaned in with an air of desperation. Plainly, he wanted to get her inside and was making his case, trying to convince her.

Sarah looked at the house, trying to see a face in the window, but she knew that was silly. They were still too far away and the angle was wrong. Besides, if Grace were a prisoner here, she wouldn't be looking out the window, would she? How were they going to walk away knowing she was probably inside? Maybe Malloy could get a beat cop to go in with him.

Maeve was shaking her head now. She'd be telling him she'd made up her mind that she just couldn't bring herself to go into a gentleman's house unescorted. That was the story they'd settled on, but Pendergast grabbed her arm. Malloy made an outraged sound, but before he could move, someone shoved them out of the way and raced past them. Malloy staggered a few steps, fighting to keep his balance and not knock Sarah over in the process, and when they both looked up, they saw the running man closing on Maeve and Pendergast.

Did he have an accomplice? Was this man going to help him force Maeve into the house? Malloy muttered what might have been a curse and started after him, leaving Sarah to fend for herself. She couldn't run in her long skirts, but she wasn't far behind, and she didn't need to be all that close to hear the running man shouting.

"Where is she? What have you done with her,

you cad?" He grabbed Pendergast by the lapels and shook him. Maeve had the good sense to jump out of the way. She cast Malloy a desperate glance as he approached.

"Stop, Livingston! Let me handle this!" Malloy cried.

Oh, dear heaven, Sarah thought. Grace's father had decided not to leave this to Malloy after all.

Livingston was still shaking Pendergast like a rat and screaming in his face, demanding to know where his daughter was. Pendergast had gone scarlet as he struggled to free himself from Livingston's grip. Malloy reached them and started shouting at Livingston to release him. "I'll take care of him," he said over and over until he finally got through. Livingston seemed to finally realize Malloy was there, and he sagged a bit as if in relief.

Pendergast's terrified gaze went back and forth between Livingston and Malloy for a few seconds, and then, taking advantage of Livingston's loosed grip, he broke free and ran. With an incoherent shout, Malloy took off after him.

Livingston would have followed, but Sarah and Maeve each grabbed an arm.

"No, Mr. Livingston, please," Sarah said. "Let Mr. Malloy worry about him. You'll only be in the way."

"Who are you?" he asked when he'd realized who was holding him.

"I'm Mrs. Brandt. I was assisting Mr. Malloy."

"I know. I followed you here. Are you with the police?"

"No." Even her old friend and well-known progressive Police Commissioner Theodore Roosevelt hadn't allowed women to serve on the police force. "I'm Mr. Malloy's fiancée."

He turned to Maeve. "Is this the house?"

"That's where he was going to take me, yes."

Before either of them realized his intent, he'd broken free, bounded up the steps, and started pounding on the front door. "Open up! Open the door!"

This hadn't been any part of their plan. Maeve was supposed to make a discreet escape without doing anything to arouse suspicion. All they wanted was to find out where this man lived. Sarah watched helplessly, wondering what she should do. Malloy would probably have told her to stop Livingston, but obviously that was no longer possible.

The door opened.

"Where is she? Where's my Grace?" he demanded of the startled maid, then pushed past her before she could answer and ran into the house shouting his daughter's name.

Sarah and Maeve hurried up the stairs.

"What's going on?" the maid demanded. "Who are you? And who was that?" she added, gesturing to where Livingston had disappeared into the house.

"He's looking for his daughter, who was kidnapped," Sarah said. "He thinks she's being held prisoner here."

The maid didn't look as shocked as Sarah might have expected. "Nobody's being held prisoner here."

"Who lives here?" Maeve asked.

The maid looked her up and down as if assessing her right to be there at all. "And who's asking?"

Before Maeve could act on the fury that question engendered, Sarah quickly said, "We're working with the police, and if you cooperate, you won't get in any trouble."

"I don't have to worry about trouble. I haven't done anything wrong," the girl said, a little haughtily for Sarah's taste.

"Then don't start now. Who lives here with Mr. Pendergast?"

This surprised her. "Pendergast don't live here."

"Then who does?"

"Just Mr. Neth and me. That's all."

So his real name was Neth.

"Then why did he bring me here to meet his mother?" Maeve asked, showing the maid she wasn't the only one who could be haughty.

Her eyes widened, and the color drained from her face. "He brought you *here?* Pendergast? Where is he?" She stuck her head out the door and looked anxiously up and down the street.

Sarah was beginning to reconsider their theories about Pendergast. "He ran away."

She turned back to Maeve. "He brought you *here* to meet his mother?"

"That's what he told me," Maeve said. "Are you sure there's no one else here? No young woman named Grace?"

"There's no one," she said faintly. "See for yourself." She stood back so they could enter.

They stepped into the foyer. Sarah wasn't sure what she'd expected, but the house was like a million others in the city. Furnished fashionably if not opulently, the home of a comfortable middle-class family. Or bachelor, if the maid could be believed.

"Mr. Livingston!" Sarah called.

A sound drew her attention, and she looked up to see Livingston stumbling down the stairs. He was sobbing uncontrollably.

She and Maeve rushed to help him before he fell.

"She's gone," he said brokenly. "My Grace is gone."

"Have you searched the whole house?" Sarah asked as they helped him down the remaining stairs.

"Grace!" he called halfheartedly. "Grace, are you here? She'd come if she was here, wouldn't she?" he asked.

"Maybe she's locked in somewhere and can't

come," Sarah said. "We need to make a systematic search. Do you have a telephone?" Sarah looked over to where the maid had been standing, but she was gone.

5

Frank didn't think he was that much older than Pendergast, but he wasn't running for his life either. That was probably the reason he'd lost Pendergast after several blocks. Gasping for breath, Frank retraced his steps, trying to figure out where his quarry had turned off. He found an alley that Pendergast could have ducked down right after turning the corner, in the moment Frank had lost sight of him. But when he ran down it, he found it let out on the next block, and Pendergast wasn't there either, at least not anymore. He could have gone anywhere, Frank knew.

Silently cursing, half-sick with fury, he made his way back to the house where he'd left Maeve and Sarah. Damn Livingston for ruining everything. Well, at least they knew where the man lived, and by now they may even have found Grace, if she was still alive to be found. They'd find Pendergast, too. If he owned a house or even just rented it, someone would know his true name. He couldn't hide anymore.

Frank had expected to find Sarah and Maeve on the sidewalk in front of the house, although why he had, he couldn't really say. In their place, he would have gone inside looking for Grace

Livingston, and that was apparently what they had done. Oddly, they'd left the front door hanging wide open.

He stepped inside. Nothing seemed out of the ordinary except for some white cloths lying in a heap by the door. "Sarah? Maeve?"

"Malloy, is that you?" Sarah called from above him. He looked up and saw her peering down the stairs from the floor above.

"Have you found her?"

"We haven't found anything up here. See if there's a cellar."

Almost an hour later, they had searched every inch of the place only to find no Grace Livingston and no one else either.

"Does he live here alone?" he asked them. They'd found only one bedroom that appeared to be occupied.

"The maid said it was just the two of them," Sarah said.

They'd gathered in the main parlor, a well-furnished room that had seen little use. Livingston sat on a horsehair chair, grim in his despair.

"What maid?" Frank asked.

"Oh, I forgot to tell you. After you went after Pendergast, Mr. Livingston ran up and started pounding on the door, and a maid opened it."

"She seemed really surprised when we told her Pendergast had brought me here," Maeve said.

"She probably didn't know that's the name he uses when he's on the prowl."

"Oh, she recognized the name," Sarah said. "That was the funny part. She knew who he was, and she said he doesn't live here, so she was also surprised he'd brought Maeve here, to this house."

"That's right," Maeve said. "She said the man who lives here is named Neth."

Frank frowned. "So Neth isn't Pendergast?"

"That seems to be the case," Sarah said.

"So which one brought Maeve here?"

"We have no way of knowing."

"Where's this maid?"

"She disappeared when we weren't looking," Sarah said.

"Well, maybe not *disappeared*," Maeve said. "She left her cap and apron on the floor, and I think she just ran out."

Frank remembered the white cloths he'd seen by the front door. "You mean she ran away?"

"Wouldn't you if a crazy man came pounding on your front door and accused you of kidnapping his daughter?" Maeve asked with a meaningful glance at the despairing Livingston.

"Joanna?" a male voice called from downstairs.

The three of them froze, eyes wide with surprise. Frank put his finger to his lips and pointed at Livingston. "Keep him quiet," he whispered. Sarah went to him, touched her fingers to his mouth, and gave him a warning look.

"Joanna, where are you?"

"Answer him," Frank whispered to Maeve.

"Here," she called.

Frank stepped out of sight of the open parlor door and flattened himself against the wall.

They could hear the man running up the stairs. "You need to pack my things. I have to go away for a while." He stopped at the top of the stairs, looking around. He was the one who had met Maeve in the park.

"In here," Maeve called again.

"What's going on?" He took a few hesitant steps toward the parlor door.

Maeve stepped forward so he could see her plainly.

"You! What are you doing here?" He started for her. "You little bitch, I ought to—"

As soon as he cleared the doorway, Frank tackled him. He fought like a tiger, but Livingston lunged up to help, and between the two of them, they got him pinned, helpless, on the floor.

"Get something to tie him up," Frank said, and Sarah was there almost instantly with some tasseled ropes she'd ripped off the draperies.

In a matter of minutes they had him trussed and in a chair. He glared up at them, furious in his defeat. He looked even less prepossessing than he had in the park, with his hair hanging in his eyes, his collar coming loose, and his nice new suit all rumpled. "Where's Joanna? What have you done with her?"

"Is that the maid? She ran off," Frank said.

"She wouldn't do that. She'd never leave me." If they'd thought he was lacking confidence when he was in the park with Maeve, he was more than confident of this fact.

"Where's my daughter?" Livingston demanded. "Where's my Grace?"

"I don't have your daughter. I don't have anybody's daughter. You can search the house and see for yourself."

"We have, so we know you don't keep them here. Are they with Pendergast? Is he the one who keeps them?"

For a second Neth's very ordinary face registered alarm, but then it vanished. "Oh, you know his name from the letter."

Frank exchanged a glance with Sarah, who took the hint. "We know it from Joanna, too. She said that's where you take the girls."

"You're lying! I never take the girls at all!"

"Oh, so you do know about Pendergast and how he kidnaps unsuspecting young women?"

"No! I don't know what you're talking about!"

"You might want to change your mind about that. I'm sure when we find Pendergast, he's going to try to blame everything on you."

"Where is she?" Livingston grabbed Neth by

his lapels and half pulled him from the chair. "Just tell us where she is."

"I'll tell you."

They all turned to the doorway. A young woman stood there. She wore a black maid's dress without the cap and apron. For some reason Frank had the impression it was a costume, although that was ridiculous. Who would dress up like a maid if she wasn't one?

"You must be Joanna," Frank said.

"Joanna!" Neth cried as Livingston released him in disgust. "Help me! Get me out of here."

She gave him a brief glance, then turned back to Frank. "If I tell you where Pendergast is, will you let him go?"

"After we get Pendergast."

"What will you do with him in the meantime?"

Frank glanced at Neth, whose eyes were now wide with renewed terror. "Lock him up at Police Headquarters for a few hours." The instant the words were out of his mouth, he realized that he no longer had the authority to lock anyone up. He only hoped whoever was on duty today would see the wisdom of it. "As soon as we find Pendergast, we'll let him go." Another promise he couldn't keep and might not even want to.

"I'll take you to him, then."

"Joanna, no!" Neth cried, but she ignored him.

"Is that where we'll find the girl?" Frank asked.

She shrugged. "If he has her."

"You can't betray him," Neth said, obviously terrified.

She had no beauty to speak of, but for a maid, she had a strange dignity, Frank realized, and she gathered it about her now as she stared at Neth. "Why did you bring that girl here?" She gave Maeve a glance sharp enough to draw blood.

Neth's anxious gaze darted around the room as if looking for an escape or at least an ally. When he found none, he turned back to Joanna. "He told me to. He said she was . . . special."

"Huh," Joanna said contemptuously and gazed around at their guests meaningfully. "He smelled trouble, and he wanted you to find it instead of him. Did he tell you to keep the girl for yourself?"

"I . . . No, of course not!" he said, desperate now and probably lying through his teeth."She was for him, same as always."

Her face tightened, as if she were in pain. She would know he was lying, and the knowledge wounded her. Frank pitied her for a moment. "Just give me Pendergast's address. We'll find him."

"I don't know the address, but I can take you there."

"Good. Are you on the telephone? I need to call Police Headquarters," Frank said.

She glared at Neth for one more moment. "Yes. I'll show you."

"Joanna, why are you doing this?" Neth looked as if he might weep.

"I'm doing it so you won't go to jail, you fool. Now shut up before you get yourself into any more trouble."

Frank exchanged a glance with Sarah, who looked as puzzled as he. Neither of them had ever heard a maid talk to her employer like that before. Apparently, things were not exactly as they seemed here in Mr. Neth's home.

The wait for the police to arrive seemed interminable to Sarah, especially because Mr. Livingston kept wanting to leave Neth's house to find his daughter. Malloy didn't want to take a chance that Neth would escape or warn Pendergast so he could get away, though, so they waited. They were all relieved by the pounding on the door.

Malloy went to answer it, Sarah at his heels.

"Officer Donatelli," she said as he entered, so happy to see him that she could have hugged him.

The handsome young man smiled, tipping his helmet. "Mrs. Brandt. What are you doing here?"

"It's a long story," Malloy said for her. Two other beat cops followed Gino Donatelli inside. Sarah noticed they were staring at Malloy.

"He don't look like a millionaire," one of them said to the other.

Malloy glared at them both, which shut them up but didn't stop them from staring.

"They only agreed to come because they wanted to see you," Donatelli said. "You're a seven-day wonder."

Malloy looked like he might explode, but he said, "Did you bring a Black Maria?"

"Of course. Who is it we need to take in?"

"He's upstairs." Malloy briefly told them the story of the missing girl and their plan to follow Pendergast here to find her. "But this fellow isn't Pendergast after all. His maid is going to take us to him. She says he's the one who keeps the girls, and it's only a few blocks from here."

The other two officers were now staring at Malloy for a different reason. They were obviously as interested in this case as he was.

"We'll load this fellow into the Maria, and one of you will take him back to Headquarters," Donatelli said. "The other one will go with me and Mr. Malloy to pick up this Pendergast."

But both of the others were shaking their heads. "You might need help with this Pendergast fellow. You don't know what you'll find there, and then you'll just have to send for us to take him in anyway. Why don't we go with you with the Maria?"

Malloy nodded. "Let's get Neth."

The other two officers followed Malloy upstairs while Donatelli waited with Sarah.

"I'm so glad you were on duty today," she said. Gino Donatelli had proved himself useful in several of the cases she had helped Malloy solve.

"They always make the dagos work on Sunday." As an Italian, Gino would be a minority on the mostly Irish police force.

"I'm sorry," Sarah said.

"I'm not. I might've missed this."

She returned his boyish smile.

The two other officers came clumping down the stairs with Neth between them. They'd replaced the curtain ties with handcuffs.

"You can't arrest me," he was saying. "I haven't done anything wrong."

"We'll be the judge of that," one of them said, giving him a friendly shove that sent him stumbling down the last three steps.

Donatelli caught him and set him on his feet again.

Malloy was behind them with Joanna, and Maeve and Livingston brought up the rear.

Gino's face brightened. "Miss Smith, I didn't know you were still here."

Maeve did not see fit to reply to this, although Sarah could tell she was pleased to be noticed.

Malloy turned to her. "Maeve, will you make sure Mr. Livingston goes straight home and wait with him there until I come?"

"I'm not going home," Livingston said. "Not when Grace is so close."

"Mr. Livingston, we know what we're doing. Let us do it."

"I know I ruined your plans earlier, but I won't interfere this time, I swear. I'll wait outside and stay out of your way, but I want to be there when you find her. I want to take her home."

Sarah knew exactly how he felt. "Maeve and I will make sure he doesn't interfere."

"And who's going to make sure you and Maeve don't interfere?" Malloy asked in exasperation.

One of the officers holding Neth made a noise that might have been a smothered laugh. Malloy sighed. "All right. Put Neth into the Paddy wagon and let's go."

Malloy set out with Joanna, not waiting for the others. Gino easily caught up with them while his cohorts threw a protesting Neth into the Paddy wagon. One of them climbed up to drive while the other trailed after Malloy and the others on foot.

Sarah and Maeve fell in on either side of Livingston, who didn't acknowledge them with so much as a glance.

Their odd procession was separated as oblivious pedestrians with their own destinations in mind failed to realize the two police officers and the other five oddly matched individuals belonged to the same group. Livingston set a brisk pace, determined not to lose them in the noisy streets. Behind them, lumbering along, came the large enclosed wagon known as a Black Maria, some-how managing to keep up in spite of the traffic.

Luckily, Joanna had not lied about the distance. They'd gone only half a dozen blocks when she stopped and pointed.

Malloy, Gino, and the other officer were discussing how best to approach the house when Sarah and her group reached them.

"What are you waiting for?" Livingston demanded.

Malloy gave him an impatient look. "If Pendergast suspects we're onto him, he might kill Grace. Is that what you want?"

Livingston blanched, and Sarah took his arm. "Let them do what they need to do," she said, leading him a few steps away.

Malloy glanced at Joanna, who seemed almost frightened now that they were here. "Gino, put her in the Maria, too."

"What! You never said anything about that!" she cried as Gino took her arm.

"I wouldn't want to lose track of you," Malloy said. They waited while the protesting woman was locked into the wagon with Neth. "Sarah and Maeve, make sure Livingston stays here. You"— he pointed to the wagon driver—"make sure nobody lets them out of there." To Gino and the other officer, he said, "Let's go."

Sarah breathed a silent prayer as the three men approached the house halfway down the pleasant residential street. Nothing set it apart from its neighbors. No one would suspect that anything untoward was going on there.

Still holding Livingston's arm, she felt him stiffen as Malloy raised his hand to knock. After a few moments, he knocked again. The three men seemed to consult, and then it looked like Malloy opened the door. Livingston bolted then, breaking free of Sarah's grasp and running toward the house.

The smell hit Frank first, the coppery scent of fresh blood that was like a fist to his gut. "Pendergast?" he shouted, his gaze searching every corner. "Pendergast, where are you?"

Silence was his only reply.

"You"—he indicated the officer—"search down here. Gino, come with me."

Donatelli followed him up the stairs. The smell was stronger here, and Frank silently willed Sarah to keep Livingston outside.

"Pendergast!" he tried again when they reached the top of the stairs, and this time he thought he heard a sound coming from the front room. One of the double doors to what must have been a parlor stood half-open, as if someone had left in a hurry.

Frank strode over and threw it wide to a scene of crimson horror.

A man lay on the floor in a position so

unnatural, he had to be dead. Beyond him, slumped against the wall and staring vacantly into nothingness, was a woman clad only in a shift and covered—no, *drenched*—in blood. Frank knew her instantly. He carried her photograph in his pocket.

"Is that her?" Donatelli asked.

Frank nodded. "Grace Livingston."

The staring eyes blinked.

"Grace?" Frank said, not trusting his own senses.

An ear-piercing sound broke the silence, a wail so tortured, it could have come straight out of hell. Frank needed a few seconds to realize it was coming from her.

"She's alive," he told Gino. "Go get Mrs. Brandt up here, but keep her father out."

Sarah and Maeve managed to catch Livingston just as he reached the porch steps. They grabbed his arms and held on for all they were worth, slowing him, but she knew they couldn't stop him for long.

Then Gino Donatelli burst out the front door, catching himself just before he would have plowed into them. "Mrs. Brandt, Mr. Malloy wants you right away. Upstairs," he added as she pushed past him. "Mr. Livingston, you've got to wait here," she heard him say as she ran inside and up the stairs.

She was almost to the top before she realized what she was smelling and what it must mean. Malloy stood in the doorway of the front room, his expression grim.

"She's alive," he said when she'd reached him. "There's blood everywhere, though. She's covered in it, but I can't tell where she's hurt."

She nodded, thinking she understood.

"It's bad, Sarah."

"I'm a nurse," she reminded him. She'd seen blood before.

He nodded and stepped aside. Only then did she understand. The smell hit her first, and then the sight: the man's contorted body, the darkening pools soaking into the oriental carpet, and the woman's half-naked body sprawled like a discarded doll. How could she be alive? Her shift was literally dyed red with the blood, her face splattered, her bare arms and legs streaked.

But then the poor creature took a shuddering breath, breaking the spell of horror, and Sarah went to her. Carefully, trying not to step in the blood, she finally reached her and knelt down beside her.

"Grace? Can you hear me?"

Slowly, the staring eyes turned to her. They held such pain, Sarah could hardly bear it.

"Grace, I'm Sarah Brandt. I'm a nurse. I'm here to help you. The police are here, too. We've come to take you home."

She shook her head, or at least Sarah thought she did.

"Can you tell me where you're hurt?"

She did shake her head this time.

"You can't tell me or you don't know?"

"Not . . . not hurt."

"But all this blood . . ."

The pain-filled gaze shifted, and one red-streaked arm lifted to point at the man sprawled a few feet away. Malloy squatted next to him, peering closely.

"His throat's been cut," he said.

From this angle, Sarah could see that for herself. That would explain the great quantities of blood, she thought.

"That's his blood on you?" she asked Grace.

She nodded.

Someone was shouting, calling Grace's name. Her eyes widened in terror.

"That's your father," Sarah said. "He wants to take you home."

"No!" she cried. "He can't see me like this!"

She struggled to rise. Sarah helped.

When she was on her feet, Sarah could see the blood was only on the front of her body. "Please," she said.

"I'll help you get cleaned up. Where can we go?"

Grace set out on unsteady legs, walking carefully, as if each step might shatter her. Sarah turned to Malloy. "Get Maeve in here. I'll need her help."

When they reached the hall, they could hear Livingston's voice more clearly as it carried up the stairwell. He was arguing with Gino, desperate to see his daughter. Grace was just as desperate not to be seen. Still stumbling, she limped for the stairs and headed up to the next floor. Sarah took her arm as they climbed.

"Do you know where you're going?" Sarah asked.

"His . . . his room."

Only one door stood open in the upstairs hall, and Grace headed right to it. Sarah caught a glimpse of a large four-poster bed, set on a dais, and an assortment of large, mahogany furniture as Grace hurried through to what proved to be a bathroom. An enormous claw-footed tub sat along one wall and a sink and commode on the other. Grace turned on the taps of the tub and inserted the stopper, moving with a speed born of desperation. The pipes rumbled and groaned before finally spewing a geyser of water.

"Mrs. Brandt?" Maeve called.

"In here," Sarah said, going to meet her.

"What on earth has happened?" she asked as she followed Sarah's voice into the bathroom. The sight of Grace Livingston stopped her dead.

"Sweet God in heaven!" she cried, nearly sinking to the floor before Sarah could catch her.

"I know it looks terrible, but it's not her blood. There's a man downstairs who's probably Pendergast. His throat's been cut."

Maeve turned away from the awful sight of Grace Livingston. "What do you need me to do?"

"I'm going to help Grace get cleaned up, but she'll need some clothes. Grace, do you know where your clothes are?"

She shook her head.

"They must be here somewhere. Get Gino to help you search, though. I don't want you going through this place by yourself. Find her something to wear so we can get her out of here. Grace, is there anyone else in the house?"

"I . . . I don't know."

"Be careful, then," Sarah said to Maeve.

Maeve nodded and hurried off.

Sarah found some towels in a cabinet, and when the water was deep enough, she said, "Do you want me to help you? If you're modest, I'll turn my back."

"It's not that. I just . . . I don't want you to see what he did to me."

"You don't have anything to be ashamed of. It wasn't your fault."

"Oh, but it was! I never should have gone to meet him. I brought it on myself."

Sarah knew many people would agree. "Is that what he told you?"

She nodded brokenly.

"Well, he was lying, then. He did this to you because he's an evil man and he tricked you. Making you feel guilty was his way of putting the blame on you, but it belongs on him. All of it. Now let's wash off every trace of him, shall we?"

Malloy looked up as Gino Donatelli came back into the bloody parlor.

"I found a telephone. The medical examiner is coming, and they're trying to find Broghan. He's going to be pretty mad about this."

"Yeah, lots of people will be. I'll probably lose my job," Frank said.

"Oh yeah. I keep forgetting." Gino shook his head. "When you think about it, I guess there's not much they can do to you, is there?"

"No." Which was, he realized, at least one reason to be happy about his change of fortune. Combined with having Sarah, it was starting to sound like a good deal after all. "Where's Livingston?"

"Outside on the front stoop. He ran out of steam and started crying when he finally understood that his girl is alive. How bad is she hurt?"

"Not at all from what I could tell. The blood was all his." He nodded toward the body.

"Is that Pendergast?"

"Probably. We'll get Joanna and Neth in here later to identify him. Are they still locked up?"

"Safe and sound. So this Pendergast character, he finds women through the lonely hearts columns, and he brings them here, and what?"

"Probably what you think and a lot more. What I don't know is what he does when he's finished with them, if he kills them or lets them go. Either way, none of them are going to go to the police."

"I guess not."

"Officer Donatelli?"

They both turned to see Maeve in the doorway. At the sight of the bloody room, she gasped and quickly turned her back.

"Miss Smith, are you all right?" Gino hurried to her. "This is no place for you."

"Mrs. Brandt asked me to look around upstairs and see if I could find some clothes for Miss Livingston, but she didn't want me to do it alone. She said to ask you to go with me."

"I would be honored. We haven't searched the upper floors yet anyway. Mr. Malloy . . . ?"

"That's a good idea. I'll wait here for the medical examiner. I'll call you if he gets here before you get back."

Frank took the opportunity to look around the room to see if he could figure out what had happened here. Plainly, someone had sliced Pendergast's throat, and Frank couldn't think of anyone who'd deserved it more. Grace Livingston certainly would have been justified in doing it. She was covered in his blood, so plainly she had also been standing in front of him when it happened. But if she'd killed him, where was the knife?

Frank had looked all over the room and under every piece of furniture, but there was no sign of a knife. Also, he couldn't figure out how a woman as small as Grace Livingston could have overpowered a man as large as Milo Pendergast. He was in his shirtsleeves and trousers, and wore socks but no shoes. Plainly, he'd been at his leisure, not entertaining or expecting company, so that meant he had most likely been alone with Grace. Frank could see he'd been almost six feet tall and powerfully built, and even the smallest man was stronger than most women. He would have seen her coming at him with a knife in her hand. She might have managed to stab at him once or twice before he wrenched the knife from her, but unless he was blinded or tied up, there was simply no way she could have had enough time or strength to slash his throat before he tried to stop her.

The blood told what had happened afterward, though. The initial gush of blood had hit her, then he'd probably shoved her away. She'd stumbled backward into the wall and slumped to the floor, probably in shock. He'd stayed on his feet for a minute or so, probably trying to stanch the flow of blood with his hands.

His sleeves were dyed crimson, just like Grace's shift, and his hands were also covered with blood, proving Frank's theory so far. The biggest pool of blood on the floor marked the spot where the attack had occurred. A short trail marked where Pendergast had staggered, probably in a vain effort to find help before he fell and died where he now lay. A smaller pool spread out from his body.

Frank would be very interested to hear Grace's story about what had happened here. He stepped out into the hallway, wanting to get away from the stench of death. From the top of the stairs he could see the open front door and Livingston still sitting on the front steps. He sat with his elbows on his knees and his head in his hands. At least he would be able to take his daughter home with him. She would be forever changed, but at least she was alive. That had to count for something.

Above him, he could hear Gino and Maeve moving around and talking quietly, probably out of respect for Grace Livingston. A few minutes later, they came down the stairs. Frank was glad to see that Maeve carried some clothing draped over her arm. Thank God they wouldn't have to take Grace out of here wrapped in a blanket. She didn't look too happy to have found Grace's things, though.

Neither did Gino, come to that. They both seemed profoundly disturbed.

"What is it?" he asked when they reached him.

Maeve looked at the clothes she held, then at Gino.

"We found Miss Livingston's clothes," he said. "In a room with a . . . a cage in it."

Frank winced. He hated that Maeve had seen that. "I'm sorry."

"It's not that," Maeve said, still looking at the clothes with a worried frown. "We found two sets of clothes."

"Two sets?"

"Yes. Could they both belong to Miss Livingston?"

"Did she think she was eloping with Pendergast?" Gino asked. "Did she pack a bag or something?"

Frank shook his head. "Her maid said the only things missing from her room were the clothes she was wearing."

Frank watched their faces as the truth dawned on them. Another woman had been here, too.

6

"Malloy, where are you?" a voice called from downstairs.

Frank walked over to the stairway. "Up here."

The officer he'd sent to search the lower floor came bounding up, taking the steps two at a time. He hesitated for an instant at the sight of Gino and Maeve, but then said, "I found something in the cellar."

"What?"

He glanced at Maeve again. "A woman."

Maeve gave a little cry of outrage.

"Oh, she's alive," he said quickly. "But . . ."

"But what?" Frank snapped.

"Well, she's locked in a cage, and she . . . well, she don't have no clothes on."

"That bastard," Frank said, not even bothering to apologize to Maeve. "Why didn't you get her out, at least?"

"She . . . I started to, but when I got close, she started screaming. I didn't . . . Well, we've got some females here, and I thought maybe they should handle it."

One glance at Maeve's face and Frank knew he couldn't send her down into that cellar. "Take those clothes up and figure out which are Miss

133

Livingston's. Then send Mrs. Brandt down here with the rest of them."

Maeve nodded and hurried away.

"What else did you find upstairs?" Frank asked Gino.

Gino shook his head. "Nothing. The other rooms are empty."

"Did you check the attic?"

"Not yet."

Frank sighed. "Go up, then, and look. If he's got any more women here, I want to find them before anybody else gets here."

The two took off, leaving him to pace the hall until Sarah came down, carrying the other woman's clothing.

He met her at the bottom of the stairs. "I'm sorry you had to see all this."

"I am, too, but I'm glad I was here. I don't know how you would have handled Grace if I weren't. Now we need to see about that poor woman downstairs." She headed for the next set of stairs.

"I'll go with you," he said.

"Do you think that's wise?"

"I'm not letting you go down there by yourself."

She gave him a tiny smile.

When they reached the foyer, Mr. Livingston jumped from where he'd been sitting on the front stoop and came to the open doorway "Mrs. Brandt, you've seen her? Is she really all right?"

"She isn't hurt. She's getting cleaned up before she sees you."

He blinked his red-rimmed eyes. "Can I take her home now?"

Sarah exchanged a glance with Frank. Frank had no idea what the police would say. Maybe the best thing would be for her to be gone when Broghan and the others arrived. He nodded.

"She's still very upset and ashamed by what happened," Sarah said. "She thinks it was her fault, that if she hadn't gone to meet Pendergast—"

"Of course it wouldn't have happened if she hadn't gone to meet him, but how could she have known the kind of man he was?" Livingston said.

"That's exactly what you need to tell Grace. Just be patient. I'm sure she'll be ready very soon. Now, we've found another . . . another woman, and we must see to her."

His eyes widened. "Another one? Dear heaven!"

"You'll excuse us," she said.

Frank realized he'd neglected to ask where the entrance to the cellar was, but they found it easily enough. The door off the kitchen stood open.

Sarah took a deep breath to fortify herself, then started down the dark stairs. The rest of the house, she'd noticed, bore a sad, neglected air, with dust gathered in the corners and a cobweb here and there. She imagined it was difficult finding servants when you kept female prisoners.

The cellar was much worse, of course. She didn't let herself think of what might be hiding in the shadows.

She saw the cage as soon as she reached the bottom of the steps. It stood just out of sight of the stairwell. She took a minute to let her eyes adjust. The light coming down the stairway only reached a few feet, and the two tiny windows up near the ceiling had been smeared with dirt, so they emitted only a feeble hint of the sunlight beyond.

Gradually, the shadow in the far corner of the cage came into focus as a body huddled on the dirt floor, knees clutched to her chest, her hair loose and tangled, her eyes wide and staring.

Sarah glanced back to see that Malloy had stopped at the bottom of the steps, and now he was looking around, everywhere except at the cage. When he'd made sure nothing else threatened, he turned his back to the poor woman. Sarah could feel his fury radiating across the small space between them.

"Hello," she said to the woman, speaking softly and slowly, as if to a frightened animal. "My name is Sarah Brandt. The police are here. We've come to rescue you."

"The police!" she echoed, her voice hoarse. "No! Don't let them take me!"

"They aren't here to take you. We're here to rescue you."

She shook her head frantically. "He won't let you. He won't let me go."

"If you mean Milo Pendergast, he's dead. He can't hurt you anymore."

"No, he's not. He can't be dead!"

"But he is. He's dead and you're free." Sarah found she could see fairly well now, and she glanced over the cage, trying to figure out how to open it. She missed it the first few times because she'd been looking for a lock of some kind. She'd thought they would need a key. Perhaps someone would have to search Pendergast's dead body for it. But in the end, she realized it was just a bolt. It slid free with only a small tug, and the door swung open.

"No!" the woman cried in terror. "Don't let him in here! Don't let him touch me!"

Sarah realized she meant Malloy. "He's not going to touch you. I told you, we're here to help you."

"That's what they always say, but they only hurt me. They always hurt me!"

Sarah stepped into the cell, noting what she hadn't let herself realize before. The only items inside it were a filthy straw mattress and a pail.

The woman cried out and drew herself in even tighter. She was, Sarah could see, trying to cover her nakedness. Her legs and feet were filthy, her straggling hair lank and greasy. Only then did Sarah remember what she'd brought.

"I have your clothes," she said, holding them out.

The staring eyes widened and she reached out a hand. Sarah took another step closer and then another, until the woman could reach them. She snatched them, using both hands now, pulling them close, clutching them to her.

"Would you like to bathe? I can take you upstairs—"

"No! I'm never going up there again!"

She picked through the clothes frantically. Finding a shift, she threw it over her head and stuck her arms through it. Then she glanced at Malloy, who still stood with his back to her. Quickly, as if afraid he might turn at any moment, she started pulling on the other articles of clothing. Only when she'd covered herself with all the pieces did she stop to button her shirtwaist, her mistrustful gaze darting to Malloy every few seconds.

At last she was left with only her stockings, and she pulled them over her filthy feet, leaving them to sag around her ankles.

"My shoes? Where are my shoes?"

Grace had asked the same question. "We haven't found them yet. But we're still looking. Come upstairs with me now. Are you hungry? Can we get you something to eat?"

"I won't go with him," she said, jutting her chin in Malloy's direction. "I told you. I won't do it anymore. I don't care what you do to me."

"You don't have to do anything you don't want to," Sarah said. "Malloy, would you go upstairs, please? Ask Officer Donatelli if he can find the missing shoes. We haven't found Miss Livingston's either."

Malloy nodded, and without so much as a glance back, he hurried back up the cellar stairs.

"Come with me now. Can you stand?" Sarah asked.

The woman struggled to her feet, ignoring Sarah's outstretched hand in favor of using the bars of the cage for support. The whole time, she watched Sarah warily. Sarah was surprised to see how tall she was, and how large-boned, too. Not fat. In fact, she was rather thin, as if she'd been starved, but no matter how thin she got, she would never be a small woman.

"No one is going to hurt you anymore," Sarah said. She backed out of the cell and pushed the door as wide as it would go. "Let's get out of here."

Sarah started for the stairs, glancing back to see if the woman was following. The woman took a tentative step, but stopped when she realized Sarah was watching. Sarah forced herself to look away and keep going up the stairs. By the time she reached the top, the woman had started up herself. Like Grace Livingston, she was unsteady on her feet, or perhaps she was just weak.

When she reached the untidy kitchen, Sarah began to rummage around in the larder. She found almost a whole loaf of bread and some cheese. She set them on the table just as the woman emerged from the stairwell.

The woman literally fell on them, snatching up the bread and tearing a hunk off the loaf before Sarah could even locate a knife. Just as she had suspected, the woman had been starved. Sarah continued her searching. She found only a paring knife, and she used it to slice the cheese. The woman devoured the pieces as fast as they fell from the knife. Sarah found a glass that looked reasonably clean and filled it from the tap. The woman drank the water down in one breath.

Only when she had set the glass down did she pull out a chair and sit, apparently drained from the effort of eating.

Sarah sat down opposite her at the table. "What's your name?"

The woman's expression transformed instantly from exhausted to suspicious again. "Rose."

"I'm Sarah, Rose. Milo Pendergast is dead. We know he contacted you through a lonely hearts advertisement in the newspaper and tricked you into coming here to meet his mother."

Her suspicion transformed again, this time into surprise. "How do you know that?"

"Because he's done the same thing to other

women. We were looking for one of them, and that's why we came here."

"You said the police are here, too."

"Yes. One of them found you. Do you remember?"

She nodded slowly, her pale brown eyes still wary and guarded.

"They came with us to arrest Pendergast, but he's dead. Someone killed him, and I suppose they'll try to figure out who did it, but that doesn't concern you. They may want to ask you some questions, of course, but other than that, I'm sure you'll be free to go."

"Free to go where?"

Now Sarah was surprised. "Back to your home. In fact, I'll be glad to take you myself, just to make sure you get there safely."

The kitchen door opened, and Rose stiffened in alarm. Gino Donatelli stuck his head in. He cast a curious glance at Rose, who looked about to bolt. Sarah laid a reassuring hand on her arm, making her flinch away. So much for comforting the woman.

Sarah smiled at Gino, hoping her reaction to him would make him less threatening to Rose. "Did you find the shoes?"

"Uh, well, Mr. Malloy asked if you could come take a look at something."

"What is it?"

He glanced at Rose again, plainly unwilling to

141

say in front of her. "I, uh . . . it won't take long, he said."

She turned back to Rose. "Will you be all right here for a few minutes? Officer Donatelli will wait outside the door so no one bothers you."

Rose considered her offer for a long moment, then nodded. "As long as he stays outside the door."

Sarah got up, wishing she didn't have to leave Rose alone. "I'll be right back. If you need anything, just call for Officer Donatelli."

Rose just stared back at her with blank eyes. Sarah wondered if the woman would ever get over what she had endured in this house. Gino held the door for her.

"Where is he?" she asked when he'd closed it behind her.

"Upstairs in the bedroom where you took Miss Livingston."

"What has he found?"

"You need to see it for yourself."

With that ominous warning, Sarah made her way to the stairs and up the two flights. There she found Malloy standing before one of three wardrobe cabinets in the large bedroom. He was frowning as he gazed around the room when she entered.

"Did you look at this place?" he asked.

"Not really. I was in a hurry to get Grace cleaned up." She followed his gaze and really looked at the wallpaper she had barely noticed before. "Good heavens!"

The figures adorning the walls were groups of satyrs and naked nymphs performing all sorts of acts, some of which Sarah was fairly certain were actually impossible.

"Where do you buy something like this?" Malloy asked.

"In this city, I guess you can find whatever you might want, no matter how depraved it is." She shuddered, then remembered why she was here. "What did you want to show me?"

"I didn't *want* to show it to you, but I need you to tell me if it's what I think it is." He opened the cabinet.

At first Sarah didn't understand what she was seeing. The interior had been divided into shelves designed to hold a large quantity of shoes. The shelves were tipped slightly with a strip of molding running the length of each shelf to catch the heels so the shoes wouldn't slip off. The lower shelves were empty, but the upper ones held about a dozen pairs of shoes.

Women's shoes.

Why did Milo Pendergast have so many pairs of women's shoes?

Her blood turned to ice as the truth dawned on her. "These belong to the women he kidnapped!"

"That's what I thought, too, but can we be sure?" he asked.

She stepped closer, loath to touch the shoes, as if doing so might violate the women who had owned them even more. "They're different sizes." And they showed different kinds of wear. Some had been stretched by wide feet. Others leaned a bit from heels worn down on one side. One showed the telltale bulges of bunions. But they were all polished brightly and had obviously been someone's "best" shoes, the ones she would have worn to meet a potential suitor. "There are so many of them," she said as the meaning of it turned in her stomach.

"I know. We have two women here, but where are the others?"

"I don't know, but I want to get the two that are here away before the detectives arrive and want to question them."

"Do you think a pair of these shoes belongs to Miss Livingston and the woman downstairs?"

"If they're arranged chronologically, then these must belong to Grace." Overcoming her reluctance, Sarah picked up the bottommost pair. "Is she still in there?" she asked, indicating the bathroom.

"Yes, with Maeve."

Sarah went to the door and knocked. "Miss Livingston, it's Mrs. Brandt. May I come in?"

The door opened a crack, and Maeve peered out. "She's not ready to face her father yet."

"Ask her if these are her shoes."

Maeve took them and, after a brief consultation, returned. "Yes, they are."

"Maeve, explain to her that they're sending a police detective over, and he'll want to question her about what happened with Pendergast and . . . well, everything that happened to her here. They'll want to talk to her at some time or other, but if she'd rather it not be today, she needs to let her father take her home right away."

Maeve nodded and closed the door.

Sarah sighed, fighting the urge to either scream or weep with frustration. How could something like this have happened to these women? What had they ever done to deserve being brutalized by a madman? And the others. Where on earth were the others?

"Sarah? I think you and Maeve better leave, too."

"I will. Just let me take Rose's shoes down to her."

"Rose?"

"The woman from the cellar." She picked up the pair that had been next to Grace's.

"Are you sure those are hers?"

They were by far the largest pair in the cabinet. "Yes. I'll send Mr. Livingston up to get Grace."

"Tell him to get a cab first, to have it waiting for them."

She nodded and made her way out of the room with its horrible wallpaper and its even more horrible cabinet full of shoes. Where were those other women? Were they dead? Or had Pendergast let them go when he was finished with them? And if so, had they returned to loving families, or had they been too ashamed to go home again? Such questions would drive her mad if she let them, but she couldn't stop asking them.

Mr. Livingston still sat forlornly on the front steps, but he ran off with the energy of a man twenty years younger when she suggested he find a cab to take Grace home.

Gino Donatelli still stood guard at the kitchen door. "Not a peep out of her," he said.

"Thank you, Gino."

"Did you see the shoes?"

Sarah nodded. "I think these must be hers."

She opened the kitchen door. "I found your—" she began, but stopped when she realized the room was empty. "Rose?" She looked around, then felt silly. The room offered no hiding places for someone as large as Rose. Could she have gone back to the cellar? The thought made Sarah shiver, but perhaps Rose found some kind of comfort in her cell. "Gino?"

"What is it?" He stepped in and looked around. "Where is she?"

"I . . . Would you check the cellar?" Sarah couldn't bring herself to go back down there.

Gino hurried down the stairs, then hurried back

up again. "There's nobody down there, Mrs. Brandt."

"Where could she . . . ?" She saw it then. The back door was ajar. She ran over and threw it wide. "Rose!" The small, overgrown yard was empty, but the back gate stood open, too.

Sarah ran out and raced to the gate, Gino at her heels, but when she reached the alley, she saw only a mangy yellow tabby cat curled up in a patch of sun between the ash cans.

Sarah thought of the poor woman, filthy beneath her hastily donned clothes, barefoot and penniless, her hair hanging wild. Where had she gone? Would she find safety before night fell? Would some conscientious patrolman arrest her, thinking she was insane or worse? She breathed a prayer for Rose's safety.

"Do you want me to go after her?" Gino asked.

Sarah shook her head. "If she was that anxious to get away, it would be cruel to bring her back. She probably wouldn't come with you anyway."

They started back inside, and Sarah realized she still held Rose's shoes. For some reason, that made her infinitely sad.

Maeve and Sarah had escorted Grace Livingston downstairs to her father, and they'd promised Frank they would leave for home as soon as the Livingstons were safely away. With no sign of the medical examiner or Broghan or anyone else yet,

Frank was left to finish searching the house. Broghan might not like it, but if Frank found some useful evidence, he should at least be grateful.

Pendergast's obscenely decorated bedroom yielded only an assortment of unpleasant-looking devices for which Frank could only guess the intended uses. He didn't think he wanted to know, either. One of the upstairs bedrooms held a cage similar to the one in the cellar. The mattress in it was cleaner, but it was the same in all other ways. Is this where he'd kept Grace Livingston? Someone would probably ask her, and he was glad he wouldn't be that someone.

Downstairs, he found a small room furnished as a study. The cluttered desk held a collection of mail, mostly bills, but one drawer contained stacks of letters, all written in female handwriting. As Frank flipped through them, he realized they were replies to Pendergast's advertisements, dating back a couple years.

If he were the detective on this case, he would take the letters with him. Since he couldn't do that, he pulled out his notebook and jotted down all the names and addresses he could find in the stack. If the police weren't interested in what had become of the missing women, maybe he could track them down or at least let their families know why they had disappeared. It would be a small way of compensating for not being able to bring the man responsible to justice.

Gino found him as he finished searching the rest of the drawers.

"Is Broghan here?"

"Not yet, but Neth and the girl are complaining about being locked up in the Paddy wagon."

Frank had almost forgotten about them. "I guess we should get them in here to identify Pendergast, at least. Broghan will probably want to question them, too, about what Pendergast was up to here. Go ahead and bring them in."

Frank waited outside the bloody parlor for Gino to bring the two prisoners upstairs. He could hear Joanna complaining about being kept locked up for so long, but she fell silent as they reached the second floor. Halfway down the hallway, she stopped dead, and Frank realized her face was ashen.

"Miss . . ." Frank realized he didn't know her last name. "Joanna? Are you all right?"

Neth, who had been walking beside her, had gone on a few steps before he realized she had stopped. He went back to her. "Joanna, what is it?"

"I . . . I don't want to be in this house anymore."

That's when Frank realized the truth about Joanna. "You were one of his victims."

The color rushed back into her face, blooming like a fever in her cheeks. "One of the stupid females who believed his lies, you mean?"

"It's nothing to be ashamed of. He tricked you."

Neth took her gently by the arms. "You don't have to stay. I'll go look at his body."

But she shook him off, furious at someone or something not present. "I need to know he's dead. Where is he?" she asked Frank.

He gestured toward the parlor. The door still stood open, and she headed toward it, determined now. Neth hesitated only a moment before following, and Frank trailed after, wanting to see their reactions.

Joanna faltered a moment in the doorway. The smell of death still hung heavy in the air, and the drying puddles of blood were daunting indeed. But she squared her shoulders and continued. Neth, however, stopped dead, covering his mouth and whispering something that might have been a prayer. Or a curse.

Joanna strode over to the body and peered down at it. "That's him." To Frank's surprise, she didn't look away, though. She just kept staring. Finally she said, "He doesn't look like much, does he? Lying there in his own blood like that." She looked up at Frank. "Did he suffer? I hope he suffered."

"I think he died pretty quick, but he'd have been choking on his own blood, so it wasn't very nice."

"Good." She suddenly realized Neth still stood in the doorway, frozen by the horror of it. She strode back to him, took his arm, and turned him, urging him back into the hall. "Don't look at him anymore. You don't even have to think about him anymore."

Neth looked like he might be sick, but he seemed to take heart at her words. "You're right. He's dead. I still can't believe it, though."

She looked over at Frank again. "Can we go now?"

"I'm afraid not. You still have to answer some questions, and there's the matter of the young lady you tried to lure into your house this afternoon."

"That was a mistake," Joanna said quickly, before Neth could speak. "He didn't mean her any harm, and you can't prove that he did. Pendergast told him to meet her in the park and make his excuses for not coming. She's the one who wanted to go back to his house with him. She was trying to trick him so that man could attack him."

Frank raised his eyebrows. "You've been out there in that Maria for hours. Is that the best you two could come up with?"

Neth had the grace to look abashed, but Joanna never batted an eye. "It's the truth. Now let us go."

"I can't let you go. We've got to wait for the detective to get here. This isn't a very pleasant place to wait, though." Frank gestured toward the gruesome scene in the parlor. "Why don't we go to Pendergast's study?"

"Yes, let's," Neth said, obviously eager to be someplace else.

Frank waited and was gratified to see Neth head down the hall to the study without the slightest hesitation. He'd been here often enough to be familiar with the house.

Neth and Joanna sat down on a small sofa that was the only furniture in the study except the desk. Frank pulled the desk chair over and straddled it to face them. "Now, Mr. Neth, let's start with how long you've known Milo Pendergast. And is that his real name?"

"It's the only name I know him by," Neth said, then glanced at Joanna as if for her approval. They obviously hadn't cooked up a story for this.

"Where did you meet him?"

"At my . . . at our club. He's a member, too. I've known him for a long time."

"What club is that?" New York had dozens of private clubs for men.

"The Fleet Street Club."

"There's no Fleet Street in the city," Frank said.

"It . . . it's named after a street in London."

So, a bunch of pretentious snobs. "When did he tell you about his little hobby of kidnapping unsuspecting females?"

"He never . . . I didn't know anything about it!" he tried, but he kept glancing at Joanna, who simply glared at him.

"All right, Mr. Neth. Let me tell you what I know. Pendergast has been enjoying his little hobby for a couple of years now, and you knew all about it. I know that because Joanna here was one of Pendergast's victims. I also know she now belongs to you. Did he give her to you when he was finished with her?" Now Joanna was glaring at Frank. "Oh, wait. Pendergast wouldn't just *give* her to you, would he? Oh no. He *sold* her, didn't he? How much did you pay, Neth? I hope you drove a good bargain."

Joanna had paled again, but Neth's face grew scarlet with rage and humiliation. "How dare you suggest such a thing."

"After what I know went on in this house, I think I can suggest just about anything. We found a naked woman locked in a cage in the cellar. Is that where Pendergast kept you, Joanna?"

"Don't talk to her like that! Can't you see she's terrified?" Neth cried, putting his arm around her.

Only then did Frank realize she was trembling, but whether from terror or from fury, he couldn't be sure. "So why don't you just tell me what you know about Pendergast, and then I won't have to talk to her at all."

Neth sighed and turned back to Frank. He looked annoyed, which struck Frank as a rather mild emotion considering what most people would be feeling under the circumstances. "I told

153

you, I met Milo at our club. He . . . he didn't tell me where the women came from, not at first. He just . . . Well, he invited a few of us to his house for some entertainment. That's what he called it. He had two women here. They . . . they did whatever he told them to. We thought they were prostitutes. I swear, I never suspected what he was doing."

"Not until Joanna told you," Frank said.

Neth glanced at her again and swallowed. "Yes."

"So, did you offer to buy her or did Pendergast suggest it?"

"I had to get her out of here, didn't I? I couldn't leave her here."

"What does it matter how he did it?" she snapped. "He got me away."

"But he didn't set you free, did he?" Frank said. "Now you're *his* slave instead of Pendergast's."

"I can leave him whenever I want to!"

"Then why are you still with him? Why didn't you go back home?"

"I couldn't go back home. They knew I'd been corresponding with a man. When I didn't come home, they would've thought I eloped. I couldn't go back after months away, alone and unmarried. I was ruined, and they never would've taken me back. They wouldn't want their friends to know how I'd shamed them."

Frank had suspected this, of course, but hearing it from her made it sound even worse. "Is that what he does with the women he kidnaps? Does he sell them to his friends?"

"Stop saying that," Neth said.

"Then answer my question."

"He . . . I don't know what he does with them. I do know that some . . ." He glanced at Joanna again, and she stared back at him in surprise.

"What do you know about some of them?" she asked, her voice crackling with outrage.

"He told me that sometimes . . . well, two times, he said . . . that sometimes they kill themselves."

"The women?" Frank said, shocked, although he shouldn't have been. Anyone who'd been treated the way he knew the woman in the cellar had been treated might well lose all hope.

"Yes," Neth said, not meeting Frank's eye. "He complained about it."

"Complained?" Frank echoed in astonishment.

"Yes, because he had to get rid of the bodies. He couldn't just call the undertaker or anything, you see. There would be questions. It was difficult, I gathered, to, uh, dispose of them."

"So he didn't kill the women when he got tired of them?"

"Oh no."

"What did he do with them, then? I know he'd had at least a dozen of them here over the past couple years."

"A dozen? Are you sure?"

"He kept their shoes. They're upstairs in a cabinet where he could look at them whenever he wanted."

Joanna made a strangled sound. "That bastard."

"You shouldn't swear," Neth said. "It doesn't become you."

She shot him a glance sharp enough to draw blood. "I heard him say once . . ."

Frank waited, knowing how difficult this must be for her. He tried to soften his expression, although he thought it was probably too late to win her confidence.

She cleared her throat. "I heard him say that he'd taken a girl to a madam once."

"Did he mention the madam's name?" Frank asked, keeping his voice calm and even so as not to alarm her.

She shook her head. "I don't think so. It doesn't matter, though. He said . . ." She had to close her eyes for a moment and draw on some inner strength to go on. "He said the madam wouldn't take her because she was too . . . too ugly. He said that was the trouble with fooling ugly women. Nobody wanted them when you were done with them."

So what did he do with them? Frank wondered. Did Neth even know?

Before he could ask, Gino Donatelli stuck his head in the door. "Broghan is here, and he's drunk."

7

Frank sighed. "Stay here," he told Neth and Joanna.

He found Broghan standing in the parlor doorway, taking in the bloody scene. He turned when Frank approached.

"A fine mess you've made here," he said.

Frank could smell the liquor on him, but aside from his bloodshot eyes, Broghan gave no other sign of being drunk. Frank suddenly realized he'd probably never seen him sober, so he really had nothing with which to compare his behavior. "I didn't make the mess."

"But you found it, which you wouldn't've done if you hadn't been interfering in my case."

"I told you I'd sent Pendergast a letter. He replied to it and wanted to meet the girl this afternoon. I didn't want to miss the chance to catch him."

"You could've told me."

This was true. Frank had no reply that didn't insult Broghan, so he made none.

Broghan shook his head. "So that's Pendergast?"

"It is."

"Do you want to tell me what happened?"

Frank told him, starting with their plan for

Maeve to meet Pendergast in the park, how Livingston had spoiled it, and how they'd ended up here to find the real Pendergast dead and Grace Livingston in shock near his body. Then he described who and what else they'd found in the house.

"So the Livingston woman killed him," Broghan said.

"I doubt it."

Broghan scowled. "From what you said, there were three people in the house—the woman locked in the basement, the Livingston woman, and Pendergast. Maybe you don't think I'm as smart as you, Malloy, but even I can figure out she's the only one could've done it."

"Did I mention the front door was unlocked? Anybody could've come in and done it, or maybe somebody else was here and left after killing Pendergast."

"You said his blood was all over the girl, though."

"Yeah, because she was standing in front of him when his throat was cut, but would you let somebody walk up to you with a knife and slit your throat? Especially somebody smaller and weaker and female? Seems like he could've stopped her pretty easily."

"Unless he didn't think she'd really do it. Would you? Expect a female to slit your throat? Maybe he just laughed at her and that made her madder and she caught him by surprise. I've seen crazier things and so have you."

"What did she do with the knife, though?"

"Huh?"

"The knife she slit his throat with. It wasn't in the room anyplace."

"You sure?" Broghan glanced around as if to see for himself.

"Yes. I haven't found it yet, anyway."

"You search the whole house?"

"Not for the knife, but if it's not in this room, Grace Livingston didn't kill him."

"How do you figure that? She could've hid it someplace after she did it."

Frank frowned. "So you really think she cut his throat, stood there while his blood squirted all over her, then ran out someplace—without managing to drip any blood along the way—hid the knife, came back here and slumped down in front of the dead body in a faint?"

"Like I said, people do strange things."

Frank knew that. Broghan was proving it. "She didn't kill him."

"She tell you that?"

"I didn't ask her. She wasn't in any condition to answer questions when I found her."

"Well, let's ask her now. Where is she?"

"She . . . Her father took her home."

Broghan raised his eyebrows.

"Like I said, she wasn't in any condition to

answer questions, and we know where to find her. You can talk to her later."

"What about the other woman? The one in the cellar?"

"She, uh, she left."

"What do you mean, she left?"

"When nobody was paying attention, she snuck out of the house."

"You didn't have anybody watching her?"

"Donatelli was outside the kitchen door, but she went out the back way. She wasn't in any shape to go very far. We think Pendergast had been starving her, and she didn't have any shoes. Nobody figured she'd leave."

"And yet she did," Broghan observed.

Frank really hated not being a cop anymore. If he were still a cop, Broghan wouldn't dare make him feel like he'd messed up. In fact, if he were still a cop, Broghan wouldn't even be here. He decided to change the subject. "We found about a dozen pair of shoes that Pendergast had apparently been keeping as souvenirs of the women he kidnapped. I also found where he kept the letters from the women. Most of them have addresses."

"Why would I need that? Can't prosecute him for kidnapping when he's already dead."

"The families might want to know what happened to the women if they never made it back home."

"And maybe they wouldn't." Broghan looked around the room again. "Did you send for the medical examiner?"

"Of course."

"Where the hell is he, then?"

"It's Sunday."

"Yeah, well, I got here, didn't I?"

"Malloy?" A voice called from down the hall. Frank looked out to see Neth and Joanna standing there expectantly. Once again he'd almost forgotten about them.

"Who's this?" Broghan asked.

Frank introduced them, choosing not to add that Joanna had once been one of Pendergast's prisoners. "They identified Pendergast's body. I thought you might want to ask them some questions."

Broghan nodded. "Were either of you here when he was killed?"

"Of course not!" Neth said.

"Then you can go."

Frank glared at him. "You might have more questions when you've finished looking around."

"If he does," Joanna said, "Andy can answer them."

"Who's Andy?" Frank and Broghan asked in unison.

"He's Milo's man," Neth said. "Takes care of the house."

Joanna gave an unladylike snort.

"Donatelli!" Frank called.

Gino came scrambling up the stairs. "Yes, sir?"

"You don't need to call him sir anymore, boy," Broghan said with a nasty smile.

Frank ignored him. "Did you find anybody up in the attic?"

"No, sir," Gino said with a defiant glance at Broghan.

"Any trace of anybody?" he continued, trying to be patient.

"Well, one of the rooms looked like somebody lived there. We thought maybe he kept one of the women up there."

"Did you look in the drawers? Check for clothing?"

"Uh, no . . ." Gino's glance at Broghan was sheepish this time.

"So where could this Andy fellow be now?" Broghan asked no one in particular. "Oh, maybe he just left like everyone else who might've helped solve this case."

"If he did, he's probably the one who killed Pendergast," Frank said. "He could've taken the knife with him, which would explain why we didn't find it."

"Or maybe he ran away when the Livingston woman killed Pendergast," Broghan said. Frank was sure he was just trying to make him mad. He couldn't possibly think Grace Livingston killed Pendergast, not with the knife missing.

"Can we go now?" Neth asked. "We've told you everything we know."

"And I assume Mr. Malloy has your address," Broghan asked with just a trace of sarcasm.

"I know where he lives," Donatelli said.

"That's convenient," Broghan said, still sarcastic. "So yes, you can go."

Neth and Joanna hurried away, down the stairs and out the front door as fast as they could go.

Broghan turned to Frank. "You can go, too."

"What?"

"I said you can go. I don't need your help, and you've already done enough damage."

"I didn't do any damage!"

"You let the two women get away when one of them might be a killer."

"If one of them killed Pendergast, it was justified."

"Only if he was trying to kill her. Do you think he was trying to kill her?"

Frank didn't even know what to say to that. "Grace Livingston did not kill Pendergast."

"And the other woman was locked in a cage. So who did?"

"Maybe this Andy fellow."

"If he turns up," Broghan said, "I'll ask him. Meanwhile, you can go, Mr. Malloy, and let the *police* do their work."

Frank thought he might choke on his rage, but he knew better than to challenge Broghan. He'd already insulted the man's pride by interfering in the case. If Broghan got mad, he might lock Frank up just for spite. He'd done that himself a time or two to annoying citizens who had needed a lesson in respect.

Gathering as much dignity as he could manage under the circumstances, Frank nodded to Broghan and Donatelli and made his way down to the first floor and out the front door. The Maria still sat where it had before, abandoned by the driver, who had probably joined his fellows in the house while they explored the horrors within. They would, he knew, find the idea of having naked females as prisoners at least somewhat appealing. Young men like them would seldom consider the horror and anguish those females must have endured. In fact, few would. Society in general would blame the women first for being foolish enough to have fallen into Pendergast's trap and then for not having the courage to take their own lives rather than endure his abuse.

Without conscious thought, Frank had instinctively headed for Sarah's house. He needed to discuss all this with her to see if they could make any sense of it at all. Then he would have to figure out if he should call on Mr. Livingston one last time or if his responsibilities to the man were complete. Would he even want to see Frank again, since he'd be a reminder of all that poor Grace had endured? Sarah could probably advise him on that. At least he hoped she could. He doubted her finishing school had taught any etiquette rules for calling on the family of a kidnap victim.

Sarah and Maeve had been sitting at her kitchen table for a long time going over and over what they had learned about what had happened at Milo Pendergast's house. Neither of them had even given a thought to fetching Catherine from Mrs. Ellsworth's house, since they needed time to recover from their afternoon's trials, and they couldn't speak about them openly with an innocent child in the house.

When someone rang Sarah's bell, however, she realized Mrs. Ellsworth's patience must have finally ended, and she had come to find out how their efforts to trap the kidnapper had gone.

Sarah gave a cry of joy, however, when she found Malloy on her doorstep, instead. She pulled him inside and threw her arms around him, absurdly grateful for his mere presence. She wanted to weep out her anger and frustration against his chest, but she'd never been the kind of woman to weep about anything. Instead she drew back and looked into his eyes. "What happened after we left?"

He looked past her, and Sarah realized Maeve had followed her out. She discreetly stepped out of Malloy's arms. "Broghan got there finally.

He heard what I had to say and then sent me on my way."

"I don't suppose he was grateful for your help," Sarah said.

"He didn't seem to be."

"Come into the kitchen. We've got some coffee," Maeve said.

When they were seated at the table and Maeve had found a cup for Malloy, he told them what little they had missed.

"Did you see the room upstairs where the Andy person supposedly lives?" Malloy asked Maeve.

"No, I didn't go up to the attic with Officer Donatelli. I stayed with Miss Livingston while Mrs. Brandt went downstairs to help with the woman they found in the cellar. Miss Livingston didn't want to be alone."

"So Gino searched the attic himself. That explains why he didn't realize a man was living in that room. He's smart, but he still has a lot to learn."

"But you think I would've figured it out if I'd gone with him?" Maeve asked, obviously pleased.

"Yes," Malloy said with a ghost of a smile. "Women are just naturally nosier than men."

Maeve stuck her tongue out at him.

Sarah shook her head. "So this Andy person might well be the killer."

"The fact that he's missing seems to indicate

166

something isn't right, at least. He could have killed Pendergast and run out, still holding the knife without even realizing it. That would at least explain what happened to it."

"But there's no explanation for what happened to the knife if Grace killed him," Sarah said. "And even if Grace did kill that man, surely no one would consider it a crime after what he'd done to those women."

"I hope not," he said.

Maeve frowned. "Does that mean that you're not sure?"

"It means Broghan is a drunk, and he's mad at me for going behind his back and trying to trap Pendergast myself. He might do any stupid thing just to annoy me."

"That's horrible!" Maeve said.

"Yes, it is, and we won't let him get away with it," Sarah said.

Malloy just took a sip of his coffee, reminding Sarah with his silence that they couldn't depend on the police to do the right thing in any circumstance.

Before anyone could think of something else to say, someone tapped on Sarah's back door. Mrs. Ellsworth had, at last, reached the end of her patience. She came in with Catherine and a roast chicken that reminded everyone it was supper-time.

No one mentioned a word about the after-

167

noon's activities during supper, and Malloy took his leave shortly afterward. He wanted to see his son, Brian, before he went to bed. Sarah saw him to the door so they could enjoy a good-night kiss in private.

"I think I should call on Mr. Livingston tomorrow," he said. "What do you think?"

"That would be very nice. He's bound to have some questions, and he won't want to upset Grace with them, I'm sure."

"I probably don't know the answers to his questions."

"No, but you can at least hear him out. He'll be angry and upset. Which makes me think I should go with you. Grace might welcome some female company who can understand what she's been through."

"That's a good idea. I'll . . ." He frowned.

"What is it?"

"I started to say I'll try to get away early, but I just realized I don't have anything to get away from anymore. It's hard to get used to."

Her heart ached for him. As much as he'd had to compromise in his job as a police detective, the position had given him a measure of pride in doing his job well. Now that the Livingston case was solved, he had nothing challenging to do anymore. She realized that she would most likely find herself in the same position after having supported herself as a midwife for all these years. "I suppose we'll get used to it, or find something to do with our time."

"I guess." He didn't look like he believed that, though.

"So we're agreed," she said briskly, determined not to worry about the future. "We'll both call on the Livingstons tomorrow. What time shall we go?"

"What time do morning calls start?" he asked with a smile.

"You know very well they start in the afternoon. We should probably give Grace time to sleep late if she can. Come for me around one o'clock."

He kissed her then, making her forget for a moment all the ugliness in the world.

Frank hired a cab to fetch Sarah for their trip to the Livingston house. They could have walked, but he wanted some privacy so they could talk on the way. In the confines of the cab, he took her hand.

"Are you sure you want to do this?"

"Of course," she said. "I can't say I'm eager to relive Grace's experiences, but reliving them is nothing compared to what she went through actually living them. I can't even imagine how horrible it was. What kind of a man does that to helpless women?"

"I hope you never find out. It really irks me that Vernon Neth is getting off scot-free in this.

He was definitely planning something for Maeve. Maybe he thought he could set up his own operation, just like Pendergast."

"I don't think he's clever enough to be as successful as Pendergast was, if *successful* is the right word. Besides, I can't see Joanna allowing it."

"She was his prisoner, or rather Pendergast's prisoner. You can't think Neth would listen to her about anything."

She gave him a pitying look. "Didn't you notice? He listens to her about everything. I have no idea what really happened, but I'm guessing that Joanna was more clever than most of the women Pendergast kidnapped. She recognized a potential protector in Neth and somehow convinced him to 'save' her from Pendergast."

"I did ask her why she hadn't gone back home when Neth took her away from him, and she said her family would be ashamed to take her back if she came home unmarried."

"That's probably true. They wouldn't care that she was kidnapped and held prisoner. They'd just worry about how to answer their friends' questions about where she'd been all the time she was missing."

"If she's got so much control of Neth, I'm surprised she hasn't gotten him to marry her, then."

Sarah smiled at that. "Maybe she doesn't want to marry him."

Frank had a difficult time believing that, since marriage was the ultimate goal of practically every female alive. "Why wouldn't she? She could at least see her family again."

"Maybe she doesn't want to see them. Maybe she wants to be free to make another choice. Who knows? But ask yourself this: Would you want to marry Vernon Neth?"

"He doesn't really appeal to me," Frank said to make her smile, "but I see what you mean. As long as she's not married to him, she can leave if she wants."

"Marriage can be another kind of bondage, if you're married to the wrong person. I think Joanna knows this."

They rode in silence for a few minutes. "What will happen if you figure out who killed Pendergast?" Sarah asked.

"If it's one of the women, the police should call it self-defense and forget about it."

"How could they call it anything else?"

He shrugged, wishing he didn't have to ruin any more of Sarah's illusions. "Lots of men get upset when a woman kills a man. They think about all the reasons *they've* given women to kill *them,* and they start to worry about what the females might do if they know they can get away with it."

"So they would deny a woman the right to defend herself and her honor?"

"A lot of them would, yes. You've seen it yourself."

She nodded, frowning at the memories. "You're right, I know, but in this case . . ."

"This case is even worse, because even other women won't sympathize with the victims."

"I know. It's horrible the way females turn on their own. I've tried to figure out why, but it just doesn't make any sense to blame the woman when a man attacks her."

"I think if they can convince themselves that the woman brought it on herself by doing something stupid—something they would never do—then they can believe they're safe from whatever happened to her."

"I'd hate to think that's true, but you're probably right, Malloy. But what will happen if this fellow Andy is the killer? Or another man?"

"I hope he confesses, because if he doesn't and it goes to trial, they'll call the women to testify."

"Why would they have to do that?"

"The killer will probably claim he was trying to protect the women, so they'll have to testify about what Pendergast did to them."

"Dear heaven!"

"Yes, and every newspaper in town will report every scandalous detail."

"And make up more. And ruin the women's lives completely! They'll never want to show their faces in the city again."

"And if they decide one of the women did it, she'll go on trial, and it'll be even worse."

"This Broghan, will he find the real killer?"

"He might, but I think the most we can hope for is that he decides Pendergast deserved what he got and catching his killer isn't worth the effort."

"I should probably want to see justice done, but I do think Pendergast got what he deserved."

"That's justice," Frank pointed out.

"I guess it is."

The cab dropped them at the Livingstons' brownstone town house, and Sarah took Frank's arm as they made their way up the steps to the front door. They had to knock several times before a maid, looking harried, opened the door for them. She stared at them blankly for a long moment, as if she had forgotten what she was supposed to do when someone came to the door.

"Daisy? It's Frank Malloy," he said. "I'm here to see Mr. Livingston."

She blinked and her expression hardened. "You're with the police. We don't need no more police here. You can be on your way." With that, she tried to slam the door in their faces, but Frank threw up a hand to stop it.

"Wait! Don't you remember? I'm the one who helped find Miss Livingston."

"And now you're here to take her to jail!" she cried, struggling mightily to close the door.

"Daisy!" Sarah said in the voice Frank had heard rich people use with unruly servants. The girl froze, responding instantly to the tone of authority. "I'm Mrs. Brandt. I'm here to help Miss Livingston, and Mr. Malloy is no longer with the police at all. What's this you're saying about her going to jail?"

The girl opened her mouth to reply but burst into tears instead. Frank took the opportunity to ease the door open wide enough for Sarah to slip in, and then he followed, closing the door behind them.

Sarah put her arm around Daisy and started crooning comforting words to her.

"Daisy, what is it? Who's there?" Mr. Livingston called from upstairs.

"It's Malloy and Mrs. Brandt," Frank called back.

"Oh, Mr. Malloy, please come up."

Daisy recovered herself enough to lead the way, using her apron to wipe her face as she climbed the stairs. Livingston was waiting for them at the top.

"Oh, Mr. Malloy, I'm so glad to see you," Livingston said. "I had no idea how to reach you."

"What's going on?" Sarah said. "Your maid said something about taking Miss Livingston to jail."

"Mrs. Brandt, it was good of you to come,

too," Livingston said. "Please come into the parlor so I can tell you what's happened."

He sent Daisy off to get them some tea, then ushered them into his parlor and closed the door behind them. "Please, sit down," he said.

Livingston was pale, and his hand shook as he gestured toward the sofa. Frank and Sarah sat down.

"Please, Mr. Livingston, tell us what's happened," Sarah said.

Livingston made his way to an armchair opposite where they were sitting and lowered himself carefully. He drew a deep breath, as if he needed to fortify himself for the explanation. "A police detective came here earlier today. He really was an obnoxious fellow, I must say. He wanted to speak with Grace, and he became very belligerent when I told him she wasn't able to receive visitors yet. He said the most awful things, Mr. Malloy. He said Grace was a cold-blooded killer and she'd cut that man's throat and that they'd be coming back to arrest her and put her on trial."

Frank wanted to swear, but he managed to swallow down his fury. "They won't do that, Mr. Livingston. He was just trying to frighten you."

"Why would he want to frighten me? My daughter was kidnapped! We're the victims here."

"Of course you are," Sarah said. "I'm sure

there's some misunderstanding, but Mr. Malloy can straighten it out."

Frank frowned at her hopeful expression. He wasn't sure he could straighten anything out. "As I told you, I'm no longer working for the police department, but I'll do everything I can to make sure Miss Livingston isn't arrested for anything." If necessary, he'd have Livingston take her someplace out of town to keep her hidden while he got this sorted out. But first: "Do you remember the detective's name?"

"He said Broghan, I think. Something like that."

Frank nodded. "Did he speak with Grace?"

"Oh no. I wouldn't allow it. She's . . . well, she's very fragile, I'm afraid. She cries if anyone even looks at her, and she hasn't left her room since I brought her home. Daisy says she . . . Well, she's had several baths since she's gotten home. She says she can't get the smell of blood off her."

"Do you think she'd see me?" Sarah asked. "I'd like to see for myself how she's doing and, well, I'm a nurse. I'd like to make sure she wasn't injured. She might be too embarrassed to say so if it means you would send for a doctor."

"I hadn't thought of that," Livingston said. "You are one of the few people I think she would agree to see. I hate for her to be all alone up there, but she says she can't bear how sad I am, so she always sends me away. I'll go up and ask her, if you'll excuse me."

He hurried out, leaving them to kick their heels in the stiffly formal parlor.

"Do you really think she's injured?" Frank asked.

Sarah's lovely face hardened. "I hope not, but I wouldn't be surprised, and she wouldn't want to explain to a doctor that she'd been assaulted."

Frank wanted to punch someone, and for the first time, he regretted that Milo Pendergast was beyond his grasp.

Mr. Livingston was smiling when he returned. "She'll see you, Mrs. Brandt. I told her you're a nurse and that you want to make sure she's all right. That persuaded her, I think."

"Thank you, Mr. Livingston," she said, rising from her seat. "If you'll tell me where her room is . . ."

"Daisy will take you," he said as Daisy followed him into the room with the tea tray.

Leaving the two men to manage for themselves, Sarah followed Daisy up the stairs to the floor above. The girl hesitated outside one of the doors.

She turned to Sarah, a desperate look in her eyes. "You can't let them take her to jail. She'll die if they take her. I know it!"

"I'll do everything I can for her," Sarah promised, wondering exactly what that might be if Broghan made good on his threat to come for Grace. Malloy would know what to do, though. They'd keep her safe.

Daisy knocked, and a faint murmur bid them enter. Daisy gave Sarah a last, pleading look and scurried away, leaving Sarah to open the door herself.

"Miss Livingston?" Sarah said, sticking her head in to test the waters.

"Mrs. Brandt, I'm so glad you've come," Grace said. She was in her narrow bed, propped up on an elbow.

Sarah came in and closed the door. "How are you feeling, Grace?"

"I . . . I don't really know," she said, her red-rimmed eyes filling with tears. "I thought I'd be happy to escape from that horrible place, but I don't feel happy at all." From what Sarah could see, she wore a plain nightdress, and she had a freshly scrubbed look about her. Her hair, still damp, had been braided and lay over her shoulder.

"Of course you don't feel happy. You've been through a terrible experience. It'll take a while before you feel normal again."

"I don't think I'll ever feel normal again," she said, her voice breaking on a sob.

Sarah hurried over to her, perching on the edge of her bed and taking the girl in her arms. Grace wept for a while, great racking sobs, as she clung to Sarah like a lifeline. When she was too exhausted to weep anymore, Sarah laid her gently back against the pillows and poured her a glass of water from a carafe on the bedside table. Grace drank it gratefully, then sank back into her pillows.

Sarah took a moment to look around the room. She didn't think she'd ever seen a girl's bedroom so plainly furnished. The lack of color and feminine touches disturbed her. Why would a young woman deny herself even the slightest trace of female indulgence?

Before she could do more than just wonder, Grace said, "Are they really going to put me in jail for killing that man?"

"Who told you a thing like that?" Sarah asked in outrage.

"My maid. She overheard the policeman who came here telling Father. Can they really put me in jail?"

"Mr. Malloy and your father are discussing how to keep you safely at home," Sarah said with as much truth as she could manage. "It would certainly help if you could tell us what happened, though."

"What happened?" she asked in alarm. "You mean all of it? I couldn't possibly! I don't want anyone to know what happened to me in that place."

"I'm sure you don't. You'd never want your

179

father to know, for example. You don't want to see how much it would hurt him."

"Exactly!"

"But what I've learned from living through some tragedies myself is that when you keep them inside of you, they just get bigger and more awful until they take over your thoughts and your emotions. But if you talk about them, if you let them out, every time you do, they get smaller and weaker and lose their power to hurt you anymore."

"But I couldn't! Who would I tell? No one wants to hear things like that."

"You're right, no one does, but some of us are willing to hear them if it helps someone else. I'm willing to hear your story—as much of it as you want to tell me. If you tell me, I promise I won't judge you or blame you or even be shocked. I'll be angry, I'm sure, at the man who hurt you, but not at you. You couldn't help what happened to you."

"But I went out and met him. I went to his house with him. I should never have written those letters. It's all my fault!"

"Why *did* you write the letters?" Sarah asked gently.

"What?"

"Why did you start reading the ads in the newspapers in the first place and then decide to answer them?"

180

Her face twisted with some inner agony. "It seems so ridiculous now!"

"I don't think it was ridiculous."

"But you don't know what my reasons were."

"I think I do. Try me."

"I . . . I wanted to be married. I wanted to be like other women. But look at me. I'm not pretty, and I'm not charming. Men never look twice at me. But when I read those ads, I thought . . . Oh, it sounds so stupid!"

"You thought there were men who were as anxious for a wife as you were for a husband. Maybe they weren't handsome or charming, so they had a difficult time winning a woman's heart in the usual way."

"It even sounds stupid when you say it like that. Men don't have a difficult time. They're the ones who do the asking. They're the ones who decide. If a man wants a wife, all he has to do is look around. It's only ugly women who don't have a choice. That's what he said."

"Who?"

"Him. Pendergast." She spat the name like it left a vile taste in her mouth.

"I wouldn't put much stock in anything he had to say."

"He said so many hurtful things. Things I can't even repeat. In some ways, his words hurt more than . . . than the other things he did. He told me I was ugly and stupid and no man would ever

181

want me and I should be glad he—" She clapped a hand over her mouth to hold back the awful words.

"Did he really think you should be grateful he'd chosen to abuse you?" Sarah asked gently.

She squeezed her eyes shut and nodded her head, her hand still over her mouth.

"Grace, Pendergast was a liar, among many other things. Nothing he said was true."

She turned her face away, and after a minute, she lowered her hand. "I'm glad he's dead."

"Do you remember what happened yesterday? Do you remember how he died?"

She turned back, her muddy brown eyes shining with fury. "Yes."

"Oh, Grace, did you see who did it? Do you know who cut his throat?"

"Yes," she said, suddenly calm and more confident than Sarah could have imagined. "I did."

8

Frank and Livingston sat in silence for a few minutes after Sarah left with the maid.

Finally, Livingston said, "They won't really arrest her? Put her in jail? I don't know how she'd—"

"I don't know what Broghan might do, but I think we'd better plan for the worst, at least until we can figure out what's going on. Do you have a place you could take her? Somewhere out of the city or at least a place where she'd be away from here?"

"When my wife was alive, we sometimes spent time at the shore. I'd rent a cottage and—"

"Do that, then. Take Grace away as quickly as possible. Today if you can. Meanwhile, I'll try to find out what the police are planning to do, and see if we can locate this fellow, Andy."

"Who's Andy?"

"He worked for Pendergast as some sort of servant, I think. He's missing, though, which makes me think he's involved in Pendergast's death."

"Do you think he's the one who killed him?"

"I won't know until we hear Grace's story, if she remembers at all. Or until we find Andy and question him."

"But you aren't with the police anymore, Mr. Malloy. Why would you do this for us?"

Frank opened his mouth to reply but found he had no answer.

Livingston smiled sadly. "I'm a businessman, Mr. Malloy. I've learned that men seldom do anything that is not in their own self-interest. I've been successful by learning to judge what men want and figuring out a way to benefit from helping them achieve it."

"I had promised you I'd find your daughter" was all Frank could come up with

"Yes, you did, and perhaps you felt honor bound to follow through on your original plan when Pendergast arranged the meeting with your young lady. But Grace is found, so your duty is discharged."

"I don't see it that way, not if she might end up arrested and charged with murder."

"A horrible possibility for me as her father, but not something that would affect you in any way. No, Mr. Malloy, don't protest. You may be a kind person at heart, but I can't depend on your kindness if I want to protect my daughter. You told me you had left the police department, but you did not say you had taken another position. Allow me to offer you one. I would like to hire you as a private investigator to find out what happened to this Pendergast and ensure that my daughter isn't prosecuted after all she has already endured."

Frank's mind was racing. Livingston had no way of knowing why Frank had left the police department, and he'd be justified in thinking Frank would need a job of some kind to replace his old one. Frank was just getting used to the idea that he no longer needed to worry about such things, and while the idea of never again having to earn a living was appealing, the prospect of having nothing to do with himself weighed heavily. This was probably the real reason he was so eager to keep working on Grace Livingston's case. The surge of emotion he felt at Livingston's offer was certainly proof of that. He didn't examine the emotion too closely, because he thought it might be joy, and that was hardly an appropriate feeling to have, considering the seriousness of Grace Livingston's situation. "I haven't really had time to consider my future employment, but I will accept your offer. I can't promise the police won't do something really stupid, but I can help you protect Grace from the consequences. I'll also do my best to figure out who really killed Pendergast to clear Grace's name completely."

"Did you say *you* killed Pendergast?" Sarah asked, trying not to let her shock show on her face.

"I must have. I was with him. His blood . . ." She shuddered and covered her mouth again, this time as if to keep from being sick at the memory.

"Do you remember what happened?"

"I remember pieces of it. I see things, a scene like a photograph and then another one, but nothing makes sense."

"What do you see in these 'photographs'?"

"He . . ." She shook her head, shuddering.

"All right, let's start with earlier in the day. Do you remember waking up that morning?"

Grace nodded. "It was . . . the same as all the other mornings. I woke up, expecting to be home in this bed, but I wasn't. I was in a nightmare that wouldn't end."

"Where were you?"

"In the cage. The one upstairs."

"You know about the one in the cellar?"

She shuddered again. "Oh yes. That's where he put me first, after . . ." She closed her eyes.

"You don't have to tell me everything if you don't want to, but remember what I told you about sharing your burdens with others."

Grace lay there, staring at Sarah for what felt like an hour. She studied Sarah's face for something. Sarah wasn't sure what Grace was looking for, but she stared back, trying to let Grace see only kindness.

Finally, Grace said, "He invited me to his house to meet his mother."

Sarah nodded. "Mr. Malloy had been investigating your disappearance, and he'd found out that was how he got women into his house."

"He brought me there. The house looks respectable from the outside."

"Perfectly respectable."

"But when we were inside . . ." She closed her eyes again.

"It wasn't your fault, Grace."

"I was so stupid."

"He lied to you. He tricked you. He took advantage of your innocence."

She shuddered again, but when she opened her eyes, Sarah saw determination in them. "He hit me. Across the face. As soon as we were in the house, he changed into a different person. Nobody had ever hit me, Mrs. Brandt."

Sarah nodded, understanding how shocked she must have been.

"He made me take off my clothes. Right there in the hallway. When I didn't do it fast enough, he hit me again. He said terrible things to me, how ugly I was and how no one would ever care about me."

"That isn't true. Many people care about you, Grace."

She didn't seem to hear. She stared at something Sarah couldn't see. "Then he . . . he raped me. I was screaming, begging him to stop, but that seemed to please him somehow. I thought it would never end. And then he dragged me down to the cellar and locked me in this filthy cage and left me in the dark." Her eyes, when she turned back to Sarah, were haunted with the horrors she had endured. "I was . . . naked. Naked and . . . and bleeding. And all alone with the rats and the spiders, and no one came for days. It seemed like days at least. I think it was two days. I didn't have anything to eat or drink, and I thought I was going to die there and no one would ever know what happened to me. My poor father . . ." Her voice broke on a sob and she wept for a bit.

Sarah marveled at how cruel Pendergast had been, and how calculating. He must have worked out how to break the women's spirits so they would be more malleable and completely under his control. Violating Grace would have completely terrorized her, and locking her in that horrible place with no food or water would have crushed her.

When she'd composed herself again, Sarah said, "You don't have to go on if you don't want to."

"You're right. It helps to talk about it. I didn't think it would, but it does. I wasn't sure anyone would even believe me."

"I saw that cellar." Sarah thought about the woman she'd found in that cell, but she'd wait to ask Grace about her.

Grace nodded. "After I had given up all hope, Andy came and brought me some food."

Sarah decided to feign ignorance. "Who is Andy?"

"Didn't you find him?"

"No, although we did find a room in the attic where it looked like a servant lived. Is Andy Pendergast's servant?"

"I suppose you'd call him that."

"He was kind to you?"

Grace's eyes widened. "Oh no! He brought me food, and by then I was starving, but he wouldn't give it to me until I . . . until I did something for him. I refused at first. I just couldn't bear the thought of . . . of doing what he wanted, so he left the tray sitting there, just out of my reach, taunting me. And then he left. The rats came and ate the food, and I had to watch them. I was so hungry and so thirsty, and I had to watch them."

Tears leaked out of her eyes, her silent weeping somehow more awful than the sobs that had racked her before. Sarah squeezed her hand, which seemed to give her courage.

"He came back. A long time later, he came back. He had another tray, and this time I . . . I did what he wanted, even though it made me sick. But I didn't want to die, Mrs. Brandt."

"Of course not. You were brave to do what you needed to in order to survive."

"I didn't feel brave. I felt like a coward."

"You survived. That took courage, Grace."

She seemed to be considering Sarah's words, weighing the truth of them. Then she said,

"Pendergast came later. He told me I was being a good girl, and he was going to let me come upstairs. I was grateful. I can't believe how grateful I was to that man, but I was so frightened in that cellar, in the dark with the rats. You can't know how frightened I was."

"Of course you were. That was his plan, to terrorize you."

"And he told me if I was good and did everything he said, he would let me go. So I was . . . good." She closed her eyes and turned her face away.

"Of course you were. You had no choice, did you?"

"I could have refused. I knew I could, because . . . But I didn't want him to put me back in the cellar. I thought I would die if he put me back in that cellar."

"So you really had no choice," Sarah insisted, trying to make Grace believe it.

She still refused to meet Sarah's eye, though, and stared at the wall instead. "After a while, he let me have my shift, so I didn't have to be naked all the time. I was pathetically grateful for that, too."

"Of course you were. How could you not be?"

"I just wanted to go home. I prayed and prayed. I didn't want to die. I didn't want my father to always wonder what had become of me."

"You were strong and brave, Grace. You

survived an ordeal that many women could not."

She just shook her head, unwilling to accept Sarah's praise. "It went on and on, day after day. I thought it would never end. I thought I'd always be his prisoner."

"What about that last day? Do you remember that morning?"

"I woke up in the cage, like I said. The one upstairs. Andy came to let me out. He took me to Pendergast and . . . Well, usually Pendergast made me do something to earn my breakfast, but he seemed distracted that morning. He didn't pay any attention to me, so I just sat down on the floor, in a corner of his bedroom, and waited until he went downstairs. I got very good at that, at sitting quietly and not drawing attention. I think he sometimes forgot I was there, which was fine with me."

"Then what did you do?"

"I waited and then followed him downstairs. He'd let me eat after he was finished. I had to sit on the floor in the dining room."

Sarah managed not to wince. She was beginning to regret the fact that Pendergast was dead. He deserved a far worse fate than that for the way he had dehumanized his victims. "Then what happened?"

"I . . . I followed him when he went to his study. He wanted me nearby all the time, in case he . . . he wanted me for something. But I was quiet and I just sat out in the hall, praying he would forget I was there. He was working at his desk. He was always reading letters, the letters he got from women. And he'd write letters, too, replies to the ones he got. I wanted to sneak in there and tear them to shreds, but of course I didn't. I thought he'd kill me if I tried. So I just sat there all morning, not moving, not making a noise."

"What was the next thing that he did?"

She considered the question for a time. "Andy came to tell him it was time to eat. He finished up in his study and put all the letters away. Sometimes he'd have a letter or two with him that he wanted to mail, but I don't think he had one this time. He went to the dining room, and I followed. I sat in the corner, waiting until he told me I could eat. But he . . . he forgot. He seemed to forget about me completely. When he went out, he didn't even look at me."

"He must have had something on his mind." Sarah realized he was probably worried about Neth. He'd sent his friend to meet Maeve, so he must have suspected something wasn't quite right with Maeve's letter. Why hadn't he just not met her at all? If he hadn't, they would have lost the opportunity of tracking the kidnapper back to his lair—even though Neth had led them to the wrong lair—and they might never have found Pendergast at all. The thought chilled her.

"I didn't know about your plan, of course," Grace said. "Father told me all about it in the cab after we left Pendergast's house. He was so impressed with the way Mr. Malloy had tricked Pendergast into meeting another girl."

"Except he wasn't really tricked, but at least we were able to find you eventually."

She nodded, but without much enthusiasm. Being found hadn't won her the kind of freedom she'd imagined, since she would always carry the memories of her ordeal.

"So Pendergast seemed preoccupied that day," Sarah reminded her.

"Yes, he went back to his office, I think. I grabbed some food and ate it before Andy could take it away. He said some nasty things to me, but I'd learned to ignore him. I just ran out and found a corner to hide in again until Pendergast remembered and called for me."

"And did he?"

"Not for a long time. I . . . I must've fallen asleep. I think I was dreaming I was home. I did that a lot. Fall asleep, I mean. At least when I was asleep, I wasn't afraid. Then something woke me up. Shouting, I think. Someone was shouting."

"Pendergast?"

"No. Wait, yes. They were arguing. Pendergast and someone else."

"Do you know who?"

She squeezed her eyes shut as she tried to remember. "I . . . I didn't know him."

"Did you see him?"

"I . . . Yes. Pendergast called me and I went in. They were in the parlor."

"Do you know what they were arguing about? Can you remember what they said?"

She shook her head as if trying to dislodge the memories. "Something about Pendergast tricking him, I think. It didn't make sense that he'd tricked a man. I thought that was strange."

Could it have been Neth? Could he have run to Pendergast when he escaped them the first time? He'd certainly had time to run to Pendergast's house, and he would've been angry. "Then what happened?"

"Pendergast was so angry with me. He said it was my fault."

"What was your fault?"

"I didn't know. I remember him shouting at me. He hit me, I think, at least once."

"What happened then?"

"I . . . That's where it all gets fuzzy. After he hit me, I mean. I see figures, but not clearly. I don't know who they are. People were shouting, but I'm not sure who or what they were saying. And I remember Pendergast grabbing me by the arms and shaking me, and the blood—" She gagged at the memory and clamped both hands over her mouth.

"Take a deep breath," Sarah said. "There, that's right." She waited until Grace was calm again. "What's the next thing you remember?"

She frowned in concentration. "You, I think. You helping me up and taking me upstairs. I didn't think you were real at first. I thought I was dreaming."

Sarah squeezed her hand again. "Do you still think you killed Pendergast?"

She concentrated some more. "Someone else was there. I remember that now."

"A man, you said."

"The man he was arguing with, yes."

"Was he still there when Pendergast grabbed you that final time? When you saw the blood?"

Grace stared back at her for a long moment, her forehead furrowed as she tried to recall. "I don't know. All I can see is his face. Pendergast, I mean. He was furious, screaming at me. I thought he was going to kill me. I . . . I'm not sure if anyone else was there or not."

"That's all right. You may remember more later."

Someone tapped on the door. Sarah got up to answer it and found Daisy, the maid, standing there, wringing her hands anxiously.

"Mr. Livingston said we was to pack up Miss Grace's things. He's taking her away to the shore, he said."

Sarah nodded. Of course. Malloy had probably

advised taking her out of the city, beyond the reach of the police if they intended to arrest her. "I'll tell Miss Livingston."

At first Grace balked at the idea of even leaving her bed, but after Sarah explained they were trying to hide her so the police couldn't arrest her for Pendergast's murder, she reluctantly agreed. Barely an hour later, she was dressed and packed, and the Livingstons were in a cab heading for the train station.

"How will they know when it's safe to come back?" Sarah asked when the cab had turned the corner out of sight.

"Livingston is going to send you a telegram telling you where they are once they get settled."

"Me?"

"I didn't think it was a good idea for him to tell me. That way I don't have to lie to Broghan, if it comes to that."

Sarah nodded. "Very clever. Now what do we do?"

"We take a cab back to your house, and on the way you can tell me what you found out from Grace."

Frank listened with growing fury to Grace Livingston's story.

"I hate the thought that you had to hear all that," he said when Sarah had finished.

"And I hate the thought that Grace and those

other women had to endure it. Do you realize how methodical Pendergast was? He must have experimented with his captives to figure out the best way—or I guess I should say the worst way—to ensure they would become completely subservient."

"I wish we'd found this Andy character. He might be able to answer some questions for us, like what became of the other women."

"He might have been the man Grace heard Pendergast arguing with, too. And if he was . . ."

"He might also be the one who killed him," Frank said, thinking how convenient that would be, if they could only prove it.

"Are the police looking for him?"

Frank shrugged. "Did you ask Grace about the woman we found in the cellar?"

"I didn't have a chance. I didn't want to interrupt her story, and then the maid came and we had to pack. She didn't mention her, but it seems unlikely they could be held prisoner in the same house and not at least be aware of it."

"That woman in the cellar—"

"Rose."

"Rose," he repeated obediently. "She kept saying she wasn't going to, uh, cooperate anymore."

"I got the idea she was being punished in some way, too. Grace said that she got rewards for being 'good,' like coming upstairs and getting to wear some clothing. I'm guessing Rose had not been 'good,' and Pendergast was trying to break her will. Oh, wait. I almost forgot. At one point Grace said she knew it was possible to rebel, but she couldn't bear the thought of going back to the cage in the cellar."

"So maybe she was aware of the woman down there and why she was down there."

Sarah sighed in discouragement. Frank hated that sound. "I wish I knew what happened to Rose," she said. "I hate to think of her alone on the streets."

"We could check with her family to see if she turned up."

She widened her eyes at him. "How could we do that?"

"I think I have her address." He pulled out the little notebook in which he'd copied the addresses from the letters in Pendergast's desk. "Rose Wolfe. She's the only Rose, so it must be her."

"What's the address?"

Frank pointed.

"Can we go there? Right now?"

"What are you going to say when they ask you what you want?"

He loved watching her expressions when she was trying to figure something out. After a few moments, she said, "I'll just ask for Miss Rose Wolfe. If they want to know anything else, I'll just say I'm a friend of hers. If she got home, she may be willing to see me. If she's still missing, maybe her family will want to talk to me. I can probably convince them to search for her, too."

This sounded reasonable to Frank, or at least as reasonable as anything about this case could be. He banged on the top of the cab, signaling for the driver to stop, and gave him their new destination.

The house wasn't too far from the Livingstons' home in Murray Hill. The quiet street was home to successful men who had provided well for their families. Frank dismissed the cab, and they climbed the front steps and rang the bell. As they had expected, a maid answered, and her eyes widened when Sarah asked to see Miss Rose Wolfe. She looked them over as if trying to judge whether they were worthy of being invited inside.

"Is Miss Wolfe at home?" Sarah asked when the maid hesitated a bit too long, using that tone servants instinctively obeyed.

"I . . . I couldn't say, I'm sure. Would you . . . ? Would you come inside and wait while I see?"

Frank didn't know a lot about being rich, but he knew that if you had servants, you could pretend you weren't home if someone you didn't want to see came to visit. The Wolfe family wasn't as rich as some. They didn't have a whole room where uninvited guests could sit while the maid asked if she should admit them or send them on their way. Instead, she left them standing in the front hall after getting their names to announce to her mistress or whoever really was at home. So they were rich enough, Frank judged.

A few minutes later, the maid returned, and although she was obviously still suspicious, she said, "Mrs. Wolfe will see you."

Frank exchanged a glance with Sarah, whose frown told him she was also intrigued. Was Mrs. Wolfe Rose's mother? The maid escorted them to the formal parlor, a room furnished with amazing restraint. Frank had never been fond of the currently fashionable "overstuffed" method of decorating, which required cramming as much furniture, drapery, and knickknacks into a room as possible. This room had an airy feel to it, with natural sunlight filtering through the sheer drapes. The furniture curved gracefully instead of squatting, as the horsehair-stuffed chairs and sofas he saw so often seemed to do. The only thing unwelcoming here was the beautiful woman standing in the center of it.

Sarah had no idea who the woman might be, but she recognized the fierce determination in her eyes. If she was a member of Rose's family, Rose would be well defended.

Mrs. Wolfe looked them over without bothering to hide her suspicion. She wore her honey brown hair in the latest fashion, and her dress had been custom-made to fit her figure perfectly. She had also been trained from birth how to handle any social situation except, probably, this one. "Mrs. Brandt, is it?"

"Yes," Sarah said. "Thank you for receiving us, Mrs. Wolfe. May I present my fiancé, Frank Malloy?"

This information only made Mrs. Wolfe more suspicious. "May I ask why you are here?"

Sarah gave Malloy a warning glance, in case he felt he should reply. Luckily, he looked less likely to speak than the table standing nearby. "I'm hoping to speak with Miss Rose Wolfe."

"And how are you acquainted with her?"

"We met recently. I was able to offer her some assistance, and I was hoping to find her here."

"And how did you know where she lives?"

"I . . ." She glanced at Malloy, but he obviously couldn't think of a logical explanation that wouldn't reveal the details of Rose's ordeal either. "Mrs. Wolfe, we know that Rose was missing from her home for a period of time. Where she was during that time is her story to tell, and I will not betray her confidence. The only reason we are here is to find out if she arrived here safely and if we can be of any further assistance to her."

"Who *are* you?" Mrs. Wolfe demanded, not bothering to conceal her fury any longer.

Sarah hesitated, not quite sure how to reply,

but Malloy had the perfect response. "I'm a private investigator. I was hired to find a young woman who had gone missing, and in the process, we located Miss Wolfe as well."

It wasn't the exact truth, but close enough. Even better, it was just the right information to allay Mrs. Wolfe's fears, if not her anger. "You found her, but you abandoned her to the streets? Do you have any idea the condition she was in when she arrived here yesterday?"

"So she *is* here?" Sarah cried, relief flooding her. "Thank heaven." For a second, she thought her knees might buckle, but Malloy grabbed her arm and supported her.

"Could we sit down?" he asked.

Seeing Sarah's distress, Mrs. Wolfe said, "Of course. I'm sorry. I should have . . ." Plainly, she wasn't at all sure she should have done anything, but Malloy helped Sarah to a sofa and helped her sit.

Sarah looked up to see Mrs. Wolfe still glaring at her. "We wanted to help Miss Wolfe, but she was so eager to get home, she left before we could do anything for her."

"You'll forgive me if I'm not entirely grateful," Mrs. Wolfe said. "I'm still not certain what your role was in Rose's disappearance."

"We weren't involved with that at all, I can assure you."

"And since Rose hasn't told us where she's

been these weeks, I can't even be sure she needed rescuing, if that is what you're claiming to have done."

"We aren't claiming anything," Malloy said, letting his own irritation show.

"And when Rose arrived here, she was filthy," Mrs. Wolfe said, unconcerned about Malloy's annoyance. "She'd run through the streets in her stocking feet. Her stockings were in ribbons, and her feet were cut and bleeding. Besides that, she looked like she'd been starved. Her hair was a mess and hanging in her face. She came to the back door and scared the servants half to death. They thought she was a madwoman and almost didn't let her in."

"I'm sure it was distressing to see her in that condition," Sarah said, having no trouble at all sympathizing.

"Particularly when we thought she had eloped." Mrs. Wolfe glared at them as if they were personally responsible for Rose's behavior. Perhaps she thought they were.

"Has she told you anything at all?"

"Just that she—" Her voice broke and along with it her composure. Tears flooded her eyes. "We were so afraid we'd never see her again!"

Sarah jumped up and went to comfort her. "I know. You must have been terrified when she disappeared." She took Mrs. Wolfe's arm and led her to the sofa where she'd been sitting.

"Can I get you something?" Sarah asked.

Mrs. Wolfe sighed as Sarah sat down beside her. "I think we could all do with some refreshment. Mr. . . . Malloy, is it? Would you pull the bell cord, please?"

Malloy did as he'd been bid, and in a moment a maid came in. Mrs. Wolfe ordered a tea tray. Before dismissing the maid, she turned to Sarah. "Do you think Rose would want to see you?"

"I don't know, but I desperately want to see her." Sarah turned to the maid. "Perhaps you could tell her that Sarah is here, the lady who helped her yesterday." The maid's eyes widened, but she scurried away obediently.

"Please forgive my manners," Mrs. Wolfe said, pulling a lacy handkerchief from her sleeve to blot her eyes. "I hardly know what I'm saying, I'm afraid."

"You're related to Rose?" Sarah asked.

"She's my husband's sister. She came to live with us last year, when their mother died. We were happy to have her. She's been a wonderful companion."

"And was she happy to be here?"

Mrs. Wolfe smiled wanly. "How perceptive you are. She didn't want to be a burden to anyone. We tried to convince her that was ridiculous, but she . . . Well, like most women, she wanted a home of her own, I'm sure, but . . ."

Sarah nodded. There was no use in mentioning

how few young men would find a woman like Rose Wolfe attractive. Men got to choose, and they always chose the prettiest girl they could.

"We found out she'd been corresponding with men who had advertised in the newspaper that they were looking for a wife," Mrs. Wolfe said. "Zachary, my husband, was horrified. He forbade her to continue, but I guess the damage was done. When she didn't come home one evening, we found a note she had left for us. She said that if she hadn't returned, that meant she had eloped with a gentleman with whom she had been corresponding. We couldn't understand why she would elope. If he was suitable to be a husband, why didn't she just bring him here to meet us? Zachary would have given her a marriage settlement and everything." She dabbed at her eyes again.

Sarah had no intention of telling her why Rose hadn't returned home that day, so she had no answers for her.

After a few minutes, the maid brought the tea tray, and Mrs. Wolfe served them. Sarah drank hers gratefully.

"Mr. Malloy," Mrs. Wolfe said after they'd been served. "You said you are a private investigator. Do you get many cases of missing women?"

"I've just started my business recently. I was a police detective before, and we saw our share, though."

"I wanted to report Rose's disappearance to

the police, but Zachary was afraid of the scandal. If she'd just eloped, there was no reason to involve the police, was there?"

"Not if she'd eloped," Malloy said.

Mrs. Wolfe's eyes filled again. "I knew she hadn't. If she'd married, she would have let us know. I told Zachary that, but he . . . I think he just couldn't allow himself to believe anything bad had happened to her, you see."

"I can understand that," Sarah said, earning a frown from Malloy that she ignored. "You must have felt helpless when you had no idea how to find her."

"We . . . Well, *I* did. I put an advertisement in the newspaper. I didn't tell my husband. It said that we wanted Rose to come home. I didn't say her last name, of course, but I thought if she read the advertisements, she might see it and know it was from me. I used my name, Franchesca. It's an unusual name, so she would have known who had placed it."

"I don't think she saw any newspapers while she was . . . away," Sarah said.

"That man she was writing to, the one she was meeting. Do you know who he was?"

Her anxious gaze darted back and forth between Sarah and Malloy. Sarah didn't know how to answer, but Malloy said, "Yes."

She stared at him for a long moment, as if willing him to say more, but he did not.

"He betrayed her, didn't he? I was so afraid of that. He didn't really want to marry her, did he? Or he changed his mind or something. What a horrible thing to do to an innocent girl."

Neither of them replied. Anything they said would be too much.

"Do you know where he is? Zachary will want to deal with him, I'm sure. He can't be allowed to get away with this."

"You don't need to worry about that," Malloy said.

"No, you don't," a voice said. "He's dead."

9

Rose Wolfe stood in the doorway. She looked much different than the creature Sarah had released from that cage just yesterday. Her hair had been washed and tamed into a sedate bun. She wore a simple dress of sprigged muslin that hung loose on her because of the weight she'd lost while held captive. Still, her height and her bearing, proud in spite of everything, made her an imposing figure. Only her eyes hinted at the horrors she had endured.

"What are you doing here?" she demanded of them.

Sarah and Malloy had both risen to their feet. Sarah resisted an urge to rush to Rose and embrace her. "We wanted to make sure you'd gotten home safely."

"How did you find me?" Her anger resonated in the room like a chime.

Sarah glanced at Malloy, who glanced at Mrs. Wolfe. "I found your address," he said, giving nothing away.

"And have they told you everything, Franchesca?" Rose said in challenge, braced for the onslaught of whatever emotions Franchesca Wolfe would unleash if she had known the truth.

"No, they have not," Franchesca cried in frustration. "Nothing more than I already knew, at least. Please, Rose. I can't bear seeing you in such pain and not being able to help you."

A spasm from that pain twisted Rose's face, but she shook her head. She turned to Malloy. "Are you a policeman?"

"No," he said. Sarah could see how much it cost him to say that word, although she doubted anyone else noticed. "I'm a private investigator."

"Then you aren't here to arrest me?"

"Arrest you?" Franchesca echoed, appalled. "Why on earth would anyone want to arrest you?"

"No," Malloy said, ignoring Mrs. Wolfe.

"But he is dead, isn't he?" Rose asked.

"Oh, yes," Malloy said.

Rose closed her eyes and swayed. All three of them rushed to her aid and, in spite of her protests, soon had her seated on the sofa. Franchesca perched beside her, chafing Rose's wrists until Rose pushed her hands away. She lifted her white face to where Sarah and Malloy stood over her.

"Franchesca, would you leave us? I'd like to speak to Mrs. . . ."

"Brandt," Sarah supplied.

"I'd like to speak to our guests alone."

Mrs. Wolfe looked crushed. "You don't have to protect me, Rose. Whatever happened—"

"Yes, I do," Rose said. "Please respect my wishes."

Sarah could see how difficult it was for Franchesca Wolfe to leave her sister-in-law's side. Plainly, she cared for Rose very much and truly only wanted to help. Perhaps eventually Rose would be able to accept her help, but not yet. Not today.

"If you need me . . . I'll be nearby," Mrs. Wolfe said, her unshed tears almost choking her as she fled before they fell.

The instant the door closed behind her, Rose covered her face and began to sob quietly, her shoulders shaking with the force of her grief.

Sarah took the seat beside her, aching to offer comfort but not sure how welcome her efforts would be. Malloy moved to the other side of the room, obviously willing to leave this to Sarah. While she waited, Sarah noticed that Rose wore slippers instead of shoes, and her feet appeared to be bandaged. If only she'd waited a few more minutes, she would have had her shoes. But of course, she couldn't have known that.

After a few moments, Rose lowered her hands and scrubbed the tears from her face with her sleeve, like a child. "Thank you for not telling her."

"It's not our place," Sarah said.

Rose stared at her for a long moment, as if taking her measure. "What were you doing there yesterday? How did you find me?"

"We were looking for the other woman who was there. Did you know about her?"

"Oh yes. I knew he'd brought in someone new."

"New?"

"She hadn't been there long. There was another woman before her, though. I knew about her, all right. Sometimes when he . . . did things to one of us, he'd make the other one watch."

Sarah winced. Every time she thought she'd heard the worst, she found out she hadn't. "Do you know what happened to her? Or even what her name was?"

"I don't know her name. She didn't talk. She . . . she'd been there awhile before I got there, and something was wrong with her. You could tell. Her eyes were . . . blank. Like she didn't know what was happening to her anymore. Even when he hurt her, she didn't react. He said she was no good to him anymore. He wanted us to be afraid of him, I guess, and she wasn't showing any emotion at all."

"What happened to her?"

"I don't know. She just wasn't there one day, and then the new woman came. I heard her screaming and begging, so I knew she'd just gotten there. You said you were looking for her."

Sarah winced again, but she forced herself to go on. "Her father had gone to the police when she didn't come home. They figured out that she had gone to meet Pendergast, but of course they had no idea where he'd taken her, so we set a trap for him."

"We?" Rose said, glancing at Malloy across the room.

"Mr. Malloy is my fiancé. I've helped him with some cases before," Sarah said, thinking this was enough information to explain the situation. "We wrote Pendergast a letter, as if we were a young woman answering his advertisement. Luckily, he replied almost immediately and set up a meeting."

"But he didn't go out yesterday."

"No. He must have suspected something, because he sent his friend, Vernon Neth, in his place. We followed him, and . . . well, eventually, he led us to you."

"That was Neth, then? The one who came in and started arguing with him?"

Sarah tried not to show her excitement. Rose had just confirmed Grace's account of a man arguing with Pendergast right before he was killed. "You heard them arguing? Even from the cellar?"

"He started shouting as soon as he came in the door. I heard that part. I couldn't understand what he was saying, but he was angry."

"And you're sure it was another man and not Andy?"

"I'm sure it wasn't Andy. It was someone who

knocked on the door, and Andy was already in the house."

"Do you know when he left? Andy, I mean. Because he wasn't there when we arrived."

"No, but if there was trouble, I'm sure he'd run. So you know who the man was?"

Sarah glanced at Malloy, who nodded slightly. "Not for sure. Do you know Neth?" Sarah asked.

"Not by name. He'd bring men home sometimes, but I never knew their names."

"Did you see him? The man who was arguing with Pendergast yesterday?"

"No."

"Tall fellow," Malloy said. "Thin, with brown hair. Going bald."

Rose shrugged. "I try not to remember them."

"Rose, we know what Pendergast did. We know how he tricked women into his house and what he did to them after. You don't have to tell us anything else."

"How do you know all that?" she asked in alarm.

"The other woman, Grace. She told us."

Another spasm of pain flickered across her face. "Is she . . . all right?"

"She's back with her family, but they've left the city, because the police have threatened to arrest her for killing Pendergast."

Her eyes widened with outrage. "And what if she did? After what he did to us . . ."

"The police might say she was there willingly," Sarah said.

"What? How could they think such a thing?"

"She hasn't told anyone her story. Anyone else, I mean, and certainly not the police. As you can imagine, she isn't anxious for it to become public."

"It would help if we knew who did kill Pendergast," Malloy said. "Then we could give the police the real killer and they'd leave Grace alone."

Rose stared at Malloy for a long moment, then turned back to Sarah. "So you came here to ask me if I know who killed him?"

"No, we came to make sure you were all right," Sarah said.

"You could have come yesterday."

"I didn't realize Mr. Malloy had your address until an hour ago. As soon as I did, we came straight here."

"And now that we're here," Malloy said, "we wondered if you had any idea what happened to Pendergast."

"And what you can tell us about Andy," Sarah added.

Her lip curled in distaste. "Andy? That little snake."

"Yes, we know all about him," Sarah said. "But he wasn't at the house yesterday when we arrived, and we only found out about him today. Could he have killed Pendergast?"

"I don't know. I don't know anything. I was locked in the cellar, as you will recall."

"But you did hear Pendergast arguing with someone."

"And I told you, I didn't see who it was, and I don't know what happened to him. I didn't see anything. And now I'm very tired. I know you'll understand if I ask you to leave."

Sarah wanted to argue. She wanted to convince Rose Wolfe that she had to help them, but how could she insist that the poor woman continue to tell them about the worst horror she had ever experienced? Besides, she knew full well that Rose had been caged in the cellar, so how could she have seen anything?

"Thank you for seeing us," Sarah said, rising. "If you think of anything or if you just want to . . . Well, if I can help in any way." Sarah fished one of her calling cards out of her reticule and offered it.

Rose looked at it as if she were offering a cup of poison, and Sarah pointedly laid it down on the tea tray instead.

"I'm glad you got home," Sarah said.

Rose refused to meet her eye, so Sarah made her way to the door. Malloy fell in behind her, and the instant she opened it, Franchesca Wolfe jumped up from where she'd been sitting in the hallway.

"Thank you for allowing us to visit," Sarah

said before Franchesca could ask a question they didn't want to answer. "Rose is tired, so we'll be going. If you need anything or Rose does, please send for me." She gave Mrs. Wolfe another of her cards, then hurried on, not waiting for the maid and not allowing Franchesca Wolfe time to gather her wits.

The maid caught up with them in time to hand Malloy his hat and open the door for them. Out on the sidewalk, Sarah turned to Malloy.

"What do we do now?"

"I think you should go home. You've done enough for one day."

"I haven't done much at all."

"You've dealt with two women who have been to hell and back, not to mention you helped them escape from hell yesterday. I think you should go home. Spend some time with Catherine. Let Mrs. Ellsworth tell you some gossip. Tell Maeve what's happened. Get some rest."

"And what will you be doing?"

"I'm going back to Pendergast's house to see if I can find this Andy fellow. He probably knows who Pendergast was arguing with, at least."

"It was probably Neth, you know. He was gone for a while after Mr. Livingston confronted him. It's logical he went to tell Pendergast and naturally he'd be furious at being used as bait like that."

"Which is why that's the first thing I'm going to ask Andy when I find him."

"What will Broghan think about that?"

"Nothing, if he never finds out."

"And if he does?"

He smiled grimly. "They can't fire me."

"They can arrest you."

He smiled. "Yes, but I realized now I can afford to bribe them, so I'm not going to worry too much."

Malloy put her in a cab, and Sarah watched him turn and start off in the opposite direction and wished she could go with him. But he was right, she was exhausted. Not so much physically tired as emotionally wrung out. She needed to spend some time not thinking about the horrible things she'd learned these past two days. She only hoped she could.

By the time Frank reached Pendergast's neighborhood, he was wishing he'd gone home with Sarah. He'd been through everything she had, plus he'd been insulted by Broghan after being unceremoniously booted off the police force. He'd earned a quiet evening at home, too, and he'd take one just as soon as he'd made this attempt at locating the mysterious Andy.

If this Andy was smart, which Frank doubted, he would have hightailed it out of Pendergast's house and the city as well as the state, just to make sure he wasn't involved in any of the backlash from Pendergast's murder. Even if he hadn't killed the man himself, and on the off chance that he also didn't know who had, he was at the very least involved in holding all those women captive. Only a fool would come back to the very house where those crimes had taken place.

In Frank's experience, however, most criminals were fools at best and idiots at worst, so he fully expected that Andy would not disappoint him.

But if Andy had returned to Pendergast's house, he wasn't answering the door. Frank knocked and then pounded and even tried the door, but it was locked tight, as were the back door and all the windows he could reach. He kept looking up at the windows, clearly visible in the evening light, but he saw no sign of life, even though he had the uncomfortable sensation he was being watched. Finally, he took his own advice to Sarah and went home to see his son. He'd try again tomorrow, and after that . . . well, after that, he'd do something else.

"So I don't suppose Malloy found Andy," Sarah said.

"He probably would've come by to tell you if he had," Maeve agreed.

They were sitting at the kitchen table. Catherine was fast asleep upstairs, and Sarah had just finished telling Maeve about her eventful day, although she had skimmed over the more horrific details of what the women had suffered at Pendergast's hands. She didn't think Maeve needed to know the true depths of depravity to which the man had sunk.

"What are you going to do now?" Maeve asked.

"Go to bed."

Maeve smiled. "No, I mean about the case. Now that Mr. Malloy is a private investigator, he'll keep working on it, won't he?"

"I'm sure he will. I think he would have anyway, but now he has a good excuse."

"And you can help him. Oh, I know you've helped him before, but now you can help him officially."

"I'm not sure any of this can be called *official*."

"And I can keep helping him, too."

Sarah frowned. "Don't we keep you busy enough taking care of Catherine?"

"Of course you do, but I can help sometimes, like when I met Neth the other day. Admit it, I was a great help."

"Yes, you were, and I know Grace and Rose would be grateful if they knew what you'd done for them."

Maeve waved away their imagined gratitude. "I just keep wondering what Neth was planning, if he thought he'd take me captive like Pendergast did with the women he met."

"I know. He certainly didn't have any place to lock someone up, unless he thought he'd just lock you in a room. And what about Joanna? She obviously didn't know what he was planning, and I doubt she would've been too happy about it if she did."

"I can't imagine she would."

"We'll probably never know what Neth was planning, though. There's so much we'll never know. But I do plan to visit all the women for whom we have addresses to see if we can find out what became of them and let them know Pendergast is dead, at least."

"Some of them died, though. What will you do about them?"

"We don't know which ones, so I guess we'll have to visit all the families and see which of the women are still missing, then deal with what we find. It won't be pleasant, but it's the right thing to do."

Maeve sighed. "My grandfather always used to warn me about men, but I never dreamed . . ."

"Not many men are like Pendergast."

"I know, and I also know many men are like Mr. Malloy. The trick is how to tell the difference before you make a terrible mistake."

"I'm glad you understand that, Maeve, although you've got plenty of time before you have to worry about making a mistake."

Maeve shrugged, as if she disagreed but wasn't

going to say so. "Which reminds me, when are you and Mr. Malloy going to get married?"

Sarah sighed, knowing they needed to make plans very soon. "We haven't really discussed it. We need to find a place to live first."

"Are you looking?"

"Well, we haven't really had time yet . . ."

"Mrs. Ellsworth is looking."

Sarah should not have been surprised. "Is she?"

"She's looking in this neighborhood."

"Has she found anything?"

"No, but I'm thinking she's not above asking someone to move out if it comes to that."

"You're probably right," Sarah said with a smile. "Maybe Malloy and I need to get busy finding a house to protect our neighbors from Mrs. Ellsworth."

"Or you could just wait to see what she comes up with. She might surprise you."

Sarah sighed. "Mrs. Ellsworth always surprises me."

Frank didn't bother to make an early start the next morning. He wanted to be sure the neighborhood had settled down and people who left their homes early were gone before he returned to Pendergast's house. He was fully prepared to break a window if necessary in order to get inside, and he wanted as few witnesses as possible.

As he turned onto Pendergast's street, however,

he saw a man standing on the front stoop of Pendergast's house. Frank slowed his steps, being careful not to look directly at the man or act at all interested in who he might be. Frank didn't think he'd seen the fellow before, but he didn't look like a servant. In fact, he looked quite prosperous in his tailor-made suit and smart new bowler hat. He glanced around nervously as he waited for someone to answer his knock, so Frank stopped a few houses away to retie his shoelace.

While he was hunkered down, the man knocked again, more loudly and very insistently. Frank retied his other shoelace before rising again. By that time, the man had tried the door, much as Frank had done last night, and to his surprise—and Frank's—he found it unlocked.

Someone had been there and had left the house unlocked since last night. Frank quickened his step. He'd sneak in behind this fellow and see what he was doing here. Then he'd ask him some questions about how he knew Pendergast.

But just as he reached the front stoop, the man came barreling out the front door as if his tail were on fire. Frank caught him before he could escape.

The man glared at Frank with eyes wide with terror. "Let me go!"

Frank took his arm and twisted it up behind him until he cried out. "Not so fast. What were you doing in there?"

"Nothing! Let me go, I tell you!"

"Were you looking for Pendergast?"

"No, no! I . . . I don't even know who that is!"

"You're a terrible liar. Now let's try this again. What are you doing here?" He gave the man's arm a little extra twist and nearly sent him to his knees.

"Stop! Stop! I'll tell you!"

Frank eased the pressure but didn't let go. "So tell me."

"I . . . Someone sent me a message."

"Who? Not Pendergast."

"No, he . . . he's dead. Andy. Andy works for him. He . . . he wanted to see me."

"Then why didn't he answer the door?"

The man stiffened. Frank tightened his grip again, and the man cried, "Because he's dead, too!"

Frank nearly shouted a protest. Andy couldn't be dead, not until he'd told what he knew about Pendergast. "Show me," he said, shoving him toward the steps.

The two men climbed them clumsily, with Frank still holding his arm. Then Frank propelled his prisoner through the front door before releasing him and closing the door behind them.

The man caught himself and straightened, turning to Frank in a fury. He was older than Frank had first thought, almost fifty, and he was already running to fat.

"Who are you?" the man said, rubbing his arm.

The words Frank could no longer say trembled on his lips, the words that would have won this man's cooperation instantly, but Frank was no longer with the police. "I'm investigating Pendergast's death."

"I didn't have anything to do with that. I hardly know the man, in fact."

"But you belong to the same club," Frank guessed, making it sound like he already knew. "Fleet Street, isn't it?"

The man's eyes widened, and he pulled a handkerchief from his breast pocket to wipe the sweat from his face. "Yes, but—"

"And you knew what he did here, didn't you? He'd invited you to his little parties, didn't he?"

"Only once! I was appalled, I assure you!"

"So why are you here now?"

"I told you, Andy sent for me. He . . . he said he needed help to leave the city."

"Help? You mean he needed money."

The man pulled himself up to his full height in a vain attempt to regain some of his dignity. "That was my understanding, yes."

"So you generously decided to 'help' the poor fellow out."

"He said he'd tell the police I was involved if I didn't, and here you are anyway," he added bitterly.

"I'm not going to arrest you," Frank said quite truthfully, although he saw no reason to explain why. "Show me where Andy is."

The man turned and pointed down the hall to where a dark form lying on the floor was visible through the open kitchen door.

Frank took a step in that direction, and the man tried to duck around him in a bid to escape out the front door. Frank grabbed him by the lapels and shook him, jarring loose a thick envelope that fell to the floor.

"What's that?" Frank asked.

"The money for Andy. You can keep it, all of it. Just let me go."

Frank picked up the envelope and found what looked like several hundred dollars inside. That was a lot of money for somebody who had only been here once.

"I didn't kill Andy. You know that. I only just got here, and he was dead when I arrived."

"Let's take a look and see if I believe you." He slapped the envelope into the fellow's pudgy hands and shoved him down the hallway toward the kitchen.

He stumbled but then righted himself, scurrying ahead, but he stopped just short of the doorway. Frank stepped around him until he could see the body lying crumpled on the kitchen floor. Andy had been a small man in his late twenties with a pockmarked face and a crooked nose. Blood soaked his trousers from a wound in his lower abdomen. He'd tried to stanch the flow with a towel, but the wound had been too deep and had bled too fast, and he'd probably fainted and bled to death before he could get help.

The staring eyes told Frank the man was dead, and when he felt his neck for a pulse, just to be sure, the skin was cold. The fat fellow was right. He'd been dead for a while. So when the fat fellow took advantage of Frank's momentary distraction to bolt for the front door, he let him go. He could always find him at the Fleet Street Club if he needed him.

Muttering a curse—he wouldn't be getting any information from Andy after all—Frank went out in search of a patrolman.

After sending for Broghan and the medical examiner, Frank spent some time searching the house again. Andy's attic room had been stripped clean of his belongings, which he'd stuffed into a cheap suitcase that Frank found lying open on his unmade bed. Besides his clothes, it contained little of interest and certainly no indication of who else he might have contacted about providing him some "help" in leaving the city.

Frank felt certain he had done so, though. It only made sense. He would have asked the men he knew had joined Pendergast for his "entertainments," and one of them had decided to shut Andy up permanently instead of trusting him to disappear. It was, Frank had to admit, the most effective way of dealing with blackmailers, since you could never depend on them to be satisfied with just one payment.

Broghan was pretty angry by the time he arrived with a couple of patrolmen in tow. Frank braced himself for a tirade, and he endured it until Broghan had to pause because he'd used up his usual store of profanity and needed a minute to think of some more.

"I know," Frank said amiably. "You've got every right to be mad, but I didn't kill this fellow and I don't know who did. I just stumbled on his body."

"Which you wouldn't've done if you'd been minding your own business," Broghan said.

"As it happens, I *was* minding my own business. Mr. Livingston has hired me as a private investigator."

"What the hell does he need a private investigator for? And what the hell do you need a job for, I might add? I thought you was a millionaire now."

"I like to keep busy," Frank said, unable to resist the urge to tweak Broghan a bit. "And Livingston is concerned that you're going to arrest his daughter, so he wants to find the real killer before you do."

Broghan humphed in outrage. "And he thinks you can do that better than me?"

"He's worried you won't try," Frank said.

Broghan started sputtering incoherently, and Frank raised both hands in a sign of surrender.

"You've got to admit, he's got a point. You did tell him you were going to arrest her before you even questioned her."

"He wouldn't let me see her!"

"Would you have, if it was your daughter?"

That shut him up for a few seconds, but no longer. He was Irish, after all. "Did he let you see her?"

"No, but Mrs. Brandt talked to her."

"And what did she find out?"

So Frank told him. He really had no choice if he hoped to change Broghan's mind about arresting Grace Livingston, even though he was taking a chance. Broghan could use the information against the women if he wanted to.

"Those women were stupid," Broghan said when Frank was finished. "You'd think they'd know better than to go off with a strange man."

"They felt like they knew him, I guess. His letters are pretty convincing. And even stupid women don't deserve what happened to them."

Broghan shrugged, obviously uncomfortable with the knowledge he had. "But if she's the one who cut his throat—"

"I told you, she doesn't remember."

"Very convenient, if you ask me. She could be protecting somebody, too. Did you think of that?"

"Another woman, you mean?"

"How should I know? Somebody. The person who killed this Andy, maybe. For all I know, Grace Livingston came back here because Andy knew she'd done it and she wanted to make sure he couldn't tell anybody."

"She's not even in the city."

"What?"

"Her father took her away, someplace quiet so she could rest."

Broghan exploded into another round of profanity. He'd managed to remember a few new phrases, and he used them liberally until he ran out of breath. "And when were you going to tell me this?"

"I just told you."

Broghan sighed in exasperation. "So where is she?"

"I don't know. I made sure I didn't know so I wouldn't have to lie about it."

"That's also convenient."

"Look, Grace Livingston didn't kill Andy, and she probably didn't kill Pendergast. Andy was trying to blackmail the men Pendergast had included in his little hobby so he could get some cash for leaving town. One of them probably killed him just to make sure he never told what he knew."

"How do you know all that?"

"One of the men he tried to blackmail arrived just before I did. He's the one who really found the body first."

Broghan looked around meaningfully. "So where is he?"

"He ran off."

"You let him go?" Broghan asked incredulously.

"I didn't let him do anything. I couldn't arrest him. I'm not a cop anymore, remember? Besides, I knew he hadn't killed Andy. I also know he's a member of the Fleet Street Club, so if you need him, you can find him pretty easily."

"I should arrest you for interfering in an investigation."

"Or you could let me keep investigating, and I'll tell you everything I find out so you'll be able to arrest the real killer."

"You think I can't find the real killer myself?"

Frank didn't think Broghan would like his answer to that question, so he said, "Do you want my help or not? Because I'm going to investigate anyway. The only question is whether I tell you what I find out."

Broghan reached into his pocket, pulled out a flask, and took a long swallow from it. Then he wiped his mouth with the back of his hand and glared at Frank. "Do you also think I should tell you what I find out?"

"I'd appreciate it," Frank said. "And I'm willing to pay for information."

Broghan snorted and tucked his flask back in his pocket. "Think you're smart, don't you?"

"No, and I'm still pretty mad about being kicked off the force, so don't try my patience. Is it a deal?"

Since he had nothing to lose and everything to gain, Broghan nodded, albeit without much grace.

"Good. Then I'll tell you what I know about Andy and his death while we wait for the medical examiner."

Doc Haynes finally showed up, long after Frank had finished his story, the sun had moved into the western half of the sky, and they'd sent one of the patrolmen for something to eat. They'd been over the house once more in the vain hope of finding something helpful, too.

"Malloy, you're like a bad penny, aren't you?" Haynes asked with some amusement when Frank greeted him at the front door.

"He's a private investigator now," Broghan reported sourly.

"Are you? That's interesting. You'll probably want to know what I found out from Pendergast's autopsy, I guess."

"Yes, I would," Frank said, pretending not to notice Broghan's disgruntled frown.

"And when were you going to tell *me?*" Broghan asked.

"I just finished him up this morning," Haynes said. "And I would've told you when you came by my office to get the report. But that can wait. Now, where's the new body?"

Frank let Broghan take charge, following at a discreet distance so he could hear what was said without being accused of interfering.

Haynes took a good look at everything, then knelt by the body and began testing the joints for rigor mortis. "When did you find him?" he asked Frank.

"I guess it was around ten o'clock, maybe a little later. Oh, and I was here last night around five or six, but nobody answered the door. He might've been dead by then, but the doors were all locked, and when I got here this morning, the front door was open, so somebody had been here between last night and this morning."

"Did you touch the body?"

"I checked for a pulse. He was cold to the touch, and the blood was starting to dry."

Haynes nodded. "So he was probably killed sometime after five o'clock last night and at least a few hours before you found him. All right. You boys can run along and leave me to my work."

10

The two orderlies Haynes had brought came in with a stretcher. They claimed the two chairs in the entry hall and started to smoke. Frank and Broghan went upstairs to wait in Pendergast's study, since Andy had apparently made no attempt to clean up the bloody mess in the parlor. Frank supposed that would be left for whoever took possession of the house next. He wondered idly who that might be. Did men like Pendergast have family? Heirs to inherit his cursed house with its cages and obscene wallpaper and bloody carpets? Or maybe he was only renting, leaving his landlord with an unholy mess.

"Where do you suppose he got those cages?" Broghan asked, lighting a cigarette himself.

"I don't know, but I hope he lied about what he was going to use them for."

"Probably. He wouldn't want to raise any suspicions."

"Do you know anything about Pendergast? How he made his living?"

Broghan shrugged. "The neighbors said he didn't seem to work. He got money every month from somewhere, according to his bank."

"Like an allowance?"

"Something like that, I guess."

"Maybe his family knew what he was like and paid him to keep away," Frank said.

"Maybe. Doesn't matter now."

Frank didn't suppose it did.

Haynes didn't take long with the corpse. He found them in the study.

"Well?" Broghan asked.

"Your fellow was stabbed with a large knife in the lower abdomen. Whoever did it was mad, because he plunged it in up to the hilt, then jerked it out again. It made quite the mess."

"How's that, Doc?" Broghan asked.

"See, if you stab someone who's conscious, it's virtually impossible to pull the knife out at exactly the same angle because the victim is going to react, instinctively jerking back, trying to get away or what have you. The knife was sharply pointed at the tip, so it went in pretty easy. No bones in that area to worry about. But the killer pulled it out, too, and the edge of the knife near the handle was big, about three inches. With the victim jumping around, the knife got twisted and came out in a new place, tearing the wound wider."

"How do you know all this about the knife?" Broghan asked.

"I could've figured it out at the autopsy, but the knife was under his body, so that made it much easier."

"Could it be the same knife that killed Pendergast?" Frank asked.

"It's possible. It's got a smooth edge, and it's sharp enough, but I don't think I could prove it. You never found that knife, did you?"

"No," Broghan said.

"If it was the same knife," Frank said, "maybe the killer brought it back with him."

"That doesn't make sense," Broghan said. "Nobody carries a butcher knife around with him."

"Or maybe the killer knew where it was hidden," Frank added.

"We searched this house from top to bottom," Broghan said. "It wasn't here."

Frank gave up on that. "So Andy bled to death?"

"Yeah. It looks like he got stabbed there in the kitchen and, instead of running out into the street where somebody might've seen him and called for help, he tried to stop the bleeding himself with a towel."

"If he'd run for help, would he have lived?" Frank asked, earning a frown from Broghan.

Doc Haynes shrugged. "A wound like that, bleeding like it was, I don't know. If he got to a hospital really fast, maybe, but the knife would've done a lot of damage inside. Maybe a surgeon could've fixed it and sewed him back up and maybe not. He probably would've died of infection eventually anyway. Not much we can do about that."

"So what can you tell us about Pendergast?" Frank asked, earning another frown from Broghan.

"His throat was cut," Haynes told them with a small smile.

"We know that!" Broghan said.

"With a large, straight-edged knife," Haynes continued as if Broghan hadn't spoken. "The cut went from his left to his right."

"How do you know that?" Broghan scoffed.

"I can tell by several factors. How deep the wound is at each end, how clean. The start of a wound like that looks different from the end, too, so it's easy to tell. The knife just nicked the jugular vein on the left side and missed the right one entirely, but it did enough damage to kill him."

"And to spray a lot of his blood all over Grace Livingston," Broghan said with a degree of satisfaction.

"Which probably means she didn't wield the knife," Haynes said.

"What? How do you know that?" Broghan asked.

"Because." Haynes took Broghan by the shoulders and turned him until the two men stood face-to-face. "We know she was where I'm standing because she was covered with blood. The cut went from here"—he pointed to a spot on the left side of Broghan's neck—"to here."

He traced a line to the other side of Broghan's neck. "Now, if I'm standing in front of you and I go to cut your throat . . ." He lifted his fist as if clutching an invisible knife and went to slash it across Broghan's throat. "You see, it would go from your right to your left, the wrong direction."

"And besides," Frank said, "how many men would let somebody slash at their throat with a butcher knife if they could see it coming?"

"Good point," Haynes said. "Especially if that person was a female who is smaller and weaker."

"She could've caught him by surprise," Broghan muttered.

"Maybe, but you've still got the problem with the cut going the wrong way. I'm going to say that I think the killer was behind Pendergast." He moved behind Broghan. "He might've grabbed him by the hair or maybe he just sneaked up while Pendergast was busy with Miss Livingston." Haynes reached over Broghan's shoulder with his imaginary knife and demonstrated how a cut made from this angle would be in the exact direction he had described.

"Being behind Pendergast has the added advantage for the killer that he wouldn't get any blood on him," Haynes said, stepping away from Broghan.

"None at all?" Broghan asked.

"Maybe a drop or two on his hand, but nothing to speak of."

"So Grace Livingston isn't the killer," Frank said, trying not to sound too happy about it.

"I'd say it's unlikely."

"Did you find out anything that would help us figure out who *is* the killer?" Broghan asked.

"Not much. I did note that his trousers were unbuttoned."

"Pendergast's?" Broghan asked with a leer. "Not surprising. We know why he kept the women prisoner here, don't we?"

"I only mention it because Andy's trousers were unbuttoned, too."

"That's not surprising either," Frank said. "He probably did it himself, trying to get at his wound."

But Haynes shook his head. "No. His trousers were unbuttoned before he was stabbed."

Sarah thought the early-morning knock at the door would be a summons to a delivery. She hadn't been called in almost a week, and she should have been worried. She supported three people on what she earned as a midwife, after all, but since she would soon be marrying a millionaire, she couldn't bring herself to be too concerned.

She was wrong, though. The visitor was a young man in a Western Union uniform, delivering a telegram.

"What is it?" Maeve asked as Sarah tore it open. She and Catherine had come to the door, too.

"I almost forgot. Mr. Livingston was going to give me their address so Malloy can contact them when it's safe to return to the city." She glanced over the cryptic message. "That's odd."

"What's odd?" Catherine asked, pulling Sarah's arm so she could see the telegram, too, even though she couldn't read.

Sarah smiled and let her see. "The address. Malloy told them to go to the shore, but this is a hotel right here in the city."

"I thought they wanted to get away so the police couldn't arrest Grace," Maeve said.

"I did, too, but . . . Well, I suppose it doesn't really matter where they are so long as the police can't find them."

"Are you going to tell Mr. Malloy?"

"He doesn't want to know, so if the police ask him, he doesn't have to lie."

They were still puzzling over the Livingstons' decision to stay in New York when Mrs. Ellsworth arrived.

"Good morning to you all," she said, breezing in with a napkin-wrapped plate. "Nelson asked me to bring you the leftover shortbread cookies so he won't be tempted to eat them himself. He's gotten very conscious of his appearance since he started keeping company with that special young lady."

"Your son might get married before Mr. Malloy

and Mrs. Brandt if they're not careful," Maeve said with a smirk.

"It's possible," Mrs. Ellsworth said, not realizing Maeve was teasing. "We were eating hazelnuts the other evening when Miss Pringle was visiting, and Nelson cracked one that had two kernels in it. He gave one to Miss Pringle and ate the other one himself."

"That's just being gentlemanly," Maeve said.

Mrs. Ellsworth smiled slyly. "It also means he's going to marry her, although I'm sure neither of them had the slightest idea it did. Miss Pringle would have dissolved in giggles and Nelson would have nearly died of embarrassment."

"So you didn't tell them?" Maeve asked.

"Of course not. I'm waiting until they announce their engagement. So, Mrs. Brandt, you and Mr. Malloy had better not wait too long if you want to be married first."

"They have to start making plans pretty soon, too," Maeve added. "Or it'll be Christmas before they're wed."

"It won't take that long. We're not planning anything elaborate," Sarah said, certain this was true even though she and Malloy hadn't discussed it. She couldn't imagine him willingly donning a morning coat and standing up in front of hundreds of strangers in a cathedral. That didn't even sound appealing to her. Widows didn't wear white gowns and veils either. No, it was a second marriage for both of them, which was more than enough reason to keep things simple.

"Which means you won't need much time to plan, either," Mrs. Ellsworth said. "Once you've found a suitable place to live, that is."

"I suppose not," Sarah said, not sure she should be admitting anything to Mrs. Ellsworth. The woman needed so little encouragement.

"In that case, I'm sure Mrs. Brandt and Mr. Malloy will precede Nelson to the altar," Mrs. Ellsworth informed Maeve. "Nelson hasn't even proposed yet."

"But they still need a place to live," Maeve said, still smirking because she knew how irked Sarah was at being discussed as if she weren't even present. "Have you made any progress with that?"

Mrs. Ellsworth pretended to take offense. "I wouldn't dream of interfering in such an important matter, although if I heard of anything suitable, I'd let them know, of course."

"Of course," Maeve echoed with a smile.

To Sarah's relief, someone did finally knock on her door, and this time it really was a summons to a delivery.

"Andy's pants were unbuttoned before he was stabbed?" Frank asked.

Haynes nodded.

"How can you know that?" Broghan challenged.

"Because his drawers have a big gash in them where the knife went through and came out, but his trousers do not."

"Which means . . . ?" Broghan said.

"Which means," Haynes replied patiently, "his trousers were open when he was stabbed."

Broghan frowned. "Why would he be walking around with his trousers open?"

"Figuring that out is your job, but maybe for the same reason Pendergast's trousers were open," Haynes said. "You said yourself, we know why Pendergast was kidnapping these women."

"But the women aren't here anymore," Broghan said. "And Andy was waiting for *men* to come and bring him some money so he could leave town."

Haynes wagged his head in despair. "I can't say for sure, but I'd guess that this Andy fellow's visitor was not a man and that he expected a much more pleasant outcome when he unbuttoned his trousers."

Finally, Broghan's eyes widened with understanding. "Then the killer is probably a female!"

Frank almost winced. He'd been hoping against hope Broghan wouldn't catch on, but trust Haynes to make sure he did.

"I think that's a possibility, yes," Haynes said.

"I knew it," Broghan said, turning to Frank. "Grace Livingston came back here to make sure he didn't tell us she killed Pendergast."

"Grace Livingston isn't even in the city," Frank snapped. "I already told you that."

"Yes, you did, but you also said you don't know where she is, so she could be anywhere. And what about that other woman, the one you let escape? She could've come back here, too. Or maybe one of the others he's had here. I knew it was a female who killed Pendergast, and now she's killed this Andy, too."

"There's no proof it was a female," Frank said, even though he had to admit it seemed likely. In fact, from what he'd heard about Andy, he would've taken great delight in forcing one of Pendergast's former victims to satisfy him. On the other hand: "Why would any of those women come back here in the first place?"

"I told you why, to make sure Andy didn't tell anybody what he knew," Broghan said as if explaining something to a particularly dull pupil. "Whoever killed Andy also killed Pendergast. You mark my words."

"I'll let somebody else mark them," Haynes said. "In the meantime, I'll take this Andy fellow . . . Does anyone know his last name?"

Frank and Broghan exchanged a glance.

"No," Broghan said.

"Well, I'll take this Andy to the morgue,"

Haynes said. "You can check back with me day after tomorrow for the autopsy results."

When Haynes had gone, Broghan turned to Frank. "You need to tell me where Grace Livingston is."

"I told you, I don't know."

"Then how are you supposed to solve this case?"

Frank sighed wearily. "Grace Livingston's father hired me to find the real killer. That makes me think Grace isn't the real killer, so I'm going to try to figure out who else it could be."

"And how are you going to do that?"

"I don't know yet, but when I do, you will be the first to know."

He bid Broghan a good afternoon and made his way out of Pendergast's house. In truth, he did know how he was going to find out, or at least where he was going to start, but first he had to get Sarah, because he was surely going to need her help.

Malloy received an enthusiastic greeting from Maeve and Catherine, and Sarah was more than happy to see him as well. She was pretty sure no one else noticed how troubled he looked, so she didn't mention it, and since they were just sitting down to supper, he accepted their invitation to join them.

"I'm glad you're here," he said to her.

"I almost wasn't. I got a call to a delivery, but it turned out to be a false alarm."

He took her hand when Maeve and Catherine hurried back to the kitchen to set him a place and held her until they were out of earshot. "Andy's dead," he whispered.

"Good heavens! How . . . ?"

"Stabbed in the stomach. Probably last night sometime."

"Any idea who?"

"Doc Haynes thinks it was a woman."

"Why?"

But before he could reply, Catherine came running back to see what was keeping them.

"I'll explain later, but I need you to go with me after supper."

They had no further chance to talk, as Catherine grabbed Malloy's hand and drew him toward the kitchen.

As soon as they'd finished eating, Sarah changed into street clothes, said good night to Catherine, and set out with Malloy into the pleasant late spring evening.

"Where are we going?" she asked.

"To see Vernon Neth."

"I thought you said a woman killed Andy."

"That's what Haynes thinks, but I need to know more about Pendergast and what he did with the women when he was finished with them. And who else was involved."

"Do you think he had *partners?*"

"We know he invited other men over to, uh, share the women. That's how Neth met Joanna. It looks like Andy was trying to blackmail the men."

"How do you know that?"

"One of them was knocking on Pendergast's door when I arrived this morning."

"I thought you were going there last night."

"I did, but no one answered the door and the place was locked. This morning, some fellow was knocking at the door and, when nobody answered, he went inside. The door was open by then."

"Maybe he killed Andy."

"He was only in there for a minute before he came running out. He'd brought some money for Andy, but Andy was dead. In the kitchen with his stomach cut open."

They'd reached the corner, and Malloy managed to hail a cab. When they were in it and on their way, Sarah said, "If Andy was blackmailing the men involved, it's likely one of them killed him, so what makes Dr. Haynes think the killer was a woman?"

"Did you notice Pendergast's pants were unbuttoned?"

"Pendergast? No. I confess I didn't look too closely at the body, though."

"Well, they were. I noticed, too, but I figured

I knew why. He had Grace Livingston in the room with him, and he was probably intending to, uh . . ." He gestured vaguely.

"I know what you mean," Sarah said grimly. "And he may have been. But you think the same thing was true for this Andy?"

"Haynes said he can't think of any other reason he would've unbuttoned his pants for his killer except that she was a female and he was expecting to be, uh, gratified."

"And we know he used to take advantage of the female captives, so that makes sense, unless you ask yourself what female would have been at Pendergast's house with him last night."

"That was my thought, too. I can't imagine any of the women who had been Pendergast's victims going back there."

"Neither can I, unless . . ."

"Unless what?"

Sarah frowned, wondering if it was even possible. "Unless Andy was blackmailing some of the women as well."

"Do you think that's possible?"

"Possible, yes. I think the women would be even more anxious to keep what happened to them a secret than the men would to hide their involvement."

"I'd been thinking about that, too, but how would he find them?"

"He probably found the letters just as you did,

and he had the advantage of knowing what had become of each of them, if Pendergast had let them go or if they'd died or whatever."

"I guess he could've done that. If he'd contacted the women or even one or two of them, that could explain who the female killer was. Broghan thinks it was Grace, but she left the city, so we know it wasn't her."

"Oh dear."

Malloy turned to her. "What?"

"Grace didn't actually leave."

"What do you mean?"

"I got a telegram from Mr. Livingston this morning. They're staying at a hotel in the city."

Malloy looked like he wanted to explode. "Why? I told them to leave town!"

"He didn't give any explanation. He just telegraphed the name and address of the hotel, which I won't tell you, so you can continue to claim ignorance."

"And I have no intention of telling Broghan she's here either. He's convinced she cut Pendergast's throat and then went back to kill Andy because he knew it."

"He's not a very good detective, is he?"

Malloy didn't reply for a long moment. "It's a logical assumption, if you don't pay any attention to how Pendergast's throat was cut, which Haynes also explained to us today."

"What do you mean, how it was cut?"

He proceeded to demonstrate as well as he could in the confines of the cab. "So you see, Grace couldn't have done it, since we know she was standing in front of him."

"And of course, you didn't find the weapon either, so the killer must have taken it with him. Or her."

"And we know Rose was locked in the cellar, so it must've been someone else."

"But she wasn't locked in," Sarah said.

Malloy turned to her in surprise. "Of course she was. She was in that cage."

"But the cage wasn't locked. Don't you remember? Oh, maybe you didn't see how I opened it," she added, remembering he'd kept his back turned to preserve at least a shred of Rose's dignity.

"I didn't even think about how you opened it."

"There was no lock, just a bolt. On the outside, but she could've easily reached it and unlocked the cell herself. I hadn't remembered that until this moment."

"If she wasn't locked in, why would she stay in that cell?"

Sarah had to think about that. "She didn't have any clothes. Even if she'd been able to escape the cage—and it looks like she could have without much effort—she couldn't have left the house. She probably didn't even want to move around inside the house with no clothes on. She wouldn't want to show herself to Andy or Pendergast, I'm sure. And remember, the moment I gave her back her clothes, she did escape."

"But she could've gotten out if she wanted to."

"Yes, she could."

"If she wanted to kill Pendergast."

"Oh my. Remember when she first saw us yesterday? She thought you were there to arrest her. Do you think . . . ?"

"I think we need to go back and talk to her again."

"But could she have killed Andy? Her sister-in-law said her feet were injured—cut and bruised—from running through the streets with no shoes. Could she have walked to Pendergast's house and back last night?"

"I don't know. She ran all the way home barefoot, so who knows? What we do know is that both Grace Livingston and Rose Wolfe had time to go to Pendergast's house and kill Andy after we left them yesterday. What we don't know is why they would and if they did."

"I just can't imagine either of them entering that house again, no matter what the provocation."

"I can't either, but if Andy had sent them a message threatening God knows what . . . People do things you'd never expect if they're desperate enough."

Sarah sighed, wishing she knew the answers. Or maybe she didn't really want to know them. No matter what may have happened, she didn't want any of Pendergast's victims to be punished for his death, guilty or not.

"So why did you want me to go with you to see Neth? Because of Joanna?"

"Yes. I want to try to separate them, so you can talk to her alone. Find out what she knows. She was a prisoner in that house, too, so she probably heard things and saw other women there, like Rose did. And I think Neth might speak more freely if she's not there. I want to find out if he went to Pendergast after Livingston confronted him and what he has to say for himself about that. He was also most certainly going to kidnap Maeve, but he's not going to admit it in front of Joanna."

"And maybe Joanna will speak more freely if he's not there," Sarah said. "Or not. She's a smart girl, and she's not going to say anything to get herself or Neth in trouble."

"Just try. I think Neth is the weaker of the two anyway. The important thing is to get her away from him. And Sarah, try to find out if Andy was trying to blackmail her. She's the one he was sure to know how to contact, so if he sent her a message, he might've also tried to blackmail the other women."

Joanna frowned when she saw them on the doorstep. "What do you want?"

"I'm here to see Neth," Frank said, prepared to

251

force his way in if necessary. For an instant, he thought it might be, but then Joanna stepped back and let them enter.

"We already told you everything we know," she said.

"I don't think so," Frank said, watching her face, but she gave nothing away.

She shrugged. "I'll tell him you're here."

She started up the stairs, and Frank indicated to Sarah they should follow instead of waiting for her to return for them. Neth might decide he didn't want to see them and slip out the back way.

Joanna rolled her eyes when she realized they were following her, but she made no protest and led them to the parlor. She pulled open the door and said, "Malloy and that woman are here."

Neth had been reading the newspaper by the front windows, and he jumped up, letting the newspaper fall to the floor at his feet. He stared at them in alarm, making Frank wonder what he had to be worried about.

"Good evening, Mr. Neth. We were wondering if you could spare us a few minutes," Frank said.

"I can't imagine why you're here," Neth said. Apparently, he was trying to be condescending, but the frightened squeak in his voice ruined his effort.

Frank smiled his own version of condescension. "I just have a few more things I'd like to ask you, if you don't mind. And maybe it would be better if we were alone, man-to-man." He winked, alarming Neth even more.

Neth glanced at Joanna, who glowered back at him. Plainly, he wanted her advice, and just as plainly, she wasn't giving it.

"Well, I suppose that would be all right," Neth said. "Oh, Mrs. Brandt, I didn't see you there." He looked back at Frank with a silent question.

"Maybe Joanna could entertain Mrs. Brandt while we talk," Frank said.

This seemed to please Joanna even less than letting Frank question Neth alone, but she left the room, leaving Sarah to follow or not. Sarah gave Frank a little smile, then followed Joanna, closing the door behind her.

Neth stood there for a long moment, his body stiff, his hands reflexively opening and closing into fists. Finally, Frank said, "Could we sit down?"

"Oh yes, of course." Neth seemed almost relieved and moved to where a sofa and some chairs sat grouped in the center of the room. Frank took one of the chairs and Neth another. Neth sat stiffly, his hands clutching the armrests. "Now, what can I do for you?" He'd made an attempt to sound hearty, but it came off pretty flat.

"I just wanted to let you know that we found the fellow Andy, the one who worked for Pendergast."

Alarm flickered over his face, but he managed to say, "Oh, good. I was worried about him, poor devil. Where has he been?"

"I don't know where he was the past few days, but I found him at Pendergast's house this morning."

"Really? I suppose he was shocked to hear about Pendergast." Neth tried to smile, to show he had no concerns about Andy at all, but the smile stopped short of his eyes, which clouded with worry. "What did he have to say for himself?"

"Have you heard from Andy since Pendergast died, Mr. Neth?"

Neth blinked in surprise. "Heard from him? What do you mean?"

"I mean heard from him. Did he come to see you or send you a letter or telephone you?"

"Andy? No, no. I don't think Andy has ever contacted me about anything."

Frank had expected him to lie about that, of course, but Neth seemed genuinely puzzled by the question and truthful in his answer. If Andy had tried to blackmail Neth, Frank was sure he wouldn't have been able to hide his apprehension, and Frank would have bet money that Neth would be the first name on Andy's blackmail list.

How very strange.

"Mr. Neth, I know a lot more about Pendergast and his little hobby now than I did the other day. I know how he used the lonely hearts advertisements to lure women into meeting him, and how he invited them home to meet his mother. I know he raped them and took their clothes and locked them in cages until he broke their wills and turned them into his slaves."

Neth shifted uncomfortably in his chair. "Really, Mr. Malloy, I don't think—"

"And I know one of his former victims lives with you here, but what I don't know is what happened to the rest of them."

"I already told you—"

"I know, I know. Two of them committed suicide, and he tried to take one to a brothel, but they weren't interested. I need to know what happened to them—the ones who survived—when Pendergast was finished with them, Mr. Neth."

"Really, Pendergast didn't confide in me about his . . . activities."

"He told you about the suicides. I consider that confiding. And what did he do with those bodies, by the way? You said he was concerned about disposing of them."

"He . . ." Neth shifted again and tried to chuckle, although it came out more like a croak. "He left them in a cemetery, I believe. Yes, that's what he said. Wrapped them in sheets and left them in a cemetery. Beside a church, you know. Someone found them, I'm sure, and gave them a decent burial."

"And notified their families?"

"Oh, well, I couldn't speak to that, I'm sure. I don't know any details, of course, not the names of the churches or anything like that. He just . . . He thought he'd been clever, you see, and wanted to brag a bit."

Frank pinched the bridge of his nose in an attempt to stave off a threatening headache. "And what about the others, the ones he didn't leave wrapped in a sheet in a cemetery?"

"I . . . I don't know. I just know with Joanna . . . Well, he wasn't finished with her yet, you see. He'd keep them until . . ."

"Until they wore out?" Frank tried when he hesitated, using Rose's expression. "Until they no longer cared if they lived or died?"

Neth blanched at that, but he said, "I didn't approve of what he did. You must believe me. That's why I took Joanna out of there. She begged me to, you know."

"I'm sure she did, and yet you'd gone to Pendergast's house more than once to visit the women he kept there, didn't you?"

"I told you, at first I thought they were whores, that he was paying them and they were there willingly. When Joanna told me . . ." He covered his face with both hands.

"And yet you were going to kidnap a woman yourself just the other day."

Neth looked up with fresh alarm. "No, that wasn't it at all."

"Were you going to bring that girl here and lock her up the way Pendergast did? Was he going to lend you one of his cages?"

"No! I wasn't going to keep her. He just . . . He said . . ."

"What did he say, Mr. Neth? Did he ask you to keep her here until he came to get her? You can't say you didn't know what he planned to do with her, Mr. Neth, not after Joanna already told you the truth."

Neth shook his head frantically.

"Or did he tell you that you were ready to start your own collection? Did you think Joanna would help you manage the women the way Andy helped Pendergast?"

"Please, please, don't tell Joanna. He made it sound so easy, but he knew something was wrong. That's why he sent me in his place. I wasn't going to hurt her, I swear!"

Frank wasn't interested in Neth's hypocritical oaths. "The other women, Neth. What happened to them?"

"I think . . . I'm pretty sure he just let them go. He'd give them their clothes and put them out."

"But not their shoes."

"What?"

"He kept their shoes as souvenirs."

"Dear God."

"Yes. He'd use them until their minds were

gone, and then he'd put them out like stray cats to find their own way home."

"I saved Joanna, though," he said, as if that excused him.

"Saved her? She's your mistress, isn't she? I hardly call that *saving*."

"What do you want from me? I've already told you I don't know who killed Pendergast. Why do you keep torturing me?"

Frank wanted to point out that he didn't know the first thing about torture if he thought that's what Frank was doing, but he said, "You must've been pretty angry when you realized Pendergast had tricked you. I guess that's why you went straight to his house to tell him."

He looked up at Frank, his eyes wild with terror. "I didn't!"

"Of course you did. The women heard you arguing, and they saw you," Frank lied, testing him.

"They didn't see me!" he cried. "They couldn't have!"

"Why? Because you didn't see them? Because you thought they were locked up in their cages? Well, they weren't. They were right there. Grace was standing right in front of Pendergast when you cut his throat."

"Then she knows I didn't do it! Why would I kill him?"

"Because you were angry. Because he tricked

you and got you caught trying to kidnap a woman."

"But I didn't. That Grace woman, she'll tell you. I wasn't there!"

"Where were you last night?"

Neth frowned in confusion at the change of subject. "Last night?"

"Yes, after five o'clock."

"I was at my club."

"All evening?"

"Yes, until about ten. Then I came home."

"Were you here the rest of the night?"

"Of course."

"Alone?"

"Joanna was here."

"So you can vouch for each other?"

"Why would we need to do that?"

"Because somebody killed Andy last night, and I was pretty sure it was you."

11

Joanna didn't even look to see if Sarah was following her as she made her way back downstairs and into the kitchen. Maybe she hoped Sarah wouldn't follow. At any rate, she didn't seem surprised when Sarah stepped into the kitchen behind her.

She crossed her arms defiantly. "What do you want?"

"I want to be sure the women Pendergast kidnapped aren't hurt any more, and that includes you."

"Then get out of here and leave us alone."

Sarah had to admit, it was tempting. "That might protect *you,* but it won't help the others."

"I can't help the others."

"I've spoken with the two women we rescued the other day. They've told me what they went through. You were very clever to have gotten away."

Some emotion flickered across her face but was gone before Sarah could identify it. "I wasn't clever enough to keep from getting caught in the first place."

"You can't blame yourself for that. Pendergast apparently had a lot of practice doing what he did. He knew what would work the best."

"Not all the women he corresponded with got caught," she said bitterly. "Sometimes one would get a bad feeling or something and would refuse his invitation to meet his mother. Sometimes they wouldn't even show up at all."

"How lucky for them. Maybe their families found out and stopped them."

"That would make him so angry," she said as if Sarah hadn't spoken. "He'd come home furious, and he'd take it out on us."

"How many women were there with you?"

Joanna's brown eyes narrowed. "Three. Not all at once. He never kept more than two at a time. He liked having two, though, because it was worse for us that way."

"Worse?" Sarah would have thought the women might comfort each other.

"Because someone else knew. We knew what he did to the other one. I couldn't figure it out at first, why that was so bad, but then I realized that when he was using the other one, I was so glad it wasn't me that I couldn't even feel sorry for her anymore. I know the others felt the same. We couldn't even look at each other after a while."

"But you can help each other now. The police think Grace Livingston killed Pendergast."

"Grace? That's the one you were looking for?"

"Yes."

"How can they arrest her? After what he did?"

"You know how men are. Or maybe you don't.

Not all men, of course, but too many, unfortunately. They don't like the idea of a female killing a man, no matter what the provocation."

"But he kidnapped her!"

"He kidnapped all of you, but some will say you deserved it because you answered his letters in the first place, and then went to meet him, and then went home with him. They'd say you were no better than you should be and got what you deserved. They might even say that you stayed willingly."

Fury bloomed in her face. "How could anyone think that?"

"People think what they want, and they think what they're told. The newspapers will say awful things about her, about all of you—"

"No! They can't!"

"They can and they will. I'm sorry. I'm only telling you what I know is true. I've seen it before, so I want to stop it. Mr. Malloy and I are trying to figure out what really happened to Pendergast and hoping we can protect all of his victims in the process."

"Why do you even care?"

"Because when men like Pendergast are allowed to prey on innocent females, no female is safe. I have a daughter, and I don't want her living in a world like that."

Joanna stared at Sarah for a long moment. "That's a good reason. I was afraid you'd pretend that you cared about me or those other women."

"I don't know any of you, not well enough to really care about you, but I do hate what happened to you. I hope you can believe that, too."

"I might," she said, still defensive. "But I can't help Grace. I can't help anyone."

"Did you know Andy was trying to blackmail Pendergast's friends? He wanted money to leave town."

Her eyes widened. "How do you know that?"

"Because Mr. Malloy caught one of them delivering money to him at Pendergast's house."

She smiled slightly at that. "Who was it?"

"Malloy didn't get his name, and Andy didn't get away because somebody had already killed him."

This seemed to please her. "He deserved it, that nasty little rat."

"They think a woman killed him."

Her eyes widened again. "Why?"

"Something about the way he was killed," Sarah hedged, not wanting to give too much information. "We were wondering if he was trying to blackmail Pendergast's victims, too."

"What do you mean?"

"The women, if they'd gotten away, they might have gone home. They wouldn't have told their families what really happened to them, or very little of it, anyway. Then if Andy sent them a message, threatening to"—Sarah gestured vaguely—"I don't know, threatening to tell their families or the newspapers or the world in general. He probably asked for money, and maybe one of them decided to get rid of him once and for all. With Andy and Pendergast dead, maybe their secret would be safe."

"I doubt Andy was that smart."

"Really? You don't think he would have thought of blackmailing the women, too?"

"I don't think he would have even known how to find them."

"He probably knew how to find you."

She stiffened. "He knew better than to bother me."

"So you didn't receive a threat from him?"

"No, I didn't. And you're wasting your time. He wouldn't even have expected women to have any money to give him. He would've only gone after the men."

"Did he threaten Mr. Neth?"

She pressed her lips so tightly together, they turned white. "He tried."

"So he did send Mr. Neth a message."

"Yes, but he never saw it. I burned it."

Sarah found herself admiring her courage. "Why did you do that?"

"Because Neth would've paid him, and I didn't want that little rat to have anything. After what he did . . ."

She looked away, seeing something dark and

ugly. When she turned back to Sarah, she said, "They're wrong. One of the men killed him, one of Pendergast's friends. You find him and punish him."

"Do you know their names?"

"Neth does. I'll make him tell you."

With that she pushed past Sarah out the door and back down the hall. Sarah followed, nearly running to keep up. When they reached the parlor upstairs, Joanna threw open the door without bothering to knock.

Neth and Malloy looked up in surprise.

"Did he tell you?" Joanna asked Neth. "Andy is dead."

Neth and Malloy rose and stared at Joanna.

"Yes," Neth said carefully. "He said Andy was murdered, and he thinks I did it."

Joanna scowled at Malloy. "Are you crazy? He couldn't hurt a flea. Besides, he was here with me all night. No, one of the others did it. One of those men Pendergast used to bring to his house. Give him their names."

"Joanna," Neth said patiently, "why would one of them have killed Andy?"

She rolled her eyes. "Because Andy was blackmailing them. Isn't that true?" she asked Sarah.

"Yes, it is."

"You see?" she told Neth. "He even tried to blackmail you."

"No, he didn't," Neth said. "He probably knew I'd never pay him," he added a bit smugly, earning a derisive snort from Joanna.

"Yes, he did. He sent you a message just like the others, but I never gave it to you. I knew you'd pay him, so I didn't tell you. I burned it instead."

"Joanna! What if he'd gone to the police!"

"And told them what? That his employer was kidnapping women and holding them prisoner and he was helping? He was stupid but not that stupid. He couldn't say a word without tarring himself with the same brush. But don't worry, because he's dead now, and all you have to do is tell Mr. Malloy who the other men were. One of them did it," she told Malloy, "but not Neth, because he didn't even know he was being blackmailed."

Neth sank back into his chair as if afraid his legs would no longer hold him. He stared at Joanna with a curious mixture of awe and terror. Then he turned to Malloy. "She's right; I didn't know. I had no idea."

Sarah believed him, and she wondered if Malloy did. Malloy hardly ever believed anyone, which was probably a consequence of having been a policeman for so long and hearing so many lies.

"You need to listen to her," Malloy said. "You need to give me the names of the other men."

"I can't give their names to the police," Neth said. "They'll be furious. They'll throw me out of the club!"

"That stupid club," Joanna snapped. "How can you care what those good-for-nothings think of you?"

"They're my friends!" He was whining now, setting Sarah's teeth on edge.

"Oh, for heaven's sake," Sarah said. "They'll never know you gave their names. Besides, Mr. Malloy isn't with the police, and if they're innocent, they've got nothing to fear."

Neth still hesitated, his eyes darting nervously while he actually wrung his hands.

Suddenly, Joanna gave an exasperated sigh and stormed out of the room.

"Joanna, where are you going?" Neth cried, jumping to his feet again. But he obviously didn't care enough to go after her and find out. Instead he turned to Malloy. "Is it true? Can you keep my name out of it? I don't want them thinking I betrayed them."

"What about those women?" Sarah said. "Didn't you already betray them?"

Neth spared her only a glance. "You understand, don't you?" he asked Malloy. "I just can't . . ." He shrugged.

Malloy looked as if he didn't understand at all. "Why did Joanna pick you?"

Neth frowned. "What do you mean?"

"Just that. I haven't met all the others yet, so maybe you really are the cream of the crop, but what made her think you were the one who'd save her from Pendergast?"

Neth took offense at the implied insult, stiffening and making a disgruntled face, but before he could reply, Joanna returned holding a booklet bound in red paper. She walked straight up to Malloy and gave it to him.

"That's a list of the members of his club. Only a few of them went to Pendergast's house, but if he won't tell you which ones, just start at the beginning and be sure to tell all of them that Neth sent you to them. I'm sure he'll change his mind when a few of the innocent ones let him know how angry they are."

"Joanna, how could you?" Neth cried. He looked for all the world as if he was going to weep.

Malloy flipped the pages of the book, then tucked it into his suit jacket when Neth tried to reach for it. "Thank you, Joanna. That's very good advice. Mrs. Brandt, I think our business here is done."

Sarah had to bite back a smile when Neth cried out in protest.

"You can't! I'll be ruined!"

"Then make me a list," Malloy said.

Neth gave Joanna a murderous glare. "Give me a few minutes," he said, then stomped out of the room much as she had done.

Only then did Sarah wonder at the possible consequences of Joanna's act. "Will he be angry with you?"

"Of course, but he won't do anything about it. He's a coward. I told you, he couldn't hurt a flea, which is why he couldn't have killed Andy."

Sarah felt sure Joanna was right, which only made her more curious as to why she had picked Neth as her savior. Even more surprising was that he really had rescued her.

"What about Pendergast?" Malloy said. "We know he was there right before Pendergast died."

"So what if he was? He didn't do that either. I'm telling you, he could never bring himself to do it."

"Even still, he'll be angry with you. If you feel you're in danger, we can find you a safe place," Sarah said, thinking about the Mission, where she did volunteer work.

Joanna gave her a pitying look. "I'm not in danger here, and I'll never be in danger from him. Why don't you both sit down? He'll be a few minutes with his list. He'll want to get it just right."

Sarah took the chair Neth had vacated and Malloy resumed his seat. Joanna walked over to the front window and pretended to stare out of it. She probably just didn't want to make conversation with them while they waited. Only when she sat watching Joanna at the window did Sarah realize she wasn't dressed as a maid today. She wore a simple dress she'd probably purchased at Stewart's or Macy's, which made her look like a middle-class matron. Was she changing her status in Neth's household from servant to . . . well, to whatever you called the lady of the house when she wasn't the wife? She would love to discuss the matter with Joanna, but she decided not to risk offending her, at least as long as they still needed her help.

They sat in silence for a few more minutes until Neth finally returned with a handwritten list. He thrust it at Malloy, his expression mutinous.

"If you so much as mention my name, I'll have your job."

Sarah wondered if he had any idea how ridiculous that threat really was.

Malloy took the paper, glanced over it, then folded it carefully into thirds and stuffed it into his inside jacket pocket. "Thank you for your help, Mr. Neth," he said.

"I don't want to see you here again," Neth said in what he probably thought was a threatening tone.

"I don't want to be here again," Malloy replied amiably. "Let's just hope neither one of us is disappointed."

Neth glowered and Malloy ignored him. "Mrs. Brandt?"

Sarah started for the door, and Malloy followed.

"Joanna, see them out," Neth said, but she merely cast him a withering glance and resumed staring out the front window.

Sarah didn't bother to bite back this smile. Joanna was going to lead him a merry chase.

Outside in the street, Frank offered Sarah his arm and she took it as they strolled away from Neth's house. "That was interesting," he said.

"Joanna is interesting. I would love to hear the conversation they're having now."

"We thought he might be a killer, but she's not a bit afraid of him," Frank marveled.

"But he's afraid of her, I'm sure. He pretends he isn't, but it's clear."

Frank was a little afraid of her himself. "I think I also believe that he wouldn't hurt a flea. I accused him of killing Pendergast, and he was more insulted than scared. He asked me why he'd even want to kill Pendergast, and the only reason I can think of is that he got really mad that Pendergast tricked him."

"So you don't think he killed Pendergast anymore?"

"I'm pretty sure he didn't. When I accused him of it, he said Grace was there and she'd know he didn't do it."

"And he doesn't know she can't remember, so I guess he didn't do it."

"That seems likely."

"Then you don't think he's the one who was arguing with Pendergast either?"

Frank had to think about that one for a minute. "I guess it's possible that was someone else, but it's also possible that Neth confronted him and then left, and somebody else killed Pendergast."

"The same person who killed Andy?"

"That would make things simpler."

She raised her eyebrows. "So you think a woman killed both of them?"

"Women had the best reason to kill both of them."

"Then I guess you won't need those names Neth gave you."

"Oh, I'll pay them all a little visit. We could be wrong. Maybe one of these men killed Pendergast, and someone else killed Andy."

"How many names did Neth give you?"

"Four. I'm thinking Pendergast wouldn't have trusted his secret to many others, and Neth would make five."

"I guess I'm relieved he only had five friends he thought would enjoy his 'entertainments.' But even though Joanna is sure one of them killed Andy, you still think a woman did it."

"Which is why I'm going to send you to see Grace Livingston and Rose Wolfe again."

"You can't expect me to ask them if they killed Andy!"

"No, but they should be warned that Broghan might decide they did. If he can't find Grace, he might go after Rose."

"Would he even know where to find her?"

"He could look through the letters the same as I did."

"I guess he could. You're right, we need to warn them."

He glanced up at the sky. The sun had sunk behind the buildings, and although the sky was still light, darkness wasn't far away. "So you can do that first thing tomorrow morning, but for now, I'm taking you home."

Sarah slept poorly that night. She kept thinking about the three women she knew who had been Pendergast's victims and wondering how she could protect them from the scandal that would surround a murder trial. When she managed to stop worrying about them, she thought about the woman who had summoned her yesterday and wondered if she would really go into labor before Sarah could get to see Grace and Rose tomorrow and, if so, if Broghan would try to arrest one of them before she was finished with the birth.

She'd finally fallen into a sound sleep around dawn, only to be awakened less than an hour later by Catherine, who was overjoyed to find her at home. The three of them made a breakfast of pancakes and bacon, and Sarah started feeling more alive after a third cup of coffee. She dressed carefully, wishing for the first time in years that she had a more extensive wardrobe. She would like to have something fashionable for her visit to Rose Wolfe, although Franchesca Wolfe was the one who would notice Sarah's utilitarian suit.

She told herself she was only concerned because she didn't want Franchesca to discount her warning because of Sarah's inferior social status. Still, she had to admit that the lovely Franchesca had made her feel a bit dowdy, most likely without intending to and certainly without realizing it. Sarah would have to tell her mother she was ready to start selecting her trousseau. She couldn't think of anything that was likely to please her mother more.

She decided to go to the hotel where Grace Livingston was staying first. She wasn't sure about the rules for visiting people who lived in hotels, but they couldn't possibly be as strict as the usual rules, where "morning" visits were actually held in the afternoon. What she hadn't figured on was the hotel's rule about unescorted females.

"I'm here to see Miss Grace Livingston," Sarah informed the desk clerk.

The middle-aged man with carefully pomaded hair and a sleek little mustache eyed her suspiciously. "Is Miss Livingston expecting you?"

"Uh, no, but if you'll let her know I'm here, I'm sure she'll see me."

He looked her over again, which Sarah found annoying. "We do not typically admit unescorted females who arrive without luggage."

Sarah managed not to sigh. "I'm not trying to check into the hotel. I just want to visit with one of your guests."

"Yes, well, that's typically what unescorted females with no luggage want to do."

Sarah glared at the man. How anyone might consider someone wearing her admittedly dowdy ensemble a female of easy virtue was beyond her. Of course, he probably just enjoyed abusing his authority to terrorize defenseless women. In his way, he was no better than Milo Pendergast and his cronies. She considered her various options and decided directness was probably the best. "Are you accusing me of being a prostitute?" she asked in a loud voice.

As she'd expected, he widened his eyes and literally jumped back a step at her boldness, glancing around to see if anyone had overheard. A well-dressed, elderly couple walking through the lobby stopped to stare in astonishment.

"Of course not!" the clerk said, not nearly as loudly as Sarah. "I didn't mean . . . I mean . . . We have to be careful. The reputation of the hotel . . ."

". . . will be ruined if it becomes known that respectable females are denied admittance," she said.

A bald-headed gentleman with a carnation in his lapel came hurrying across the lobby. "Are you having a problem, madame?"

Sarah recognized his worried frown as that of a businessman concerned over a dissatisfied customer. Probably a manager of some sort. She gave him a disgruntled frown in return. "I want to visit my friend, who is staying here, but the desk clerk has refused to—"

"Not refused," the clerk interrupted with a nervous smile. "I was merely, uh . . ." He consulted some papers. "Miss Livingston is in room three twenty-four. May I escort you up?"

"And solve the problem of my being *unescorted?*" Sarah asked with just the slightest hint of sarcasm. "No, that won't be necessary. Thank you for your assistance," she added to the gentleman who had come to her rescue, leaving him to demand an explanation from the desk clerk and making her way to the elevator.

As she walked down the third-floor hallway to Grace Livingston's room, she couldn't help thinking that the supercilious desk clerk was probably just the type of man who would take great delight in reading about Milo Pendergast's debauchery and who would blame the women for being victimized. She needed a few moments to tamp down her anger before knocking on the Livingstons' door.

Mr. Livingston answered her knock. "Mrs. Brandt, what a pleasant surprise. Please, come in." He glanced down the hallway when she'd stepped inside. "Is Mr. Malloy not with you?"

"No. He still doesn't know where you are, although I had to tell him you hadn't left the city, I'm afraid."

"Then you aren't here to tell us it's safe to return home?"

"No, on the contrary, I'm here to tell you that Grace needs to remain hidden for the time being."

Their room was a suite. The parlor was comfortably furnished and beginning to look a bit lived-in. A newspaper lay scattered across the sofa, and a cart with dirty dishes left from breakfast stood in the corner. Mr. Livingston, she noticed, wore a dressing gown over his shirt-sleeves and house slippers.

"Please excuse the mess," he said, hastily gathering up the newspaper to make room for her to sit down. "I wasn't expecting anyone. May I order some tea or coffee for you?"

"No, don't go to any bother. Is Grace up to a visit?"

"I . . . She spends most of her time in her room. I'll tell her you're here."

He knocked on one of the connecting doors

of the suite and called out the information of Sarah's arrival. She heard a response, although she couldn't understand the words.

"She'll be right out," he said with an uncertain smile.

When Sarah had taken a seat on the sofa, he perched on one of the stuffed chairs.

After a moment of awkward silence, Sarah said, "I was surprised that you decided not to leave the city."

He frowned. "I was, too. I thought Grace would want to be as far away as possible, but she decided she wanted to be close in case she was needed."

"Needed?"

"I know. I didn't understand it either, but she was so upset over the prospect of leaving that I thought it best to humor her. So long as the police don't know where we are, I don't suppose it matters."

"I don't suppose it does."

The door to Grace's room opened, and she stepped out. She wore a wrapper and slippers. Her hair hung in a long braid and, except for the haunted look in her eyes, she might have been fourteen.

"Grace, I'm so glad to see you," Sarah said.

"I don't suppose you've come to tell us we can go home, have you?" she said.

"No, I haven't, and not only that, I have some more unpleasant news to tell you."

Grace closed her eyes, and for a moment Sarah thought she might faint, but she opened them again and said, "Then we'd better get to it, shouldn't we?" When she sat down beside Sarah on the sofa, her eyes were bright with determination.

Allowing herself a small sigh of relief, Sarah said, "The fellow who worked for Pendergast, Andy, well . . . he's dead."

Father and daughter gaped at her in shock. "How . . . ?" Mr. Livingston said.

"Someone murdered him. The police believe it was a woman."

"How can they possibly know that?" Mr. Livingston scoffed.

"The circumstances of his death were a bit odd," she said, trying to be tactful. "The police believe only a female could have been responsible."

"And now they think I killed Andy as well as Pendergast," Grace guessed.

"I'm not sure what they think at this point," Sarah said, "but I felt you should be warned. I must tell you, Malloy was relieved when he thought you'd left the city, because they couldn't possibly accuse you of Andy's murder, so I had to tell him you were still here."

"And they think I traveled through the city alone and returned to the house where I'd been assaulted and tortured and held prisoner, and killed a man . . . How did he die?" Grace asked.

"He was . . . stabbed."

"And I stabbed a man to death," she concluded bitterly.

"I know. It doesn't make any sense, but you see, apparently, Andy had sent messages to some friends of Pendergast's who had been his guests and who knew about the women."

"Dear heaven," Mr. Livingston said. "You mean to tell me other people knew and no one did anything about it?"

Sarah tried to guess if Grace knew that the men had abused the victims as well, but her expression revealed nothing. She'd been there only a short time, so perhaps Pendergast hadn't had any "entertainments" while she was there. "What did Andy want from these men?" she asked.

"Money, of course. He wanted to leave the city, and he needed some assistance."

"Then surely it was one of these men who killed him," Mr. Livingston said. "That makes much more sense than trying to accuse some poor woman of the crime."

"Yes, it does," Sarah said, not wanting to tell Mr. Livingston exactly why the police thought it was a woman. "But until Mr. Malloy can figure out what really happened, you should stay here."

"You'll keep us informed?" Mr. Livingston said.

"Of course." She turned to Grace. "We didn't talk about it before, but are you aware that Pendergast had another woman at his house while you were there?"

"Yes." She looked down at her hands clutched tightly in her lap. "I . . . I'd seen her."

"I'm not sure you know this, but as soon as we released her, she left the house. She didn't wait to see if we would help her, and I guess I can't blame her for not trusting us. In any case, we located her, and I thought you would like to know that she is safe."

"Is she? I'm so glad to hear it. How did you find her?"

"Malloy went through Pendergast's papers, and he found the letters Pendergast had received from his advertisements. We found her address, and we went there. She was very distressed when I told her the police might arrest you for Pendergast's murder."

Grace looked up at that. "Did you tell her I don't remember what happened?"

Sarah tried to remember. "Yes, I did, and she says she was locked in the cellar and didn't see anything."

"So neither of us can help you."

Sarah frowned. "I'm not the one who needs help. We're trying to find the real killer so the police won't arrest the wrong person."

But Grace didn't seem to understand that she

was one of the "wrong" people Sarah was trying to protect, or if she did, she didn't seem very concerned. "Will you see the other girl again?"

"Her name is Rose, and yes, I was going to try to see her today."

"Please tell her again that I don't remember what happened."

Suddenly, Sarah realized what Grace was doing, what the real meaning behind her message was. "I'll tell her. And I'll be sure you know of any developments."

"And when it's safe for us to go home," Mr. Livingston said.

She had almost forgotten he was there. "Of course."

Sarah was so preoccupied with reviewing her conversation with Grace Livingston that she completely forgot to cast the rude desk clerk a haughty glance on her way out. The doorman, obviously unaware that she might be a potential source of embarrassment to the hotel, secured a cab for her. She rewarded him with a tip and a smile, then sank into the hansom cab to think some more.

What did they know for sure about Pendergast's death?

They knew there had been at least three other people in the house that day: Andy, Grace, and Rose. They knew a fourth person, probably Vernon Neth, had come in, angry and shouting.

Grace had been with Pendergast when he died but claimed to remember little. Sarah had believed her the first time she'd said it. Perhaps she had even been telling the truth then. She'd had a terrible shock after a week of accumulating horrors from being kidnapped by a monster, so who could doubt her when she claimed amnesia?

Now, however, she'd had some time to calm down and think about what had happened. And now when she said she didn't remember, Sarah sensed some calculation in her tone. But what did that mean? Did that mean she'd remembered killing Pendergast and was claiming not to remember to protect herself? Or had she remembered seeing the real killer and was trying to protect him? Or her?

Perhaps Grace had killed Pendergast, but Malloy had already discarded that theory. The angle of the cut was wrong, and besides, what had become of the knife?

So that meant she was protecting someone else, assuming she did remember. Who would she protect, though? Not Andy. None of the women would have protected Andy. His being the killer would explain why he'd fled the house and what had become of the murder weapon—he could have taken it with him and disposed of it or brought it back with him when he returned, and his killer would have had it ready to hand. Andy would have been a logical choice, and

Grace would have accused him in a heartbeat if his had been the face she'd seen over Pendergast's shoulder. But Grace wasn't the type of person to falsely accuse someone, even someone as despicable as Andy.

Neth also could have been the killer, but would Grace have protected him? Not likely. She had most probably never set eyes on him before that day, and if she had, she would have had no kind feelings toward him. She might not have known his name, but if she'd seen his face and his hand wielding the knife, she would have said so. The same could also be said for some other stranger—one of Pendergast's friends for instance—who might have stopped by to murder Pendergast.

That left only one person whom they knew had been in the house: Rose Wolfe. She claimed to have been locked in the cellar, but Sarah knew she could've gotten free if she'd chosen to do so. She could have come up to the kitchen, gotten the knife, and proceeded upstairs to where Pendergast was preparing to have his way with Grace. Or perhaps he'd even brought her upstairs to watch. And Grace wanted Rose to know that Grace could not remember seeing the killer. Both Rose and Joanna had told her how Pendergast had turned the women against each other, but Grace hadn't experienced that particular horror yet. No, she might still be sympathetic to her fellow prisoner, or perhaps she was simply grateful enough for being free to be willing to protect her.

Then Sarah remembered how Rose had thought Malloy had come to arrest her. Why would she fear that unless she had done something wrong?

Sarah shivered from a chill at the thought of what would happen if Rose Wolfe were accused of murdering Pendergast. And would she have killed Andy as well?

And could Sarah help Grace protect her if she had?

12

Frank spent a few fruitless hours trying to run Pendergast's cohorts to ground. The first three weren't home, which ruined any advantage of surprise he might have had. He'd already known that once he spoke to one of the men, that one would warn the others, but now their servants would warn them, too, or at least warn them some strange man had been asking for them, which would put them on guard. If this last fellow wasn't home, Frank would miss his opportunity to catch even one of them by surprise.

Luckily, Isaac Traynor was at home and, also luckily, he was curious enough about Frank to receive him. Frank had been hoping this fellow wasn't the one who had discovered Andy's body, and he wasn't. Traynor stood in the middle of his well-appointed parlor, obviously ill at ease and trying to pretend he wasn't.

Just the way a man who was being blackmailed should look.

He was younger than Frank had expected, not even forty yet, and he sported a luxurious mustache that was a shade darker than his honey-colored hair. He rubbed it as he stepped forward to greet Frank.

"Mr. Malloy, a pleasure to meet you," he said heartily, offering his hand.

Frank shook it. "Thank you for seeing me, Mr. Traynor."

"Not at all. Whatever can I do for you, my good man? The girl said you were bringing me news from one of the members of my club."

"That's right. Milo Pendergast."

Surprise and alarm flickered over Traynor's rather florid face, but he recovered quickly. "Pendergast, is it? I . . . I must confess, I hardly know the man, so I can't imagine why—"

"You know him well enough, Traynor. You've attended his little 'entertainments,' so don't pretend you're innocent."

He flushed scarlet. "I have no idea what you're talking about. In fact, I think I must ask you to leave."

Frank had no intention of leaving. "Don't worry, I'm not here about that. I'm here investigating some blackmail. I understand Pendergast's servant, Andy, contacted you asking for money."

"Blackmail? Heavens, no, I haven't received any contact at all—"

"I just wanted to know if you'd actually paid Andy any money, because if you have, I'll make sure it is returned to you."

Traynor started blinking rapidly as he tried to make sense of what Frank was saying. "I . . . You'll . . . *return* it?"

"Then you did give him some money?"

"Well, he seemed in a rather bad way. He told me Pendergast had died suddenly. It was a shock to me as well. And he wanted to go visit his elderly mother, so naturally, I . . . well, I thought I'd help him out. He'd always seemed like a nice fellow."

"Nice?" Frank asked with a frown. "That's not what I'd heard about him."

"Well, a good servant to Pendergast, I mean."

"When did you see Andy?"

"I . . . Well, let's see, I think it was . . . yes, Monday afternoon, I believe. I received a note from him in the morning mail, and I . . . uh, I didn't see any reason to delay. The sooner he had the means, the sooner he could see his poor old mother."

"Yes, I'm sure you wanted him to leave town as quickly as possible." The sarcasm was lost on Traynor, though. "About what time was this?"

"I don't know exactly. I went from there straight to my club. It must have been around four when I got there. Why, what does it matter?"

"It matters because somebody killed Andy that day."

"Killed him? Are you sure?"

"Positive."

"But I just saw him . . . Good heavens, you can't think I had anything to do with that! He was perfectly fine when I left him. And the money I paid him, he would've had that. It was over two hundred dollars. That will prove I didn't . . . I wouldn't have left the money if I'd killed him!"

That made perfect sense to Frank, except: "We didn't find any money on him."

"But you said you were going to return it!"

"I lied about that."

Traynor started blinking again. "Really, what is this about?"

"It's about trying to figure out when Andy was murdered and who might've killed him. Oh, and who killed Pendergast, too, while I'm at it."

"I don't know anything about that either!"

"So you did know Pendergast was murdered."

"Andy's letter said so. He even hinted that he knew who had killed Milo, but since it wasn't me, I didn't give it too much thought."

Now Frank was blinking. Joanna hadn't mentioned that. Had Andy really known who had killed Pendergast? It seemed possible, but it also seemed foolish to say so if one of the men he was contacting was actually the killer, because what would stop him from coming to kill Andy, too? Of course, Frank already knew Andy hadn't been very smart. On the other hand, if he really had known who the killer was, why would he have bothered to mention it to a man he knew was *not* the killer, like Traynor here? No, he wouldn't have done that if he'd really known who the killer was. So he'd been guessing, hedging his bets. And tempting fate in baiting the killer.

And wasting his time if the killer was a woman, since Andy probably hadn't even tried to blackmail the women.

"Mr. Traynor, did you happen to keep Andy's letter?"

"God, no! I burned it. Can't have the servants finding something like that, can one? Next thing you know, *they'll* be blackmailing me!"

Taking note of the fact that Traynor had just admitted that he had been blackmailed, Frank managed not to sigh in frustration. "Can anyone verify the time you arrived at your club on Monday?"

"I'm sure. The doorman would probably remember, and I saw several people there." He named two of the men on Neth's list and someone else Frank hadn't heard of.

"What about Vernon Neth?" Frank remembered he had claimed to be at his club that night, too.

"He was there, but he came after I did."

"What time?"

"How should I know?"

"Try to remember," Frank suggested in his most menacing tone.

"I, uh, it was about an hour after I arrived, I'd say."

"And did he stay long?"

"I think he left when I did. Around ten, I believe."

So Andy had probably been alive when Traynor left him before four o'clock, because he had also probably been alive when Frank pounded on Pendergast's door around five, because the doors were locked then. He would've been watching for his victims and deliberately hadn't answered Frank's knock. Frank remembered all too well the sensation of being watched that evening as he made his way around the house, trying the doors and windows. Andy had let someone else in the locked door at sometime after five, though—maybe more than one *someone else*—and one of those visitors had killed Andy and left the door unlocked when he fled.

And Neth really had been at his club that evening, even though Joanna had claimed he'd been home with her.

Sarah couldn't help thinking she would like to be anyplace except Rose Wolfe's front steps as she rang the bell. She found that she no longer wanted to know who had killed Milo Pendergast and Andy, because she was pretty sure she did know, and she didn't like it one bit. She didn't have the luxury of walking away, however, because the police were probably going to arrest someone for the crime, and Sarah wanted to at least be able to protect the innocent.

The maid ushered her right in this time, and put her in the front parlor to await Miss Wolfe.

Rose Wolfe looked a bit better today. The color was returning to her face, and she had obviously slept a bit.

"Mrs. Brandt, do you have news?" she asked as she hurried into the room.

"Bad news, I'm afraid."

"Then I'm glad I told them to bring us some tea. Let's sit down, and you can tell me while we wait." She took her place beside Sarah on the sofa.

"Andy is dead," she said, seeing no reason to gloss over the facts. "Someone murdered him Monday night."

"How? Where?"

Good. Rose didn't know the details of his death. She felt a small sense of relief. "At Pendergast's house on Monday. We think he'd returned there after the police had left."

"That makes sense. He wouldn't have known where else to go."

"At any rate, he was trying to blackmail Pendergast's friends." She told Rose about the messages he'd sent and about Malloy finding his body after one of the men had gone into the house yesterday morning.

"That sounds like something he would do."

"Tell me, Rose, did he send you one of those letters?"

"Me? Why would he have tried to blackmail me? And how would he even know where I was?"

"We thought, Mr. Malloy and I, that perhaps Andy had found all the letters Pendergast had received and that he might have found the addresses of the women he'd kidnapped and thought you'd be anxious to keep him from telling what had happened."

But Rose started shaking her head even before Sarah had finished. "I doubt he was smart enough to figure that out. Besides, how could he know who would be back at home?"

"You're probably right. I just needed to be sure because . . ." Sarah found herself reluctant to tell her the rest of the story.

"Why, Mrs. Brandt? You can't think you'll shock me, not after what I've been through."

Sarah drew a deep breath. "The police think a woman killed Andy."

"Why? For the same reason they think we deserved to be kidnapped by Pendergast?" she snapped.

"No, because Andy's trousers were . . . were undone when he was stabbed in the abdomen."

Rose's eyes widened.

"So, you see," Sarah continued doggedly, "they think a woman was there and Andy was planning to take advantage of her, so she stabbed him."

Rose's frown was puzzled. "She just happened to bring a knife with her?"

"It happened in the kitchen, and they think . . . well, they think it was the same knife that killed Pendergast, that his killer had brought it back or at least knew where to find it."

"Which means a woman must have killed Pendergast, too."

"I believe that is their reasoning, yes."

Rose continued to frown, and Sarah would have given a lot to know what she was thinking.

"I've been to see Grace Livingston," Sarah continued. "The woman who was there with you?"

"Yes, I remember. You told me about her."

"She was quite traumatized by Pendergast's death. She was standing in front of him when his throat was cut, so she was covered with his blood."

Rose flinched but she didn't object, so Sarah continued.

"She says she doesn't remember what happened. She said . . . She especially asked me to tell *you* that she doesn't remember what happened."

Sarah watched closely as Rose considered her words for a long moment. "And she wanted me to know? Me, particularly?"

"Yes."

"Mrs. Brandt, I should very much like to speak with Miss Livingston."

Before Sarah could answer, a knock signaled the arrival of the maid with their tea and also the arrival of Franchesca Wolfe, who came in behind the maid.

"Mrs. Brandt, how nice to see you again. Don't you think Rose looks much better today?"

"Yes, she does." Sarah knew better than to say more in front of a servant, so they waited until the girl had set the tray down and taken her leave.

When the door was closed behind her, Franchesca took a nearby chair and began to pour tea for them. "Rose has told me a little," she said as she handed Sarah a cup. She glanced at Rose, as if seeking silent permission for something, and when Rose did not object, she said, "She told me she was held as a prisoner and unable to leave. I know she was mistreated. Anyone can see she was mistreated." She glanced at Rose again, this time with compassion. "But she won't say more than that. I think you can imagine my anger and frustration, but she says the man responsible is dead."

"Yes, he is," Sarah said.

"And yet here you are again." Franchesca handed Rose a cup. "You cannot be trying to enlist Rose's help in bringing that horrible man to justice, so I must conclude that you are here for another reason."

"Mrs. Brandt is just concerned about my health," Rose said.

"Nonsense," Franchesca said. "I know you think I'm some helpless female who needs to be coddled, but just because I was lucky enough to be born with a pretty face doesn't mean I'm weak."

"I never thought you were," Rose said.

"Of course you did. You're as bad as your brother. You'd both keep me wrapped in cotton wool and protected from every possible unpleasantness, but I'm not weak or helpless, Rose, and I won't be crushed by your troubles. And I'm also not stupid, which means I might be able to help you sort out whatever it is that Mrs. Brandt came here to sort out." She turned to Sarah, righteousness burning in her lovely eyes. "If Rose is in some sort of trouble, at least let me help with that."

Rose started to speak, but Sarah cut her off. "Let me tell it. As you know, the man who held Rose prisoner was murdered. The only people in the house at the time—at least that we know of— were Rose, another woman who was also being held prisoner, and the man's servant, Andy."

Franchesca turned to Rose, but Rose refused to meet her gaze. "What about this other woman?" she asked Sarah after a moment.

"She didn't . . . Well, the police are fairly sure she didn't kill him."

"Then it must have been the servant," Franchesca said.

"Except that he has also been murdered."

"Good heavens."

"Yes," Sarah said. "And it appears he was killed by a female."

"How can they possibly know that?"

"Because," Sarah continued doggedly, "his clothing was . . . It appeared he was in the process of taking advantage of her when she stabbed him."

"Then no one could blame her for that!"

"And no one should blame whoever killed his employer either," Sarah said. "Yet sometimes the world judges females by a different standard and seeks to punish them unjustly."

Franchesca really was smart. Sarah could see she instantly understood. "So we must protect Rose and . . . What about this other woman? Does she have family?"

"Yes. Her father had hired Mr. Malloy to find her, which is how we became involved in the first place. She was present when Pendergast—that's the man's name—was killed. I was just telling Rose that she can't remember what happened."

"Is that possible?" Franchesca asked. "I'd think something so horrible would be burned into your memory."

"If she says she can't remember, I don't think anyone can prove she can," Sarah pointed out.

Franchesca nodded, understanding immediately. "She's going to protect"—she glanced at Rose—"whoever killed that horrible man."

"I can't speak for her," Sarah said. "I only know what she told me."

"But you don't think that will be enough to keep the police from . . . from bothering Rose," Franchesca said.

"Mrs. Brandt," Rose said, startling the other two women, "will you take me to see her?"

"Really, Rose, do you think that's wise?" Franchesca asked.

"I don't care if it's wise or not. I need to speak with her. Will you take me?" she asked Sarah.

"Of course. *She* might not want to see *you,* though," Sarah said.

"I think she will. Can we go now?"

"Right now?" Francheca echoed.

"I'll need to change my dress, but yes, as soon as possible." Rose was already on her feet. "I'll only be a few minutes."

She left before either of her companions could even think to raise an objection. Franchesca turned to Sarah. "Please, let me help."

"I'm not sure what you can do, but if there's anything . . ."

"Will she need an attorney?"

"It's possible."

"Then I'll speak to one. I don't think she wants me along on this visit, so I can do that this afternoon."

"What will your husband say about you consulting an attorney?" Sarah asked.

"A lot, I'm sure, but none of it will be of any importance at all. Luckily, he's in London on business, so he isn't likely to find out until everything is settled. Oh, I cabled him the minute Rose turned up, and he's on his way home, but I don't expect him for days. In any case, he'll want to protect Rose, too."

Rose was as good as her word and returned in a few minutes, dressed for the street. Sarah could see traces of the young woman she had been before Pendergast had gotten to her. Her skirt and bolero jacket were simple and plain over her slightly wrinkled shirtwaist, and she'd put on a hat several seasons out of style. Beneath it, her hair was a bit untidy, as if she had more important things to do than worry about her appearance. She looked like hundreds of other maiden aunts who lived off the generosity of their families and tended to other people's children and lived and died alone because they lacked the beauty and charm to attract a husband. Not for the first time, Sarah felt the urge to cut Pendergast's throat herself for the crime of betraying such a simple human need as wanting to be loved.

"May we go?" Rose asked, pulling on her gloves. One finger, Sarah noticed, had been mended.

"Of course." Sarah preceded her out of the room, leaving Franchesca Wolfe to wish them good luck. Sarah resisted the urge to return the wish. Franchesca would be just fine.

Out on the sidewalk, Sarah had to hurry to keep up with Rose's long strides. She stood nearly a head taller than Sarah and probably taller than many men. Another strike against her. Rose shortened her steps when she noticed Sarah was having difficulty keeping up.

"How are your feet?" Sarah asked, amazed that she seemed little the worse for her ordeal.

"Better, but I probably shouldn't walk very far."

"We'll get a cab, then," Sarah said as they reached the corner and, without a word, Rose raised her arm and hailed one. Obviously, her height could sometimes be an advantage.

When they were in the cab, moving haltingly through the afternoon traffic, Rose said, "Tell me about Grace Livingston."

So Sarah told her everything she knew about Grace.

"I hated her," Rose said when she'd finished.

"Hated her? Why?"

"Because she didn't stand up to that devil. I wanted her to refuse to . . . to obey him." She stared out at the street as if trying to catch a glimpse of something not there.

"She said he was punishing you."

"Yes. I . . . I was like her at first. I thought if I just did what he wanted, he would let me go, but . . . Well, he didn't let me go, and it got worse and worse. I thought he might kill me if I rebelled, but by then, I didn't care. I wanted him to kill me."

"Oh, Rose!"

"I did, because I couldn't stand the thought of being there for the rest of my life. If it was never going to end, I wanted to end it. Can you understand that?"

"I think so."

"I don't think Franchesca would understand. I don't want her to know I was a coward."

"You weren't a coward! You were incredibly brave to defy him like that."

"Do you really think so?"

"Yes, I do! Don't ever think you were a coward. Not many women could have endured what you did and come out stronger."

"I'm not stronger."

Sarah looked her straight in the eye. "Yes, you are."

As usual, they probably could have walked the distance to the hotel faster than the cab carried them, but at least they weren't tired and Rose's feet weren't taxed.

This time, Sarah didn't stop at the front desk. She did glance over and saw the desk clerk who had challenged her earlier staring at her in surprise, but she spared him only a condescending glance before reaching the elevator.

As they walked down the third floor hallway, Sarah noticed Rose fidgeting. It would be a wonder if she wasn't nervous. She was about to confront a woman who may have seen her commit murder.

Mr. Livingston answered their knock, obviously surprised to see Sarah back again. "News, Mrs. Brandt?" he asked.

"I'm sorry, no. May we come in?"

Only then did he notice Rose Wolfe standing off to one side. "Oh, yes, of course."

Sarah introduced him to Rose, and when he realized who she was, he grew a bit flustered. Luckily, Grace emerged from her bedroom to distract him before he made everyone uncomfortable. She'd dressed in the meantime, although Mr. Livingston still wore his dressing gown and slippers. Her outfit was even plainer than Rose's. She gazed at Rose for a long moment, then said, "You're very tall."

"Grace," her father scolded with a puzzled frown at such an odd remark. "Please come in and sit down."

Rose and Sarah sat on the sofa, while Grace and her father took the chairs. Grace and Rose never took their eyes off each other. They seemed to be communicating silently in some way, although Sarah couldn't imagine what could be passing between them.

Then Grace nodded, as if something had been decided between them, and turned to her father. "Papa, would you mind leaving us? Perhaps you'd like to go for a walk or something."

He started to protest, but something in Grace's expression stopped him. "Yes, of course. I . . . I'll just be a few moments."

He went into the other bedroom and soon emerged wearing shoes and his suit coat. "I . . . I won't be long," he said with a worried frown.

When he was gone, Sarah said, "I told Miss Wolfe that you said you couldn't remember what happened when Pendergast was killed, and she asked me to bring her here so she could speak with you."

"What *do* you remember?" Rose asked.

"I . . . Nothing," Grace said firmly.

"I'll tell you what I remember, then," Rose said. "I remember the house was quiet all morning. I heard Andy in the kitchen preparing dinner. He left the cellar door open so I would smell the food."

"Weren't they feeding you?" Grace asked.

"Of course not. You only got fed if you . . . cooperated."

Grace winced but said nothing.

"Then it was quiet again. I don't know how long. You can't judge time down there in the dark, but a while. Then someone started pounding on the front door. Not knocking, pounding."

"I remember that, too," Grace said, straightening in her chair.

"He must have come inside or someone let

him inside, because then I heard him shouting."

"Did you hear Pendergast shouting back?" Sarah asked.

"No," Grace said, surprising them. "He was . . . trying to calm him down, I think."

"Did you hear what they were saying?" Sarah asked.

Grace looked at Rose, who said, "They must have gone upstairs. The man stopped shouting and I couldn't hear them anymore."

Sarah turned to Grace. "What were they talking about?"

"Me."

"You?" Rose said.

Grace dropped her gaze to study her hands twisting in her lap.

"The man was angry because Pendergast had tricked him," Sarah guessed. "He said your father had followed him."

"Someone's father. I didn't know it was *my* father," Grace said, still not looking up. "But I hoped. I knew he'd look for me when I didn't come home, but I couldn't imagine how he'd ever find me."

"The man was Vernon Neth, then," Sarah said, glad they could be sure now. "Pendergast sent him to meet Maeve, the girl who supposedly wrote him the letter."

"What else do you remember?" Rose asked, leaning forward.

Grace shook her head, and for a moment Sarah thought she wouldn't reply, but she said, "They kept talking, but he wasn't shouting anymore, the other man, so I couldn't hear. I was out in the hallway, hiding, trying to keep out of sight so he'd leave me alone."

Rose nodded. Of course she'd understand.

"I moved closer to the door, hoping to hear something else, but I couldn't make out what they were saying."

Sarah glanced at Rose, whose expression was either eager or anxious. Sarah couldn't be sure which. "What do you remember, Rose? What were you doing?"

"I . . . I was listening, trying to figure out what was happening. I . . . Then, right after the shouting stopped, I heard the back door."

"The back door?" Sarah echoed.

"Yes, it . . . it opened and closed. I waited, but it got very quiet, so I knew Andy had gone out."

"Yes," Grace said almost eagerly. "He wouldn't have stayed around if there was trouble."

Sarah watched Rose's face, trying to read her expression and wondering what she was thinking and what she knew and was holding back. "That's when you left your cell and went upstairs, isn't it?"

Rose looked up in surprise. "How did you know that?"

"What did you see?" Sarah asked, ignoring her question.

Rose frowned. "Not much. I got to the top of the stairs, but I still couldn't hear anything."

"So you went on upstairs," Sarah said.

But Rose shook her head. "No, I . . . I couldn't."

"She was naked," Grace explained. "She didn't want anyone to see her."

The two women exchanged a look of complete understanding that made Sarah want to weep. "So you just stood there at the top of the stairs?"

"Until I heard him leave," Rose said. "The man who'd been shouting, I mean."

Sarah turned to Grace. "When he left, was Pendergast still alive?"

She smiled bitterly. "Oh, yes. He walked the man out, patting him on the back and telling him not to worry. As if he had anything to worry about."

"And then?"

"Then he came looking for me," Grace said. "He was furious. I tried to hide."

"You did hide," Rose said, nodding. "I heard him banging around, looking for you."

"But I couldn't leave the house, not in just my shift, and he knew that. So he found me." Grace closed her eyes, squeezing out a tear.

"Don't cry," Rose said. "He's dead. Don't forget that!"

Grace raised her chin and dashed the tear from her face. "Yes, he is."

"So he found you," Sarah prodded. "What did he say to you?"

"He was furious, like I said. I guess he was pretty sure it was my father who had followed that other man."

"My father is dead," Rose said. "I told him that in my letters."

"I'm sorry," Grace said automatically, good manners demanding the response.

Rose waved away her concern. "What did he do when he found you?"

"He . . . he slapped me. More than once, I think. He . . ." She shook her head.

"I know," Rose said. "You don't want to remember, but I can guess. He told you how ugly you are and how grateful you should be that any man looked at you."

Grace nodded miserably. "I wanted to cover my ears, but he pulled my hands away, and he just kept talking, saying the most horrible things about me and how it was all my fault that he was going to have to get rid of me." She looked up, her eyes wide. "I thought he was going to kill me."

Her eyes filled, but this time she pressed her fingers against them, stopping the tears before they could fall.

"But that's not all, is it, Grace?" Sarah said.

Grace lowered her hands and stared back warily. "What do you mean?"

"I mean that Pendergast had opened his trousers. That's how we found him. He was going to assault you, wasn't he?"

Grace looked down at her hands again. This time they were closed into fists.

Sarah turned back to Rose. "And that's when you went upstairs, isn't it?"

"No, I didn't."

Sarah blinked in surprise. "You didn't? What did you do, then?"

"I went back to the cellar because I heard someone coming."

"Who?"

"I don't know. I didn't see because I ran back downstairs when I heard someone at the back door. I thought it was Andy returning."

"Someone came in the back door?" Sarah asked, trying to make sense of this.

"Yes, while Pendergast was looking for Grace. I heard footsteps on the porch and I ran, so I didn't see who it was."

"And you didn't go upstairs?" Sarah asked again.

"No, not at all. I went back into the cell."

Sarah believed her. "So, if you didn't go upstairs, it must have been the person who came in the back door who killed Pendergast."

"It must have been, because I didn't remember you being so tall," Grace said again.

The other two women stared at her for a long moment.

"What do you mean?" Sarah asked.

"Just that. I remember . . . I remember some-one standing behind Pendergast and a flash of light and then the blood. So much blood." She shuddered.

"But the person standing behind Pendergast wasn't tall?"

"No. I couldn't see her face."

"Because she was behind him," Sarah said. "And she wasn't tall enough, so you couldn't see her face."

"I thought you killed him," Grace said to Rose, her shoulders sagging.

"I know. That's why I came, so you'd know it wasn't me, although I wish I had. I wish I'd thought of it. I . . . I wish I'd been brave enough."

"But if you didn't kill him," Sarah said, "and we know Grace didn't, then who did? Grace, do you remember anything else about the killer at all? Anything that would help? You said you couldn't see 'her' face. Do you think it was a woman?"

Grace frowned. "It sounds silly, but it's some-thing I remembered today. At least I think I remembered it. It's so odd that I can't be sure I really saw it, though."

"What is it?"

"I . . . I think the person who cut Pendergast's throat was a maid."

13

The hairs on Sarah's neck stood up. "A maid?"

"I know, it sounds ridiculous, but when I try to remember, that's what I remember."

"But Pendergast didn't have a maid," Rose said.

"No, he didn't," Sarah said. "But someone else did. I think I know who killed him now."

"Who?" the other two women said in unison.

"She . . . Well, she was another one of Pendergast's victims. He'd . . ." Sarah hesitated. She didn't want to tell them Pendergast had sold Joanna to Neth. No use adding to the list of horrors they must try to forget. "He'd released her. She lives with Vernon Neth, the man who argued with Pendergast right before he died."

"What will happen to her?" Grace asked.

Sarah had no idea. Would Neth help her? Pay for an attorney? Pay bribes to the police? What about her family? She'd been sure they wouldn't want her back, so what would they do when she was charged with murder? "I don't know what will happen to her, but if the police try to arrest either one of you, we'll have to tell them about her. And if they charge her and bring her to trial, the whole story will come out, and you two will probably have to testify in court."

"Testify? You mean tell what happened to us?" Rose asked.

"In public?" Grace added.

"Yes," Sarah said, feeling sick as she saw the reality of it dawning on them. "The newspapers will report it, too. They'll make it sound even worse than it was, and everyone in the city will know what happened to you."

The two women exchanged a look, and instead of dissolving into tears, as Sarah expected, they appeared to come to another silent agreement. When they turned back to Sarah, Rose said, "Then we have to figure out how to keep her from being arrested."

Frank wasn't sure where he could find Sarah, but he knew that, eventually, she'd return home, so that's where he went. Maeve and Catherine greeted him enthusiastically and insisted on feeding him, since he admitted he hadn't eaten all day. He spent a happy hour with them until Sarah got home.

Catherine beat him to the front door, but Sarah smiled her beautiful smile when she saw him.

"Malloy, I'm so glad you're here. I've got so much to tell you."

He wondered if she'd reached the same conclusion he had, but they couldn't talk until Catherine had adequately welcomed Sarah home and Maeve had made her a sandwich and then enticed Catherine upstairs so the grown-ups could talk.

"When we're married, I hope you'll be easier to find," he said as she sat down with him at the kitchen table to eat her sandwich.

"At least we'll always be coming home to the same place."

"If we ever find a house," he added with a smile. "Have you made any progress?"

"I haven't had time. Besides, I'm waiting to see what Mrs. Ellsworth comes up with first."

"Is she looking?" he asked in amazement.

"Oh, yes. Maeve thinks that if she finds the right house, she might even ask the current owners to move out to make way for us."

Frank didn't doubt it for a moment. "So what do you have to tell me?"

"I think I've figured out who actually killed Pendergast."

"Not Grace Livingston or Rose Wolfe," he guessed.

"How did you know?"

"Because Joanna did it."

She gaped at him. "How did you figure that out?"

"How did you?" he countered.

"It was easy. When I spoke with Grace, she asked me to tell Rose that she had no memory of who killed Pendergast. That made me think Rose had done it."

"Which she could have, because she wasn't really locked in the cellar."

"Yes, but when I delivered the message to Rose, she realized the same thing, that Grace thought she'd done it, but she knew she hadn't, so she asked me to take her to see Grace."

"You've had a busy day," he marveled.

"I certainly have. So I took Rose back to the hotel where Grace is staying, and as soon as Grace saw her, she knew Rose wasn't the killer."

"How did she know that?"

"Because Rose is so tall. That's the first thing Grace said when we walked into the room. She told us that she couldn't see the face of the person who had killed Pendergast because that person was too short. Rose's face would have been visible above Pendergast's shoulder."

"But if she didn't see the killer's face, how do you know it was Joanna?"

"Because Grace remembered an impression she had of the killer, one that didn't make any sense to her. She thought the killer was a maid."

"And Joanna was dressed like a maid that day," Frank remembered.

"Yes. She'd taken off her apron and cap, but that black uniform dress is unmistakable. So what made *you* think Joanna was the killer?"

"I tried to see the men Andy had been blackmailing. I found only one at home today, but that turned out to be enough. He told me Andy's letter had mentioned that he knew who had killed Pendergast."

"But he wasn't even in the house when Pendergast was killed," Sarah said. "Rose heard him run out when Neth got there and started shouting at Pendergast."

"Then we're sure it was Neth?"

"Grace heard them arguing. She said the man told Pendergast someone's father had followed him to his house. That could only be Neth."

Frank nodded. "So, even though he couldn't have, Andy's letter said that he knew who the killer was, which I thought was odd, because this fellow I visited, Traynor, didn't kill Andy, so he probably didn't kill Pendergast either."

"How can you be sure?"

"Because he went to see Andy earlier in the day, before I got there, and when I got there, the door was locked. That means Andy locked it behind Traynor and whoever else had visited him that day, but when the killer left, it was unlocked because it couldn't be locked from the outside."

Sarah nodded. "That makes sense, I guess, but why was it odd that Andy told him he knew who the killer was?"

"You mean besides putting himself in danger from the real killer? He was obviously too stupid to realize that part, but he may have thought the killer would pay more or something.

So I'm guessing he put that in all the letters he sent, hoping to scare the real killer."

"Including the letter he sent to Neth."

"*Especially* the one he sent to Neth, because he must have known it was Neth who'd come to the house and was furious at Pendergast for getting him in trouble."

"So Neth was the most likely prospect," Sarah said.

"And he would've been for us, too, except we knew Neth never even saw Andy's letter."

"But Joanna did and, unfortunately for Andy, she believed him when he said he knew who the killer was."

"When we were there, she told me Neth was home with her all evening," Frank recalled. "He'd already told me he was at his club, though. At the time, I just thought she was trying to protect Neth, but she was really trying to give herself an alibi."

"And she may not have thought she needed one for Pendergast's death, because Grace wouldn't have known who she was, so she couldn't identify her."

"What I don't understand is why she killed Pendergast in the first place. I can understand why she'd want to, of course, but why do it then, when she was already free of him?"

"I've been thinking about that ever since I figured out she was the one," Sarah said. "I think she must have been trying to protect Neth."

"Neth? Why would she want to protect him?"

"He's certainly no prize, as you've pointed out, but he'd gotten her away from Pendergast. Joanna seemed very sure that her family wouldn't have taken her back after what happened to her, so she must see Neth as her salvation."

Frank snorted his disgust.

"Well, think about it. If her family wouldn't take her back, what would have become of her? Neth gave her a home. She probably felt safe there, at least until we barged in telling her Neth was trying to kidnap a young woman."

Frank could see it now. "She must've been furious at Pendergast for putting Neth in a position to get caught by the police."

"Or maybe she was just furious because Pendergast seemed to have convinced him to start his own kidnapping operation. I think that might have been more threatening to her even than seeing Neth arrested."

"You think she was jealous?"

"Not jealous." Sarah thought about it for a moment. "She must have convinced herself Neth was a better man than Pendergast, which is why she could stay with someone she knew had participated in humiliating the women Pendergast had kidnapped. If Neth was going to start kidnapping his own women, though, she'd have to admit he was no better than Pendergast."

Frank sighed. "So now we know who killed Pendergast and his man, but what are we supposed to do about it?"

Sarah sighed, too. "I know. We wanted to protect Grace and then Rose, but doesn't Joanna deserve to be protected, too? She was a prisoner in that house, just like they were. Besides, if Joanna is tried for murder, the other two women will be dragged into it along with her. They'll be ruined just as thoroughly as if they had actually killed Pendergast themselves. And for what? Didn't Pendergast deserve to die?"

"Mrs. Brandt," Frank said in mock outrage, "since when did you become so bloodthirsty?"

"Since I've seen how seldom men like Pendergast get the punishment they deserve and how often women like his victims get blamed for his crimes."

Frank had to admit she was right. Too often, the law didn't provide true justice. "All right, but do you have any idea how we can manage to protect all three of them?"

Sarah smiled apologetically. "You're rich now. Could you bribe Broghan?"

"I honestly don't know. His nose is out of joint already because he thinks I butted into his case."

"Probably because you did."

"Well, yes, but he might be mad enough about it that he wants to show me up more than he wants me to bribe him."

"And if you make him an offer and make him madder . . ."

"He'll take it out on those poor women."

"What are we going to do?"

Before Frank could answer, someone rang Sarah's front doorbell.

"Maybe it's Mrs. Ellsworth, come to tell us she found a house," Sarah said with a small smile, although they both knew it was probably a summons to a birth.

They heard Maeve and Catherine clattering down the stairs to answer it, but no one called her to the door. Instead, Maeve and Catherine came into the kitchen.

"This came for you," Maeve said, handing Sarah an envelope bearing her name and address but no stamp.

"Someone delivered it?" Sarah asked, tearing it open.

"Yes, and he's waiting," Maeve said.

"It's from Mrs. Wolfe. Franchesca," she added, in case Malloy was confused. "I completely forgot to tell you, she was going to see an attorney this afternoon."

"An attorney? What for?"

"For Rose, in case they tried to arrest her for killing Pendergast."

"That was probably a good idea. What does she say?"

"She says she found out something very important and wants to tell me about it. She also says she sent her carriage to bring me back."

"That was thoughtful," Frank said. "Am I invited, too?"

"She doesn't say, but I'm sure she would be glad to see you."

"I hope so, because I'm going."

In a few short minutes, they were in the Wolfes' carriage on their way to see Franchesca Wolfe.

"Oh, Mr. Malloy, how fortunate that you're here, too," Franchesca Wolfe said as she welcomed them into her parlor.

Frank didn't think anyone had ever greeted him like that, so he smiled, then nodded to Rose Wolfe, who stood beside her and looked almost as delighted to see him.

Franchesca invited them to be seated, served them tea, then sent the maid away.

"Rose tells me that you think you know who killed that horrible man and his servant," she said to Sarah when the door was closed.

Sarah glanced at him. "Yes, and Mr. Malloy agrees. In fact, he'd reached the same conclusion himself today for entirely different reasons."

"And this woman was also deceived by the dead man the way Rose was?"

"Deceived and held prisoner, yes," Sarah said.

Franchesca nodded. "Mr. Malloy, did Mrs.

Brandt tell you that I went to see an attorney today?"

"Yes, she did."

"He was very informative."

"That's unusual for an attorney," Frank said.

"Perhaps you've never seen an attorney as a paying client," Franchesca said with a smile.

"Not often," he conceded.

"Mr. Pennyworth had many questions for me, some of which I was unable to answer because I don't know all the details of Rose's ordeal, but he did grasp the importance of protecting Rose —not only from being charged with murdering that awful man but also from being called as a witness if some other poor female is charged."

"Franchesca didn't know that we had figured out who the killer was," Rose added, "but she did know that there were at least two of us who might be suspected, so Mr. Pennyworth's advice still applies."

"It will depend upon Miss Livingston's willingness to assist us," Franchesca said, "but of course it is in her best interest to do so."

"And Joanna will also have to agree," Rose added.

"She might be more difficult to convince, since she's actually guilty," Franchesca said. "But on the other hand, she has the most to lose, too."

Frank nodded. "So we're all agreed we need to

do something, but you haven't told us what it is yet."

"Oh my, yes," Franchesca said. "Let me explain."

When she was finished, Frank gaped at her. Sarah was gaping, too. It was fiendishly clever, just what he should have expected from an attorney. Justice could be maneuvered in so many ways if you had the mind for it.

Sarah turned to him. "Do you think it could work?"

"Yes, I do. I think it could work even if Joanna doesn't want to cooperate. If she doesn't, this could save her from herself, in fact. We have to convince Grace Livingston first, of course."

"Will her father object?" Rose asked. "He's very protective of her."

"I'll convince him," Frank said. "When he understands it's our only hope for keeping Grace's name out of the newspapers, I think he'll go along."

"Then our next step is to see Grace," Rose said.

"Shouldn't we wait until morning?" Franchesca said.

"I think Grace will have a better night if she knows our plan," Rose said.

In the end, they convinced Franchesca not to accompany them. She longed to see the fruits of her efforts, but she had to finally agree that the presence of a complete stranger wasn't likely to put Grace Livingston at ease.

She did insist they take her carriage, though, so they traveled in comfort through the warm evening. Sarah noted with regret that the desk clerk who had given her so much trouble wasn't on duty this evening to see her enter the hotel with a proper escort.

Once again, Mr. Livingston opened the door to their hotel suite. "Mr. Malloy! Does this mean our ordeal is over?"

"Soon, I hope," he replied, allowing Sarah and Rose to enter ahead of him. Grace waited for them inside, her hands twisting anxiously, a silent question burning in her eyes.

"Mr. Livingston, the ladies need to discuss some things among themselves," Malloy said. "Maybe we could go downstairs to the hotel bar, and I'll tell you what's going on."

"Grace?" Livingston said.

"Go ahead, Father. We'll be fine."

Malloy escorted a reluctant Mr. Livingston out, leaving the three women staring at each other.

"We have a plan," Sarah said.

"It's brilliant," Rose said. "My sister-in-law, Franchesca, went to see an attorney today, and he suggested it."

"Well, don't keep me in suspense," Grace said. "Please, sit down and tell me all about it."

When they were seated, Rose gave Sarah a questioning glance.

"You tell her," Sarah said.

"As I said, Franchesca went to speak with an attorney. Before I saw you yesterday, I was afraid I might be arrested for killing Pendergast, and she thought I would need some legal help."

"But what could he have said that would help *me?*" Grace asked.

"His idea is so clever and yet so simple: He said we should both confess to killing Pendergast."

"What? How could that help?" Grace asked. "Especially since neither of us did it."

"You see, the police like it when a person confesses to a crime," Sarah explained. "That means they don't need to have a trial where the person might get judged not guilty and go free."

"I can see that, but . . ."

"But," Sarah continued, "if more than one person confesses to the same crime, they can't charge both of them with it because both of them can't be guilty."

"And," Rose continued, "if they have a trial for me, for instance, you would testify that you killed Pendergast and I would go free. Then if they tried you, I would testify, and you would go free."

"But we don't want this to go to court at all," Grace reminded them.

"And it won't," Sarah said, "because if you both confess, they'll know this would be the outcome, so they wouldn't charge either of you for the murder."

"But what about this Joanna, the one who really killed Pendergast?" Grace asked. "How does this help her?"

"Well . . ." Rose glanced at Sarah.

"We'll need to convince her to go along with us," Sarah said. "She might not be as anxious as you both are to escape a trial, since she's really guilty. She might be afraid that if she confesses, they'll simply throw her in prison, but if she goes to trial, she could be found not guilty."

"But won't she be as terrified of a trial as we are?" Grace asked. "Having to tell everything that Pendergast did to us?"

"A destroyed reputation might not seem as bad to a woman who has been living as a man's mistress as it does to the two of you, especially when you weigh it against a prison sentence," Sarah said.

Rose nodded. "So we'll have to convince her to go along with us."

"She's not likely to trust us, though, is she?" Grace asked.

"She's not likely to trust anyone," Sarah said. "But we've got to try. None of us want to see her punished, do we?"

"Of course not! She may have saved our lives,"

Grace said. "I think Pendergast might well have killed us both so we couldn't tell what he'd done to us."

"And she definitely avenged us," Rose added. "Nothing the law could have done to him would have been enough."

"Then we must see her and convince her," Sarah said. "Unfortunately, she lives with Neth. He's one of the men Pendergast used to invite to his house." She didn't have to add that he may have been one of the men who'd raped Rose. "You probably don't want to see him, Rose."

She stiffened. "No, I'd rather not."

"Could Mr. Malloy get him out of the house somehow?" Grace asked.

"Perhaps, but how? Without alerting her that something was going on, that is," Sarah said.

"Or could we get Joanna away from the house somehow?" Rose asked.

"I don't know. Is she likely to go anywhere with us without knowing what we want from her?" Sarah asked. "And don't forget, she's killed two men, so she's going to be wary of being caught."

"Do you think she might attack us?" Rose asked.

"I can't imagine why she would, unless she feels threatened."

"We'll just make sure she doesn't have a knife handy, then," Grace said with a sly smile. It was the first time Sarah had seen her smile.

• • •

By the time Frank had finished explaining the plan to Mr. Livingston, he was frowning.

"I don't know, Mr. Malloy. It all sounds rather dangerous to me."

"Grace won't be in any danger, I promise you."

"There are different kinds of danger, as you well know. I managed to get her back from that man, but the only way she'll ever get over what happened to her is if she can live the rest of her life in peace."

"Which is why we need to keep her story from being made public."

"And yet you propose that she confess to a murder she didn't commit, which could result in her going to prison for the rest of her life."

Frank could understand the man's concern, but he didn't want Grace to go to prison either. "As I said, if both she and Miss Wolfe confess and we can get Joanna to confess as well, none of them will be bothered again."

"And Miss Wolfe has already agreed to this?"

"Yes."

"Do you really think this Joanna woman will also agree? She has no reason to trust Grace and Miss Wolfe. She doesn't even know them."

He had a point, of course. "I think when she understands what it will mean for her, she'll agree."

"But you can't be sure."

Frank managed not to sigh. "No, not until we talk to her."

Livingston did sigh. "I must confess, I'm having a difficult time accepting a plan that allows a woman who killed two men to go free."

"One of those men was attacking your daughter," Frank reminded him. "If Grace had been the one with the knife, would you have difficulty allowing her to go free?"

"Of course not!"

"Well, Joanna stopped him from attacking Grace in the same way. And as for Andy, he was attacking Joanna or intended to."

"Did she tell you that?" he scoffed.

"No, but . . . his trousers were open when she stabbed him. Plainly, he was planning to take advantage of her."

"You really have no idea what happened," Livingston said. "Perhaps she enticed him to get him to lower his guard."

Frank almost smiled at how easy Livingston was making this for him. "Now you're doing exactly what we're afraid other people will do."

Livingston drew back, offended. "What's that?"

"Blaming the victim. We know this Andy fellow had his way with all the women. He'd raped Joanna when she was at Pendergast's house, and he'd raped Miss Wolfe and your daughter, too."

The blood drained from his face. "I didn't know."

"You're afraid that people will judge Grace for meeting a man she didn't know and allowing herself to be kidnapped. You're afraid they'll say she's no better than she should be and deserved what happened to her. Maybe they'll even think she was with Pendergast by choice."

Livingston covered his face with his hands. "Please, don't . . ."

"I'm sorry, but I can't let you protect Grace and condemn the others. All of them were victims."

"You're right, of course. Forgive me. But I still don't see how you're going to convince this Joanna to cooperate. I think when she realizes you know she killed Pendergast and that other fellow, she'll disappear. What's to stop her?"

Livingston was right, of course. They'd have to figure out how to keep her from running away. She wouldn't care about Grace and Rose. She might care about Neth, but she would surely care about herself the most, so they'd have to convince her their plan was the only way to save herself.

Sarah and the other women were still trying to figure out how and where to meet with Joanna when Malloy returned with Mr. Livingston.

"Grace, have you agreed to this plan?" her father asked.

"Yes, Papa, I have. Our only problem now will be convincing Joanna."

Malloy caught Sarah's eye. "Have you figured out how to approach her?"

"No. In fact, we know that we don't want Neth around when we do, but we can't figure out how to get her away from the house without alarming her."

"Mr. Livingston pointed out that, if we do alarm her, she might well just disappear, too."

"Oh dear, we hadn't thought of that possibility at all," Rose said.

"And yet," Sarah said, "if she did disappear and the police couldn't find her, they couldn't bring her to trial, so the rest of you wouldn't have to worry."

"But we'd worry all the time," Grace protested, "because someday they might find her, and just when we thought we could forget it ever happened, we'd be plunged back into the nightmare again."

"That would be horrible," Rose agreed. "No, we must settle this now so it's over and done with."

"So I guess we all agree," Sarah said. "We need to see Joanna and convince her to go along with our plan, except, short of kidnapping her ourselves, how can we get her to meet with us?"

"Actually," Malloy mused, "I think we will have to kidnap her."

"We can't do that," Sarah said.

"No," he said, "but the police can."

"It's about time you showed up," Broghan said when Frank found him in the detectives' room at Police Headquarters the next morning. "Did you figure out who killed those fellows?" He was sitting at one of the battered desks, his feet up, smoking a cigar. Since it wasn't yet ten o'clock in the morning, he was relatively sober.

"Not yet," Frank lied, "but I've got it down to one of three people."

"*Three?* I had it down to *one* person before you got mixed up in it!"

"I know you did, but I wanted to make sure you had the *right* person."

Broghan made a rude noise. "So who are these three people, and why do you think they did it? And most important, why can't the high and mighty Frank Malloy decide which one it is?"

Frank smiled, trying to disarm Broghan. This wasn't going to be easy. "Let's see. First of all, that woman in the cellar, the one who ran off. Her name is Rose Wolfe."

"How do you know that?" he asked in surprise.

"I got her address from the letters in Pendergast's desk."

"Oh, that's right. You had some notion of visiting the families so you could see if the women came back home."

330

"And telling the family what happened to them if they didn't," Frank added, refusing to let Broghan make him feel foolish. "I haven't had time to visit all the families yet, but I did manage to locate Miss Wolfe."

"But she couldn't be the killer. You said she was locked in the cellar. In a cage, if I remember right."

"Yes, but the cage wasn't actually locked."

Broghan snorted again. "What's the point of having a cage if you don't lock it?"

Frank wasn't about to explain that Rose couldn't escape because she had no clothes. "You'll have to ask Pendergast about that."

"And how do you know it wasn't locked?"

"Mrs. Brandt opened it to release Miss Wolfe. She said it only had a bolt holding it shut and Miss Wolfe could easily have opened it."

Broghan shrugged. "All right. I suppose that's possible. She snuck upstairs, picked up a knife in the kitchen, and sliced Pendergast's throat when he was busy with the other girl."

"That's what I was thinking."

"What did she do with the knife?"

"Hid it, I guess."

"So why did she go back to the house to kill that Andy fellow? Or did somebody else do that?"

"He was blackmailing people. He sent her a note, just like he did those men, telling her he knew who the killer was, so she went back to the house to get rid of him."

Frank could tell Broghan was impressed, even though he'd probably die before he let on. "Sounds like she's the one, all right, but you said you had three suspects."

"Yes, the woman Joanna who lives with Vernon Neth. You met her at Pendergast's house."

"That can't be right. Why would she kill Pendergast?"

"She was one of the other women he'd kidnapped. Neth bought her away from Pendergast."

"You don't say." This time Broghan did allow himself to look impressed, although Frank thought he was more impressed with the idea of buying a female than Frank's detecting skills.

"When we followed Neth to his house that day, he ran off. In fact, he went to Pendergast's house to tell him what had happened. He was pretty angry that Pendergast had tricked him into getting involved with his schemes, but Joanna was angry, too. She apparently cares for Neth and was even more furious at Pendergast for involving him. She sneaked into Pendergast's house and got the knife and cut his throat."

Broghan was frowning. "How do you know she went to his house?"

"She ran off when we went in to search Neth's place. It's only a theory that she killed Pendergast, but I do know that Andy tried to blackmail Neth. Joanna told us she saw the letter."

"So maybe this Neth killed him. You said he went to see Pendergast right before he died."

"But Grace Livingston said Pendergast was still alive when Neth left."

"So she does remember what happened!"

"Parts of it," Frank hedged. "So if Joanna killed Pendergast and saw the letter from Andy saying he knew who the killer was, she went to meet him and killed him, too."

"How do you know what the letter said?"

"One of the other men Andy tried to blackmail told me."

Broghan frowned. "Is there anybody in New York you didn't see?"

Frank bit back a smile. "A few people."

"And who's this third person? And don't say Neth, because you already told me he didn't do it."

"No, not Neth. Grace Livingston."

Broghan swore. "You already convinced me she didn't do it! I would've arrested her days ago!"

"I . . . well, I've come to think that maybe she's hiding something when she says she can't remember."

This seemed to make Broghan very happy. "Well now, I guess you don't know everything, do you?"

Frank took the insult with good humor, because

of course he did know everything. "I never claimed to."

"So now that you've made a muck of this, what do you expect me to do?"

Frank tried very hard to look sincere or at least not like he was lying through his teeth. "I think if you bring these women in and question them —scare them a little—and tell them what you think happened and how each one did it, the guilty one will break down and confess."

14

Frank convinced Broghan to leave the Black Maria they'd brought to Neth's house down the street, out of sight, when they went to get Joanna. She hadn't been too happy the last time he'd locked her in one, and she'd probably run for sure if she saw it now.

Joanna answered their knock. She wore her maid's outfit and a scowl. "What do you want?"

"I'd like to see Mr. Neth," Frank said. This was, of course, probably the only reason they could give in order to get inside.

"And if he's not here?"

"We'll wait," Broghan said.

Joanna turned her scowl on him. "And I see you've brought your little copper friend with you this time."

Broghan opened his mouth to reply, but Frank said, "If Neth's not here, tell us where he is, and we'll go find him."

"Oh, you'd like that, wouldn't you? Showing up at his club to embarrass him," she said. "Well, he's here, but he doesn't know anything more than he did the last time you talked to him. When are you going to leave us be?"

"Just one or two things we need to ask him," Frank said cheerfully.

She didn't look like she believed him, but she let them in and escorted them upstairs. Neth was in the back parlor, the less formal room where the residents of the house would spend most of their time.

He looked up when Joanna came in and jumped to his feet when she announced them. "What the devil? What are you doing here again, Malloy?"

Frank thought he might have to ask Joanna to stay, but she wasn't really a maid, so she didn't leave. Instead she went over and stood by Neth. Maybe she thought she could protect him somehow. Maybe she thought she could kill Frank and Broghan like she'd killed Pendergast and Andy. The thought made the hairs on his arms stand up.

"I need to talk to Joanna," he said.

Neth looked at her, but she was staring at Frank. "*Me?* What for?"

"We want to ask you some questions about when you were with Pendergast."

She didn't believe it. Frank could see it in her eyes. "All right. Go ahead and ask me."

"Not here. We need to take you to Police Headquarters so it's official."

"See here," Neth said, "there's no reason to take her anywhere. You can ask her whatever it is right now."

"No, it's all right," she said. "They're just trying to scare me into telling them something, but I don't know anything to tell them, so it won't work. You want me to go to Police Headquarters, you say?"

"Yes. We've brought a wagon."

"I know about your wagons," she sniffed in disgust. "I need to change my clothes. I can't go looking like this." She gestured toward her maid uniform.

"I'll go with you, then," Frank said.

She stiffened at that, and Neth said, "You can't do that!"

"If she goes off somewhere, how do we know she won't try to run away?" Broghan asked.

"I'll give her privacy while she changes," Frank said, "but I'll be right outside the room."

"All right, then," she said with a toss of her head, "but if you think you can look in through the keyhole, I'll poke your eye out."

She stalked out.

"Stay with him," he told Broghan, and followed her out.

Conscious of what Joanna had endured from Pendergast, Frank followed at a distance, staying just close enough that he could catch up to her if she tried to run. She went up the stairs and into one of the bedrooms without even looking back at him, closing the door behind her with a decisive click.

Frank heard the key turning in the lock, and he noticed she didn't remove it. She must really think he might look through the keyhole. He stopped outside her door and leaned against the wall opposite. The wait seemed long, but Frank recalled that waiting for a woman always seemed long. Their clothes, he knew, were much more complicated than a man's, and they had to fix their hair and such. Still, Joanna seemed to be taking an exceptionally long time considering she was dressing to be questioned by the police and not to attend a fancy dress ball.

He waited some more, starting to think something might be wrong. In fact, he hadn't heard any sounds of movement from the room in some time.

Then he saw the smoke curling up from under the door.

Sarah met Grace and Rose at Daughters of Hope Mission, just down Mulberry Street from Police Headquarters. The plan was that Frank would send word as soon as he and Broghan arrived at Headquarters with Joanna. Broghan thought they'd be dropping Joanna off and going after the other two women, but they were going to appear voluntarily. Frank and Sarah had agreed there was no reason to subject them to a ride in a Black Maria in police custody. He'd just explain that Sarah had convinced them to come in of their own accord.

She could tell the two women were tense, and

who could blame them? Knowing they would soon be questioned by the police and confess to murder was a daunting prospect at best.

"I've read about these missions," Rose said when they were seated in the parlor. The room in the large, old house was furnished with a hodge-podge of furniture that people had discarded, but it was spotlessly clean. "What kind of work do they do here?"

"It's a refuge for girls who don't have homes or families or whose families have turned them out," Sarah explained. "We teach them to read and write if they don't know how, and how to operate a sewing machine and cook and how to conduct themselves."

"How did you get involved with it, Mrs. Brandt?" Grace asked.

Sarah smiled, not wanting to tell the whole unpleasant story. "Oh, you know how women get asked to do things by their friends."

Mrs. Keller, the matron, bustled in. "Mrs. Brandt, how nice to see you."

Sarah introduced her to Grace and Rose. "I hope you don't mind. We're meeting Mr. Malloy later, and this was a convenient spot to wait."

"Not at all. After all you've done for the Mission, you're always welcome here. Can I get you some refreshment? It'll be good practice for the girls to serve you tea."

Sarah readily agreed, and several of the older

girls nearly tripped over themselves in their eagerness to serve their guests. Grace and Rose seemed to enjoy their attention, and Sarah sensed them relaxing a bit as they drank their tea and ate the cake the girls brought them.

Waiting was difficult, of course, and time passed so slowly, but when Sarah checked the watch pinned to her jacket, she couldn't believe how long they'd actually been there. Surely, Malloy could have collected Joanna by now. What was taking so long?

Frank started shouting for Broghan the instant he saw the smoke. The room was on fire, of that he was sure, even though it made no sense. Why would she set the room on fire?

To kill herself, you fool, an inner voice said, but his common sense rebelled. Nobody would choose to burn themselves alive.

He tried the knob, but of course it was still locked. The knob was cool, though, so he raised his foot and kicked the door as hard as he could. By then he could hear Broghan and Neth running up the stairs.

Frank kicked the door again.

"What are you doing?" Neth demanded.

"She's set the place on fire!"

He kicked again, and this time the door splintered. Broghan put his shoulder to it, and it gave. Smoke filled the room, and Frank saw with a quick glance that the heavy curtains were on fire, although the fabric was smoldering more that flaming, even fanned by the breeze from the open window.

But more importantly, Joanna was gone.

"Where is she?" Neth cried. "What have you done with her?"

Broghan had the presence of mind to tear down the curtains and begin stamping on them. After a moment, Neth joined him. Frank stuck his head out the window, but all he saw was the roof over the back porch, a little over a story below. Could she have risked it? Of course she could have, if the alternative was prison.

"She escaped," Frank said to no one in particular, and headed out the door and down the hallway as fast as he could run.

He took the stairs two and three at a time, nearly falling more than once, until he reached the ground floor, and tore through the house until he found the kitchen. He ran out the back door. The yard was empty, the gate hanging open. Frank ran through it into the back alley. Scanning the area in both directions, he saw no sign of her. She could have ducked into another yard to hide, but Frank figured she'd want to get as far away as possible. But which way would she have run?

Right seemed right, so he raced down the alley in that direction, emerging on the side street where they'd left the Maria. He shouted to the driver.

"She got away! Did you see a woman come out of this alley?"

"No! Nobody's come out of there while I've been here."

"Come with me."

The driver hopped down and loped after Frank as he ran back down the alley.

"Check in all these yards to see if she's hiding anywhere," he told the man, then headed down the alley in the opposite direction.

As he ran, he tried to calculate how long she might have been gone before the smoke had alerted him. Long enough that she'd had time to get out of sight, he decided when he reached the other end of the alley and saw no trace of her in either direction.

Where would she go? The train station, maybe, if she really wanted to get away, although she could probably disappear just as effectively in the city itself if she chose to. By the time he got back to the house, Broghan was on the back porch waiting for him.

"No sign of her?" he asked.

"No. I've got Murphy searching the yards, but I doubt she'd bother hiding. She's long gone. What about the fire?"

"We got it out. She didn't do a very good job with it."

"She didn't want to burn the house down, just slow us up a bit, I figure."

"It worked well enough, then. I'm thinking you can forget about the other two females," Broghan said with a grim smile. "This one's your killer."

Sarah checked her watch again.

"What time is it?" Rose asked.

They'd long since finished their tea and cake. The girls had tried making polite conversation with them, as an exercise in deportment, Mrs. Keller explained, but the strain of waiting soon began to tell on Grace and Rose. Sarah dismissed the girls and sent Mrs. Keller back to her duties.

"It's been much too long. I'm going to walk down to Police Headquarters. The doorman there knows me. Maybe Mr. Malloy has sent word or something."

"We'll go with you," Grace said.

Sarah didn't know if it was a good idea to bring her two charges with her or not, but she decided it would be cruel to make them sit here with nothing to do but worry. She told Mrs. Keller they were going to check on Malloy, and they made their way to the front door.

Just as they opened it, however, a cab stopped at the curb outside, and Frank Malloy stepped out.

Neth came out onto the back porch. He had a streak of soot on his cheek, and he was flexing his right hand absently, as if it hurt him. "Where is she?"

"Gone," Frank said.

"She can't be gone. Why would she go anywhere?"

"Because she killed Pendergast and that other fellow," Broghan said, "and she knew I was going to arrest her for it."

Neth glared at Broghan in outrage. "Joanna couldn't kill anyone."

Frank sighed. "Whether she did or not, she's escaped. Broghan, I think she might go to the train station."

"Why would she do that?" Neth asked, still outraged.

"To get away," Frank said patiently.

"But she can't go anywhere. She doesn't even have any money."

"Yes, she does," Frank remembered. "Traynor told me he gave Andy two hundred dollars, but Andy didn't have it when we found him."

"Ah," said Broghan. "She took it, then. Smart girl."

"So maybe you can catch her before she gets on a train," Frank said, still trying to be patient. "If you hurry," he added, in case Broghan didn't understand the urgency.

"Oh, yeah. Murphy!" he called, heading down the back stairs toward the alley. "Come with me."

Neth watched him for a minute, looked at Frank, and then looked back at Broghan. "I'm going with you! I won't have you mistreat her!"

Frank stood on the porch until the three of them had disappeared down the alley in the direction of where they'd left the Maria. Then, with another sigh, he went back into the house.

So much for their plan, although if Joanna really could get away and with Broghan convinced she was guilty, Grace and Rose wouldn't have to worry about being arrested. Still, they'd never be able to completely forget about their ordeal, knowing Joanna was still out there somewhere.

Frank closed the kitchen door, wondering if he should lock it. Neth had left in a hurry and might not have remembered to take his key. That's when he remembered: the back door had been ajar when he'd gone chasing after Joanna.

Why would the door have been open?

He turned slowly, quietly, and looked around the room. Joanna kept her kitchen clean. Everything was in its proper place. He saw no cellar door. No, the cellar entrance was outside, he remembered. The only door in here led to a small pantry. That door had a latch that could only be opened from the outside. The door was closed almost completely, but not quite enough for the latch to catch.

Slowly, carefully, hoping his shoes wouldn't squeak, he moved toward the pantry door. Listening, straining, he thought he heard something, a slight rustle, but maybe not. Oh no, he really heard nothing at all until he reached the door and took hold of the latch and in one swift motion threw open the door.

She screamed in terror and surged to her feet, the knife clutched in both her hands, raised high to strike, then plunging downward, almost before he could register her intent. Instinctively, he grabbed for it, catching her wrists, wrestling her for the blade. Her strength doubled by desperation, she fought him, but he twisted and pulled, jerking her out of the narrow pantry and throwing her to the floor. She cried out as he wrested the knife from her, sending it clattering across the floor. She lay sobbing with fury.

"Why did you stop me?" she demanded.

"You don't have to kill yourself, Joanna. We've got a plan that will save you."

Malloy," Sarah called. "What are you—?" She stopped when she saw Joanna emerge from the cab behind him. This wasn't right. They were supposed to take Joanna to Police Headquarters, not here.

Malloy took Joanna's arm, and Sarah realized she was limping as they made their way across the sidewalk to the Mission's front steps.

"What is this place?" Joanna asked with a suspicious frown.

"A refuge for homeless girls," Malloy said with a trace of irony.

Joanna rolled her eyes.

"What happened?" Sarah asked. Behind her Grace and Rose stared down at Joanna in openmouthed wonder.

"Joanna set the house on fire and escaped," Malloy said.

This couldn't possibly be true, of course, since Joanna was standing right in front of them. Or, more accurately, was limping her way up the front steps. Sarah herded Rose and Grace back inside, and whispered, "I think we may have our chance to speak with Joanna after all."

Hearing the disturbance, Mrs. Keller and some of the girls came to see what was going on. "Mrs. Keller, perhaps Mr. Malloy and our new guest would like some refreshments," Sarah said, sending her off to the kitchen while Malloy assisted Joanna inside and into the parlor.

"How did you hurt yourself?" Sarah asked, giving Malloy a chastening glance.

"Don't look at me," he said, seating Joanna in the closest chair, an old wing-backed relic with stuffing protruding from the arms. "I told you. She set the house on fire. Well, the bedroom anyway. She'd gone up to change her clothes, and then she climbed out the window to escape.

She figured the fire would slow us down."

"You climbed out a window?" Rose asked in amazement.

"That copper was going to arrest me for killing Pendergast," Joanna said crossly. "What was I supposed to do?"

"And you hurt yourself climbing out the window," Sarah guessed.

Joanna's lip curled in disgust. "I sprained my ankle when I dropped off the edge of the porch roof."

"Oh my," Grace said.

"She couldn't run away with the bad ankle," Malloy added. "So she went back in the house and hid. But we all thought she'd run off, so I sent Broghan to the train station to see if he could catch her before she left town. Neth went with him. Then I found her."

"Did you tell her about our plan?" Sarah asked Malloy.

"It's a wonderful plan," Grace said.

"It's an excellent plan," Rose added.

Joanna looked up at the four people hovering over her, and Sarah saw the anger and bitterness melt away into something that looked very much like amazement. "You were telling the truth," she said to Malloy.

"Yes, I was." He turned to Sarah and the others. "I told her all about the plan, but she didn't believe me."

"Why would you lie for me?" Joanna demanded of Rose and Grace.

"Let's sit down and explain everything, shall we?" Sarah suggested.

They did just that after Sarah had closed the parlor doors.

Rose spoke first. "We're not really doing it for you."

"Well, we don't want you to be punished, of course," Grace said quickly. "You may have saved my life."

"Both our lives," Rose said. "And nobody should be punished for killing those two bounders."

Grace smiled apologetically. "But we're mostly concerned about ourselves, you see."

"If someone is charged with killing Pendergast," Sarah explained, "the newspapers will report the story. They'll send reporters to find out everything that happened in that house, and what they can't find out they'll make up. They'll accuse the three of you of all sorts of horrible things."

"They'll make us out to be trollops," Rose said.

Grace nodded. "And everyone in the city will know what happened to us and believe the very worst."

"We'll be ruined," Rose added. "And so will you."

"No, I'll be in prison," Joanna said.

"Which is even worse than being ruined," Grace said.

Joanna frowned. "But if you claim you were the one who killed Pendergast—"

"And Andy, too," Rose said.

"And Andy, too, won't that ruin you just as much?"

All of the women turned to Malloy. "The police aren't going to charge any of you with murder or bring any of you to trial if you all claim to be guilty."

"The police can do anything they want," Joanna scoffed.

Malloy shrugged, conceding the point. "But the district attorney is the one who decides what cases go to trial, and he isn't going to want to look like a fool when three women all claim to have committed the same crime."

"You seem pretty sure of all this," Joanna said.

"My sister-in-law has hired an attorney," Rose said. "He's the one who thought of this, so he'll be sure the district attorney understands and makes the right decision."

"And then they'll just let me go?"

"They'll let all of us go," Rose said.

Joanna stared at each of them in turn, as if trying to judge their trustworthiness. Finally, she shrank back in the chair, closed her eyes, and clapped a hand over her mouth.

Sarah was up in a moment. "Are you in pain? I almost forgot about your ankle."

Mrs. Keller arrived at that moment with more tea and cake, and Sarah sent her for some bandages. She checked Joanna's ankle and determined it was probably just sprained, as she had said. She wrapped it and found a stool for her to rest it on. If tears were leaking from her eyes during this process, everyone chose to think it was because of the pain.

Malloy had taken the opportunity of Mrs. Keller's arrival to slip out and walk down to Police Headquarters to have someone get word to Broghan that he could stop watching the train station and that all his suspects were gathered conveniently in one place.

"I didn't believe him when he first told me," Joanna told Sarah as she wrapped the bandage around her ankle. Rose and Grace had gone to the kitchen with Mrs. Keller to give Joanna some privacy.

"I'm sure," Sarah said. "It's difficult to believe, but then everything about this situation is difficult to believe."

"He told me you'd come up with this plan and I wouldn't be arrested for killing those men, but I knew no one would do that for me. People only do things to help themselves."

"That's not always true," Sarah said. "Many people are unselfish and generous."

"They are when it suits them, but what would Mr. Malloy get out of helping me? Or you? Or those other girls?"

Sarah wanted to argue with her, but Joanna didn't give her the opportunity.

"No, nobody does something like that for a complete stranger, and when I asked him why, he told me it was because he'd been hired to do it."

"That's right," Sarah said. "Miss Livingston's father hired him to find her."

"So then I started to believe him because that made sense. Someone was paying him."

"Oh, Joanna, I hope you don't think that people only help others when they're paid to."

Joanna smiled grimly. "And I hope you don't think they do it out of the goodness of their hearts."

A little more than an hour later, Malloy returned with an exasperated Broghan in tow.

"Where have you been?" he demanded of Joanna, who gazed up at him with remarkable calmness.

"I was hiding in the pantry until you'd gone, but this one found me before I could get away," she told him, unrepentant.

"That's a fine thing. You set the house on fire and then leave. You could've burned down the whole city."

Joanna simply shrugged.

Only then did Broghan glance around to see Grace and Rose standing nearby with Sarah. "Well, Miss Livingston," he said. "I thought you'd left town."

To Sarah's delight, Grace lifted her chin in silent defiance. "My father thought I needed some time to recover from my ordeal," she said.

"You should've told me where you were going," he said, holding his temper with difficulty.

"Why?"

The guileless question left him speechless. In desperation, he turned to Rose. He seemed to resent having to look up to meet her eye. "And who are you?"

"Rose Wolfe."

"Oh, the woman in the cellar."

A reaction flickered across her face, but she didn't flinch.

"You ran away, too, just like this one." He flicked a hand in Joanna's direction.

"I didn't run away. I simply went home."

"You should've waited until I got there to question you."

"Why?"

Broghan obviously didn't like being questioned in return. "So I'd know where to find you."

"Mr. Malloy didn't have any trouble finding me."

Broghan turned to Malloy. "Am I supposed to put up with this?"

"I thought you wanted to question these ladies about what happened when Pendergast was killed. Oh, and Andy, too."

"They're more than willing to talk to you," Sarah said.

Broghan ran a hand over his face. "All right. Who's first?"

"Since she's injured, let's let Joanna go first," Rose suggested. "Miss Livingston and I will wait in the kitchen until you're ready for us."

The two of them went out, closing the parlor door behind them. Broghan cast Sarah a questioning look.

"Joanna has asked me to stay with her while you question her," she said.

"And I'm staying because I want to," Malloy said.

Broghan glowered at him, but not for long. After glancing around, he retrieved a straight-backed chair from the corner and set it right in front of the chair where Joanna sat resting her injured ankle on a stool.

"Where's Neth?" she asked before Broghan could speak.

"He's kicking his heels at Police Headquarters. He thinks we're in the basement questioning you."

She nodded, satisfied.

"Now Miss . . . What is your name? I don't think I've ever heard it."

"That's because no one knows it," she replied.

"I need to know it," Broghan said.

"No, you don't. Even Neth doesn't know it."

"Why all the secrecy?" Broghan asked, exasperated.

"I don't want my family to find out what became of me."

Sarah's heart ached for her, but Broghan just snorted his disgust. "They'll get your name when you go to the Tombs," he said, using the nickname for the city jail. "So, how'd you end up at Pendergast's house the day he was killed?"

She drew a deep breath, as if to fortify herself. "I was at home. At Neth's house. He'd gone out for a walk, he said. It was Sunday afternoon."

"I know what day it was."

She ignored his interruption. "There was a commotion, someone pounding on the door, and when I opened it, a crazy man came in saying all kinds of things. That's when I realized that his daughter had been kidnapped, and he thought she was in Neth's house."

"And you knew about this because you'd once been kidnapped yourself."

"Yes."

He waited, but she said nothing else.

"All right, then. What happened next?"

"These people came in." She indicated Sarah

and Malloy with a wave of her hand. "They had a girl with them. She said Neth had invited her there to meet his mother." Her lip curled again.

"What's wrong with that? Besides the fact that Neth's mother doesn't live there?"

"Because that's how Pendergast got women to go into his house. He invited them to have tea with his mother, so they thought he wanted to marry them."

"And Neth does this, too?"

"No!" she snapped, angry now. "Neth never did it, or at least he never did it before that day, but I guess he'd met this girl and he'd brought her to his house. He'd run off when he realized he'd been tricked, and I could guess he'd gone to Pendergast to complain, so I went there, too."

"To kill Pendergast?"

"That's not why I went, but when I got there, I heard him upstairs with a woman."

"What woman?"

"I don't know. But I heard him. She was crying and begging him not to hurt her. I couldn't stand it. I couldn't let him hurt anybody else ever again, so I grabbed the big knife from the kitchen and I ran upstairs. He was in the parlor with this girl, shaking her like a dog and saying horrible things to her."

"What kind of things?" Broghan asked with interest.

She just glared at him in contempt. "So I went

up behind him and grabbed him by the hair and sliced his throat open."

Broghan jerked back a little at her vehemence. "What made you do that? Cut his throat instead of just stabbing him, I mean."

"Because that's what he always said to us. He always said he'd cut our throats if we didn't do what he wanted. It would be easy, he'd say. Just one slice with a very sharp knife. So that's what I did to him."

Broghan considered her words for a moment. "Then what did you do?"

"I ran out. I didn't want anyone to see me."

"What did you do with the knife?"

"I didn't realize I was still carrying it until I got out in the backyard. I didn't want to go back, so I stuck it in the ground behind the ash can out in the alley, where nobody would see it."

Broghan nodded as if this made perfect sense. "Why did you kill Andy?"

"He sent Neth a note. He said he knew who'd killed Pendergast. I thought he'd try to blackmail Neth. Neth might've paid him not to betray me, or he might not. I didn't know, but I didn't want to take the chance, so I went to Pendergast's house and I killed him."

"You got the knife from behind the ash can?"

"Yes. I went to the back door so no one would see me."

"Why were his pants undone?"

She did flinch at that. "He wanted me to . . . to pleasure him one more time, so I pretended to go along. I figured he'd be distracted if he thought he was going to have some fun. He never thought for a minute I'd hurt him. He was pretty surprised."

That left Broghan speechless for a few seconds. "And you took the money that Andy had on him?"

"I don't know what you're talking about," she said, although Frank was pretty sure she was lying about that. "I didn't see any money, and I certainly didn't go through his pockets after I stabbed him. He wasn't even dead when I left. I had to go out the front door because he was in the kitchen and I didn't want to try to get by him."

Broghan nodded, then turned to Malloy. "You see, I told you she was the one."

Malloy shrugged. "I guess you're right. Mrs. Brandt, would you tell the other women they can go?"

Sarah caught Joanna's eye and saw the flash of fear. For a second, she doubted. For a second, she thought they'd tricked her. But Sarah gave her the smallest of smiles before opening the parlor door to go fetch the others. To her surprise, they were waiting right outside the door.

"I'm next," Grace said, striding purposefully past Sarah into the parlor.

"We don't need to see you, Miss Livingston," Broghan said. "You can go."

"You most certainly do need to see me. I need to tell you how I killed Pendergast."

Broghan frowned in confusion. "This lady here just told me how she killed him, so you couldn't have—"

"She's just trying to protect me. I killed Pendergast. He was attacking me, so I killed him."

"All right," he said, willing to humor an obviously hysterical female. "Where did you get the knife?"

"I'd snuck down to the kitchen and stolen it. I'd hidden it in the parlor in case I had a chance to catch him unawares."

"And did you?"

"No, not exactly, but he was furious, because my father had found me. He was beating me and I thought he was going to kill me before my father could get there, so I managed to get the knife from where I'd hidden it and slice it across his throat like he was always threatening to do to me."

Broghan gave Malloy a long, knowing look. He knew Grace was lying, because they both knew from the way Pendergast's throat was cut, from left to right, that his killer had been standing behind him. "Maybe you could show me how you did it, Miss Livingston."

"How I did it?"

"Yes. Just pretend you've got a knife and that I'm Pendergast, standing in front of you, and show me how you did it."

Grace looked down at her hands and closed one into a fist around the handle of an imaginary knife. Then she lifted it and pretended to draw the imaginary blade across Broghan's throat . . . from left to right.

His eyes widened in shock. "You're left-handed."

15

Grace looked down at her fisted hand, then up at Sarah, obviously afraid she'd done something wrong.

"You're left-handed," Malloy said quickly. "So you held the knife in your left hand when you cut Pendergast's throat. Isn't that exactly how the medical examiner said his throat was cut, Broghan?"

Broghan simply nodded, never taking his gaze off Grace Livingston. Sarah was beginning to feel sorry for him.

Grace opened her fist, as if dropping the imaginary knife. "In school, they made me learn to write with my right hand. The teacher would smack me with a ruler if I forgot and used my left, but I still do most things with my left hand."

"We'll have to tell Doc Haynes he might've been wrong," Malloy said.

Broghan shook himself, as if suddenly remembering why he was here. "What did you do with the knife?"

"I . . . I hid it."

"Where? We searched that house top to bottom."

Grace didn't even blink. "I hid it very well."

Broghan made an exasperated sound. "All right, why did you go to see Andy?"

"He sent me a note. He said he wanted money. He said he knew who'd killed Pendergast."

"How did he know where to find you?"

"How should I know?"

A very good question, Sarah thought, resisting the urge to say so and upset Broghan even more.

"What happened to the note?"

"I burned it."

"Of course you did." He turned to Joanna, who stared at Grace with open admiration. "I suppose you burned your note, too?"

"Of course. I didn't want Neth to see it."

"So how did you kill Andy?" Broghan asked Grace.

She hesitated a moment, and Sarah held her breath, but Grace was only gathering herself. "I went to see him. I didn't have any money to give him, so I thought I'd try to convince him not to betray me. He said . . . he said he'd think it over if I . . . if I did something. I knew he was lying, though, so luckily I'd gotten the knife from where I'd hidden it, and when he came at me, I stabbed him."

Broghan stared at her for a long moment, then looked at Joanna again. Then he turned to Malloy. "I suppose this other woman has her own story."

"I don't know," he said quite honestly, since Sarah was the one who had prepared the women. "Let's ask her."

362

Sarah helpfully opened the parlor doors and invited Rose Wolfe inside. She gave everyone in the room a quick glance and, apparently satisfied with what she saw, she said to Broghan, "I killed Pendergast."

"Let me guess," Broghan said, making no attempt to hide his disgust. "You got out of the cage, which wasn't really locked. You got a knife from the kitchen, and then you went upstairs and cut Pendergast's throat from behind."

"He was busy beating Miss Livingston, so he didn't hear me come in. Would you like me to show you how I did it?"

"No. So this Andy fellow, he sent you one of his notes, too?"

"Yes, he did."

"But you burned it."

"Of course I did. I didn't want anyone to find it."

"Did you give him any money?"

"A few dollars. That was all I had."

"And he tried to take advantage of you, so you stabbed him. Where did you get the knife?"

"I'd hidden it after I killed Pendergast, but I got it before I met with Andy."

"Where did you hide it?"

"In the cellar. I stuck it down the drain pipe."

Broghan frowned at this. "How did you get it back out?"

She held out her arm, which was as long as a

man's but very slender. "It wasn't far down. It had lodged where the pipe turns."

"And he was going to take advantage of you?" Broghan asked without much enthusiasm.

"He started unbuttoning his pants and telling me what he wanted, so I waited until he came toward me, and I stabbed him."

Broghan let his gaze drift from one woman to the next until he'd studied them all, including Sarah. Then he turned to Malloy. "You, come with me."

Malloy followed him out of the room and out of the house.

When the front door closed behind them, Sarah realized she'd been holding her breath, and she let it out with a whoosh.

"Did it work?" Rose asked. "Do you think he believed us?"

"I think he didn't have any choice," Sarah said. "He knows two of you are lying, and he may even have a good idea which two, but as long as you stick to your stories, there's nothing he can do about it."

"I thought I would die when Mr. Malloy told you to send these two packing," Joanna said.

"I'm sorry about that," Sarah said.

"Are you all right?" Grace went to Joanna and knelt beside her chair. "You've been through a lot today."

"Not so much," she said, trying to smile.

"Well, it's over now," Rose said. "For all of us. Isn't it, Mrs. Brandt?"

"I think so."

"You're trembling," Grace said to Joanna.

"I'll be fine." She turned to Sarah. "When can we leave?"

"Now if you like," Sarah said. "But you won't get far on that ankle. Let us find a cab for you."

"Nonsense," Rose said. "Franchesca sent me in the carriage. We'll take her wherever she wants to go."

But Joanna shook her head. "I can get a cab."

Sarah wasn't fooled. "Where will you go, Joanna?"

"You wouldn't understand."

"Would you go back with Neth?" Rose asked in astonishment.

Joanna glared at her. "I knew you wouldn't understand. He was good to me."

"Of course he was good to you," Rose said. "You're his mistress."

"We can't judge her," Grace said.

"No, you can't," Joanna said. "You've got families who took you back. Neth took me out of that place. God knows what would've happened to me if he hadn't."

"I'll find you a cab, Joanna," Sarah said.

"You'll never find one in this neighborhood," Rose said, and Sarah knew she was probably right. Cabs might drop someone off here, but they'd think twice about picking someone up so near the notorious Mulberry Bend. "I'll get the carriage, and we'll take you wherever you want to go, Joanna. Grace is right. We can't judge you, and I'm sorry for doing so."

Rose went out, and the three women sat in awkward silence for a few moments.

"Someone should tell Neth," Joanna finally said. "He'll wonder."

"I'll go as soon you leave."

"He's not evil," Joanna said. "He's just weak."

"You don't have to settle for that," Sarah said.

Joanna's lips curled into a bitter smile, and she turned to where Grace still knelt beside her. "Look at her, telling me I don't have to settle."

Grace dropped her gaze and shook her head.

Joanna's eyes were bleak when she turned back to Sarah. "You're pretty. *You* don't have to settle for anything. But the rest of us, we have to take what we can get. As long as Neth wants me, I'll have food to eat and a roof over my head, and I'll never have to open myself for any other man."

Sarah hated the truths behind her words. "And what happens when he no longer wants you?" she asked as gently as she could.

"I'll face that when it comes. It can't be worse than what I've faced before."

Sarah thought that might well be true, and she had no other arguments to make.

Rose returned, and she and Grace helped Joanna out to the carriage. When they were gone, Sarah thanked Mrs. Keller for her help, then walked down to Police Headquarters.

Broghan was heading in the direction of Police Headquarters, but Frank wasn't nearly as angry as he was, so he had a little trouble keeping pace. Broghan didn't even look back to see if Frank was coming until he reached the front stoop and Tom the doorman opened the door for him.

Satisfied Frank was still behind him, he went inside.

"Good afternoon, Mr. Malloy," Tom said. "Good to see you again."

"Thanks, Tom. I wish I could say it's good to be back."

"You got some business with Detective Sergeant Broghan?"

"Sure do. And do me a favor. If I'm not out of here by nightfall, would you call an attorney for me?"

Tom chuckled at that, although Frank wasn't positive it was a joke.

Inside, he found Broghan embroiled in a conversation with Neth, who had been waiting for them, thinking they were questioning Joanna inside.

"Malloy!" Neth cried when Frank entered. "What have you done with Joanna?"

"Nothing. In fact, she's probably already on her way back home."

"Home? Why didn't you tell me you'd released her?"

Luckily, he didn't wait for a reply, because Frank wasn't sure he had a good one.

"Come with me," Broghan said, even more furious now that Frank had saved him from Neth.

Broghan marched upstairs and went straight to the chief of detectives' office, ignoring the sputtering protests of O'Brien's secretary. O'Brien looked up and frowned at the interruption. Then he saw Frank and actually groaned aloud. "Malloy, I thought I was rid of you."

"So did I," Frank said with an apologetic smile.

"What's this, then?"

"Ask Broghan. He brought me here."

"He's trying to put one over on us," Broghan said. "The Pendergast case."

O'Brien frowned. "The pervert who kept females in cages?"

Frank managed not to reveal how pleased he was at O'Brien's description. The chief was a notoriously pious gentleman. "That's the one."

Broghan glared at him, then turned back to O'Brien. "He's interfering."

O'Brien raised his eyebrows. "In what way?"

"He's gotten three of those females to confess to killing Pendergast."

"Three? Malloy, is that true?" O'Brien asked in amazement.

"It's true that three of them confessed, but it's not my doing."

"Whose doing is it, then?" Broghan demanded. "That woman of yours?"

Frank had already drawn back his arm to give Broghan a lesson he wouldn't forget, when O'Brien jumped to his feet. "That's enough, Broghan! You'll show some respect in my office. Mrs. Brandt is a lady, and you'll treat her as such, even when she isn't present. Now apologize at once."

Broghan looked like he would much rather swallow broken glass, but he said, "I didn't mean to be disrespectful to Mrs. Brandt." Then he turned to O'Brien. "But she was with them when I questioned them this afternoon."

"That true, Malloy?" O'Brien asked, taking his seat again.

"This has been a very sensitive situation, after what the women went through. Mrs. Brandt has been doing what she can to help them."

"And exactly why are you still involved with these women at all?" O'Brien asked.

"Because Grace Livingston's father hired me as a private investigator to find her after I left the force."

O'Brien ran a hand over his face. "Maybe you two should sit down and tell me exactly what's been going on."

Frank let Broghan do most of the talking, stopping him only to clarify or correct when necessary.

"And then all three of them tell me exactly how they killed Pendergast and the other fellow," he concluded.

O'Brien considered the matter for several minutes. "Broghan, you told me about all the people Malloy talked to. Who did you talk to?"

"What do you mean?"

"I mean, what did you do to investigate this case and figure out who the killer is?"

"I told you. I thought it was Grace Livingston until Doc Haynes said it couldn't be her."

"So you left it to Malloy to investigate?"

Broghan squirmed a bit in his chair. "He was getting paid to do it."

O'Brien frowned. "Don't we pay you to investigate crimes, too?"

"That's not what I . . . You know what I mean!"

"I'm afraid I do. So you're telling me you made no effort to figure out who killed this Pendergast character, and now you're complaining because Malloy has found three killers who have even confessed?"

"Yes, I am, because we can't bring three people to trial for the same murder!"

"That's true," O'Brien said. "So you think

the women got together and decided to all confess so we wouldn't know which one really did it?"

"Of course they did," Broghan said. "And Malloy put them up to it."

"Malloy, is that true?"

Frank shook his head. "I'd already figured out which one I thought it was, and then one of the women hired a lawyer. After that, they all claimed to have done it."

"A lawyer," O'Brien said. "I should've known. So, Broghan, how important do you think it is to punish one of these women for killing a piece of scum like Pendergast?"

Broghan straightened in his chair. He might have been a worthless drunk, but he wasn't stupid, and no one could have mistaken O'Brien's unspoken message. "Well, when you put it like that, sir, not important at all."

"That's exactly how I'm putting it. So you'll pigeonhole this case, and if anybody ever asks you about it, you send them to me."

Broghan shot Frank a black look, but he said, "Yes, sir."

"And Malloy?"

"Yes, sir?"

"Are you going to keep interfering in police investigations?"

"Not if I can help it, sir."

"That's too bad."

• • •

"Mrs. Brandt, how nice to see you," Tom said as he opened the door for her at Police Headquarters. "Are you looking for Mr. Malloy?"

"Is he here?"

"Oh, yes, ma'am. He came in with Detective Sergeant Broghan. He said to send for an attorney if he wasn't out by sundown," he reported with a smile.

"The same goes for me, then," she told him, smiling back. "I'm really looking for a man named Vernon Neth. He was waiting for his lady friend."

"Nicely dressed gentleman? Kind of a weak chin?"

"The same."

"He ran out of here just after Mr. Malloy went inside."

"Well, then, I'll just wait inside for Mr. Malloy."

Inside, the desk sergeant greeted her and asked how she was doing. They were still chatting when Malloy and Broghan came back downstairs. Broghan didn't look quite as annoyed as he had earlier, although he didn't linger to chat.

When they were back out on the street, Malloy told her what had happened.

"O'Brien actually said he was sorry you wouldn't be interfering in any more police cases?" she said.

"He might've just been joking."

"Is he a joking man?"

"Not that I've ever noticed."

Sarah smiled. "So Broghan is going to let it drop?"

"He doesn't have any choice, but I told him he could have my fee from Livingston as a reward, so he's not as disappointed as he might've been."

"That's generous of you."

He shrugged. "Like you said, I'm rich now. I can afford to pay bribes."

"I don't think I said it like that."

"Yes, you did. But let's not argue. I'm starving, so I'm going to take you to a nice restaurant."

"I'm not dressed for a nice restaurant."

"Then I'll take you to a not-so-nice restaurant, and you can tell me what happened to our three confessed killers."

"So she went back to Neth?" Maeve asked when Sarah had finished telling her the whole story that night after Catherine was safely in bed.

"She feels like she doesn't have a choice. She's convinced her family won't want her back, and she doesn't think she's likely to find a husband to provide for her."

"I don't ever want to be that dependent on a man."

Sarah sighed. "I wish we lived in a world where

women had other choices besides getting married or slaving in a sweatshop for starvation wages or selling herself in the street."

"You supported yourself all this time since your husband died."

"Yes, but few women can do that. I was lucky."

"So, are you going to try to find the other women that Pendergast kidnapped?" Maeve asked after a moment.

"Yes. I feel obligated, and Malloy refuses to let me go alone, so he's going with me. We already know that two of them are safe and two of them died."

"And one of them is with Neth."

"I'm not sure we know which family is Joanna's, but I'm going to visit them all, even if I figure it out, because maybe I can find out if she's wrong about them not wanting her back. Then for the families whose loved ones didn't come home, I'll have to break the news that they might be dead."

"But at least they'll know what happened."

"That's true. Malloy is going to try to find out if any unidentified women's bodies were found in churchyards, as Neth claimed Pendergast had told him. Maybe the families can identify and claim them."

Maeve shuddered. "I thought I knew just how evil men could be, but now . . ."

"I know. I just hope the women who were

Pendergast's victims can recover from what he did to them."

"Knowing he's dead should help. I just wonder . . ."

"What?" Sarah asked when Maeve hesitated.

"I just wonder how well Vernon Neth will sleep at night knowing Joanna has already killed two men."

The next few days were difficult, as Sarah and Malloy visited the addresses in the letters Frank had found in Pendergast's desk. Frank had found the churches where Pendergast had left the bodies of the two of his victims who had committed suicide at his house. The police had kept descriptions of the bodies and the clothing they were wearing. Still, the descriptions could have fit thousands of women in the city.

Of the ten houses they visited, they found that only five of the victims had made it back to their families. Sarah was able to tell those five women that Pendergast and Andy were dead, at least. They were enormously relieved to know they needed never fear encountering them again. None of them had told their families exactly what had happened to them, preferring to hide behind a story of having been seduced and abandoned by an unscrupulous man. The shame of that was bad enough, but it was something their families could understand. Of the other five families, one of them belonged to Joanna and the others, well, she had to tell them about the two women who had died. They would probably never learn what had become of the two women who had simply never returned home.

As Sarah had hoped, they were able to identify which family was Joanna's, though her name, they determined, was actually Joan Marie. They had decided that the best strategy was to ask for the missing woman at each home, as they had when they'd called on Rose Wolfe's family. That way, if the woman had made it safely home, they would know instantly and could simply meet with her alone. If she had not, the family would demand to know who they were and why they had come asking for a woman who had been missing for months or even years.

Joanna's family was no different. Her father turned out to be a minister, judging by his clerical collar, and he met them in the parlor with a woman who appeared to be no older than Joanna herself. Neither of them looked happy to see them.

"Who are you and what do you want?" the man asked, more angry than concerned.

Malloy introduced himself and Sarah, explaining he was a private investigator. "Mrs. Brandt and I were investigating the disappearance of a young woman, and we discovered a man named

Pendergast had lured her to meet him through one of those lonely hearts advertisements."

The woman said, "I told you that's what she'd done." She was a woman Joanna would judge "pretty" enough not to have to settle for what she could get.

Reverend Alexander paid no attention to her remark. "What does this have to do with our missing daughter?"

"Pendergast had no intention of marrying this woman, and in fact he'd been holding her against her will. After rescuing her, we discovered he had done the same to several other females."

"And you think Joan Marie was one of them?" her father asked.

"We found the letters she had written in response to his advertisement. That's how we got your address," Frank hedged.

"But you didn't find her?" he asked, betraying the first trace of actual concern.

"We didn't find her at Pendergast's house," Malloy said quite honestly.

"May we sit down?" Sarah asked.

"Oh, yes, of course," Reverend Alexander said. "Forgive me. It's just . . . hearing news of Joan Marie after all this time. It's quite shocking."

When they were seated, Sarah said, "We have been calling at the addresses we found to see if the women returned to their families and, if they had not, to tell the families what happened to them."

"So, is she dead?" the woman asked baldly.

"Patricia!" Alexander cried.

"Isn't that what you were hinting?" Patricia Alexander asked Sarah, unrepentant.

"We do not believe she is dead, no," Sarah said.

"But she didn't come home. What could have happened to her?" Alexander asked.

"Any number of things," Sarah said.

"None of them anything we'd like to hear about, I'm sure," Patricia said. "I told you, Stephen, she isn't worth a moment of concern. She's like a cat; she'll always land on her feet."

Malloy made a sound of disgust, and Sarah didn't bother to hide her dismay. "Are you not Joan Marie's mother, then?" she asked, having decided she deserved to be insulted.

"Of course not!" she said, suitably insulted.

"Patricia is my second wife," Alexander said. "Joan Marie's stepmother."

What a trial she must have been to Joanna. No wonder she had sought an escape in the lonely hearts column.

"Joan Marie and I were more like sisters," Patricia claimed. "And she took great delight in looking after my children."

Sarah doubted this very much. More likely, Patricia took delight in having someone available to look after her children.

378

"That's why we were so puzzled when she simply disappeared one day after hinting she might be married soon," Patricia continued, unaware of Sarah's opinions. "I mean, really, we knew she had no suitors, so how was she going to marry?"

"Do you have any idea where she could be?" Alexander asked. "I would hate to think of her being in want."

Patricia sniffed in derision. "If she were in want, she would have come crawling back here for a handout."

Alexander frowned his disapproval but did not rebuke her.

"If we encounter her, we'll certainly tell her about your concern," Sarah said.

"Yes, please do," Alexander said.

They took their leave, and when they were back on the sidewalk, Sarah tucked her arm into Malloy's and sighed. "I was hoping Joanna was wrong about them."

"I think the father might've taken her back, but the stepmother would've made her life miserable."

"Yes, even a life with Neth doesn't seem so bad by comparison."

When they'd finished the last of the visits, Malloy hailed a cab to take them back to Sarah's house. The last visit had been particularly difficult, because the parents strongly believed one of the dead girls had been their daughter, based on the description of her clothing. Sarah had wept with them, and now she was exhausted.

When they were ensconced in the cab, Sarah felt the sting of tears again. She wanted to weep for all the women, both those lost and found, but she was afraid there weren't enough tears in the world for that.

Malloy took her hand in both of his. "You did all you could."

"I hope so, but I keep thinking about the ones we didn't find. Where are they? What happened to them?"

"You can't think like that. If you try to grieve for every missing female in New York, you'll go crazy."

"But there must be something I can do." She looked up at him with a watery smile. "I'm going to marry a millionaire. He should be able to help me."

Malloy sighed dramatically. "Yes, I guess he will."

Neither of them was surprised to find Mrs. Ellsworth was visiting with Maeve and Catherine when they arrived back at Sarah's house.

The girls were always happy to see Malloy, but today they seemed especially so. Catherine could hardly stand still. They kept exchanging glances with Mrs. Ellsworth, who shared their air of suppressed excitement.

"What's going on?" Malloy demanded good-naturedly after about five minutes of secret smiles and furtive glances.

"We have a house," Catherine announced, then clapped a hand over her mouth in case she shouldn't have said so.

"What do you mean, 'we have a house'?" Malloy asked, picking her up so he could look her straight in the eye. But Catherine only shook her head, keeping her hand securely over her mouth.

"What she means," Mrs. Ellsworth said, "is that I've located a house that you might be interested in. It will need some modernizing, of course, but—"

"Where is it?" Sarah asked.

"Not too far," Maeve said with a wicked little smile. "Not too far *at all*."

"What does that mean?" Malloy asked.

"It means that I thought you might want to stay in the neighborhood," Mrs. Ellsworth said brightly.

"Near familiar neighbors," Sarah suggested.

"Exactly! And when I was chatting with Mrs. Martin—"

"Mrs. Theda Martin? Who lives on the corner?" Sarah asked in surprise.

"Yes. Do you know how large that house is?

Much larger than I would've guessed. She raised five sons there. But they're all married now, and they've moved away. The oldest boy wants her to live with them out on Long Island."

"So this was her idea?" Malloy asked, not bothering to hide his skepticism.

"Oh no," Mrs. Ellsworth admitted. "She hadn't thought a thing about it until I explained your situation. She wouldn't sell to just anyone, but when I told her it was Mrs. Brandt, well . . ."

Sarah exchanged a glance with Malloy, who shrugged.

"The wallpaper is horribly old-fashioned," Mrs. Ellsworth continued, "and you'll probably want to add a bathroom or even two—"

"How long will that take?" Malloy asked suspiciously.

"Oh, I'm sure it could be done in a month."

Sarah looked up at Malloy again. "I don't suppose it could hurt to look at it."

"No," he said with a long-suffering sigh. "I don't suppose it would."

"And," Mrs. Ellsworth added, pulling a newspaper from behind her back, "you'll probably want to move as soon as possible, because this newspaper article about Mr. Malloy's inheritance also mentions where he lives."

Author's Note

When researching the Gaslight Mysteries, I've often encountered instances where the issues people were concerned about at the turn of the last century were the same issues we are concerned about today: spirituality, finding Mr. Right, alternative medicine, the immigrant's role in society, etc. One issue I'd been thinking about a lot lately was the potential dangers of social media and the way predators use it to deceive unsuspecting innocents. Not surprisingly, I learned this isn't a new problem. As long as personal ads have existed, predators have used them for evil. The only thing that has changed is the technology.

Interestingly, I already knew that several historical serial killers had lured their victims through lonely hearts advertisements, and I had already come up with the idea for this book when the contemporary story about the Cleveland kidnappings broke. A man had kept three women hostage in his house for nearly a decade in much the same way I'd had Pendergast doing. This was an unfortunate confirmation that human evil hasn't really changed over the past century.

Please let me know how you liked this book

by contacting me through my website, victoriathompson.com,

or "like" me on Facebook, facebook.com/Victoria.Thompson.Author,

or follow me on Twitter: @gaslightvt.

I'll send you a reminder when the next book in the series comes out in the spring of 2015.

Center Point Large Print
600 Brooks Road / PO Box 1
Thorndike ME 04986-0001 USA

(207) 568-3717

US & Canada:
1 800 929-9108
www.centerpointlargeprint.com